MORE LIVES
THAN ONE

Books by
CHARLES BRACELEN FLOOD

Love Is a Bridge
A Distant Drum
Tell Me, Stranger
Monmouth
More Lives Than One

MORE LIVES
THAN ONE

CHARLES BRACELEN FLOOD

1967

HOUGHTON MIFFLIN COMPANY BOSTON

THE RIVERSIDE PRESS CAMBRIDGE

This Book Is Dedicated

to

Captain Jack R. Chagnon

United States Army Security Agency

May you live in interesting times. — Old Chinese Curse

MORE LIVES
THAN ONE

CHAPTER ONE

July, 1950

"This telegram of yours is from the Pentagon." The woman at the draft board in Ellsworth, Maine, looked at the papers which had been spread before her by the worried young man standing on the other side of the counter. "It doesn't have anything to do with us." She could tell from the accents of his husky voice that he was one of the summer people, and she did not care what happened to him.

Harry Purdick cleared his throat and asked politely, "Do you think it might be a mistake?"

The woman looked at the telegram again. "They're calling you back in because you enlisted when you were in before, instead of waiting to be drafted."

"But that was in *1945*," Harry protested. "It was right at the end of the war. They were going to draft me anyway, so I enlisted to get it over with. I was in for twenty-two months. Here're my discharge papers right here."

The woman looked at his discharge papers, and then at the telegram. "If you enlisted, that means you're technically eligible for recall to active service. This telegram says you have a critical specialty they need. What's that?"

Harry shrugged his shoulders. "Oh, they sent me down to a place when I was in Germany. I had four months with counter-mortar radar. But since I got out in 1947 I haven't been in a reserve unit or anything. I'm a student. I'm supposed to go back for my senior year at Harvard in September. I'm planning to be married next June when I graduate."

"We can't help you here." The woman pushed the papers back at Harry. "That telegram says for you to report at Camp

Kilmer, New Jersey. You better show up there and see what you can work out with them. Maybe they'll make you an instructor on whatever it is you know about. Maybe this Korea thing'll be over in a few weeks and you can still get back to school in September."

Harry picked up the papers, slid them back into a manila envelope, and stood uncertainly before the information counter. The woman had turned her attention to something else. "Thanks," he said without conviction, and walked out of the brick building.

His brother was waiting for him in the old Ford convertible they knocked around in during these summer vacations in Maine.

"How'd it go?" Bill asked, sliding over as Harry got behind the wheel.

"That old bitch in there was measuring me for a uniform right across the desk." Harry tossed the manila envelope into the back seat, and shook his head as he started the car. "This is a real screwing. She says the Army can pull me back in because originally I enlisted instead of being drafted. That makes a *lot* of sense, doesn't it?" The car rolled along the main street, past farmers in red pick-up trucks, and women in flowered cotton dresses carrying shopping bags.

"How long would you have to be in?" Bill asked.

Harry glanced over at his brother, his anger dissipating as he saw the concern on the long, handsome face beneath the dark crew-cut hair.

"I don't know, Bill. Nobody knows *anything*." He stopped for a red light, and drummed his fingers on the plastic steering wheel. "A week ago I'd never heard of Korea. I don't know. That woman in there said maybe it'll be over in a few weeks and I can still get back to school in September."

"Boy, I hope so." Bill twisted his long body into a different position on the seat. "Do you think I ought to enlist or something?"

"Are you crazy?" Harry's gray eyes glared at Bill as he speeded the car up on the bridge leading out of town. "Dad got killed in the last war, and I've been in once. I think this family has just about done its bit."

Bill looked at this brother's usually friendly face. "But Harry, *I've* never been in. Because you had to go before, I got ahead of you at college. Maybe it's my turn to do something."

Harry shook his head. "Listen, Bill. If they need you, they'll get you. You're set to go to law school this fall. You *go*. Besides, how do you think Mother would like it if we *both* got in this?"

They drove on under elms, with blue glimpses of salt water inlets through the spruce to their left. A right-hand turn took them towards Woodruff Pond, the lake where they stayed, right next to Penobscot Bay.

"Harry, how are you going to tell Anne?"

Harry looked hard at the road. The lively, shy face of his fiancée Anne Wiley came before him. "I guess when we get back to the house I'll walk over to the Wileys and she'll take one look at me and say, 'What's the matter, Harry?' and I'll tell her."

*   *   *

Constance Purdick turned from the stove as she heard the convertible stop behind the cottage. She walked to the screen door, and saw her sons piling out of the car. Harry came first, his stocky body moving faster than usual, carrying the manila envelope.

"Harry," she said, pushing a lock of gray hair away from her blue eyes, "what did they say?"

"They say it doesn't have anything to do with Selective Service." Harry came through the screen door, with Bill behind him, looking the more worried of the two. "I guess it's just between the Army and me. It looks as if the only thing I can do is get down to Camp Kilmer and talk to them there."

Bill folded his long, muscly arms across his T-shirt. "The woman in Ellsworth said maybe they'd make him an instructor on this counter-mortar radar."

Constance stepped towards Harry. "Then you'd stay inside the country?"

"I guess so." Harry went over to the ice box and took out a bottle of ginger ale. "That'd be sort of a chuckle, if they made me an instructor. I've forgotten everything I ever knew about those machines."

Bill tossed Harry the bottle opener. "Harry says the woman said maybe this Korea thing'll be over by fall. Maybe Harry can get back to school in time."

Harry put the green bottle to his mouth. As the sweet ginger ale fizzed in his throat, he thought of how perfectly everything had been going until today. Anne was going into her junior year at Radcliffe, right around the corner from Harvard. The plan was that they would marry when he graduated next June.

Constance backed towards the sink, looking from one of her sons to the other. Of the two, Bill looked more like a soldier. Harry was healthy as a horse, but Bill was the athlete in the family. Gazing at Harry's brown curly hair, the bad posture, his usually smiling face, she could not believe it.

Not again, she thought. Not Harry in the Army again. "When do you have to go?"

Harry looked down at the bottle of ginger ale in his hand. "I guess about tomorrow. That telegram was forwarded from the apartment in New York, and it only gave me a week to wind up my affairs, and it'll take me a couple of days to get down to New Jersey from here."

Bill said, "I'll go down with you."

"Uh uh. You stay put right here. Maybe it's all a mistake. Maybe I'll be back next week."

Constance asked hollowly, "What do you need to take with you?"

"Not much." Harry smiled. "I guess my gray suit, and some underwear, and my shaving stuff."

*　　*　　*

The afternoon was turning hot, and the grass along the path to the Wiley's house put a sweet smell in Harry's nostrils. The Wiley's catboat, in which he and Anne and Bill had virtually grown up, lay silent at her mooring in the lake before the big brown-shingled cottage. Harry heard Anne's light laugh coming from under the porch, and he paused by its wooden lattice-work door. In the flecked sunlight under there, Anne was helping her mother load up their new electric washing machine.

"But I thought it was a fixed proportion," Anne was saying in an amused voice. "I mean, more dirty clothes, more soap powder."

"It doesn't seem to work that way," her mother said. "Not with this machine, anyway. One cupful is plenty."

Harry looked for another moment, a sad smile on his face. Anne was wearing white shorts and a blue and white striped blouse. Her arms and legs were tan, and the sun had bleached her shining brown hair.

"Hi," Harry said, coming into the concrete-surfaced area.

A pleased smile crossed Anne's face. "How are you? Where have you and Bill been all day?"

Anne's mother said, "Harry, there's some iced tea in the ice box if you'd like some."

"No, thanks," Harry said. "I just had some ginger ale at my house." He stared at Anne, at the happy, relaxed expression on her face. "When you get that washer loaded, I have to talk to you about something."

Both women stiffened.

"I can come right now," Anne said. "What's the matter, Harry?"

*　　*　　*

Harry was sitting on his front steps after supper, listening to the quiet, worried voices of his mother and Anne and Bill as they washed the dishes in the kitchen, when he saw Clarence Wiley's big frame coming along the path beside the strip of beach. Harry's lips tightened. His future father-in-law's head was set forward at its most businesslike angle. It occurred to Harry that he should have gone over there again, when Mr. Wiley came in from fishing, to explain the situation and to say good-bye.

Harry rose as Clarence Wiley stepped off the path onto the little square of lawn.

"Good evening, Harry."

"Good evening, Mr. Wiley."

"I know you just want to be with Anne and Bill and your mother tonight, naturally, but I just wanted to come over and say good-bye."

"I was going to come over after a little while," Harry said, not sure of whether he really would have.

"Look here, Harry." The big, gray-haired man sat on the steps, and Harry backed up against the railing. "I'm sure this is a mistake. It's not fair for you to have to go again, particularly with your father being lost the last time."

Harry opened his mouth, but Clarence Wiley bore on. "You know, I was in Washington during the war. I still know quite a few people down there. In the Pentagon, and with friends in the Pentagon. I'd like to get on the 'phone with a few of them and straighten this out."

"Well, that's kind of you, but I think I'll just go down to Camp Kilmer and see what the situation is."

"Well, we *know* what the situation is." Clarence spoke with the authority of thirty years spent practicing law. "All of a sudden this Korea thing has them in a stew down there, and they're grabbing everybody they think they could possibly need for anything. You're twenty-three, Harry. Because you had to be in before, you haven't been able to get through college yet.

They ought to leave you alone, and I'm not sure they have the authority to do this to you. At least let me look into it."

Harry could feel his stomach tightening. "I appreciate it," he said, "but I'm going down there and see what the situation is."

The quick Maine night was falling on the lake, and Clarence's gray-haired square head glowed in the last light.

"I wish you'd let me do this, for Anne's sake, too."

"I understand that. I may need your help after a while, but let me try to work it out."

"All right. But let's not wait too long." Clarence rose gracefully from the steps. The door above them opened, and Harry's mother came onto the porch.

"Hello, Clarence. Won't you come in?"

"Good evening. No, thank you. I know you all want to be together this evening. I just was hoping that Harry would let me 'phone a few people I know in Washington."

Constance Purdick looked at Harry in the dusk, and Harry said, "I told Mr. Wiley that I appreciated it, but I'd prefer to straighten it out myself if I can."

Constance smiled in the chilly Maine evening. "Thank you, anyway, Clarence. Please tell Mabel we liked the cookies she sent over with Anne."

"Of course." The big man shook hands with Harry. "I certainly wish you luck."

"Thank you. I'll probably be back in a few days."

*   *   *

Harry and Anne got down to the store just before it closed, and bought two ice cream cones. They walked back along the road by the lake, their nearer hands clasped in slow, swinging unison, and their outer hands bringing the ice cream to their mouths. Harry's was chocolate and Anne's was strawberry, and occasionally they stopped in the misty pine night and offered each other a nibble of the other flavor.

"Oh, Harry," Anne said in her soft voice when they kissed,

and her body came surrenderingly towards him. He gazed at the silver oval of her face in the darkness, hearing her sudden passionate breath. Her quick, tender responses were their secret.

"Can you telephone from Camp Kilmer?" Anne asked.

"I imagine so. Don't worry. I'll be in touch as soon as I can."

Anne kissed him, and there was that look again, a hungry helpless adoration in her eyes. Harry held her to him.

"Don't worry, Anne. We have something special. I'll be all right as long as I know you're there."

*   *   *

The last light burning around the lake was in Constance Purdick's room. She stared at the photographs set into the tall bookshelves, and repeatedly her gaze returned to the photograph of her husband. Stephen Purdick smiled at her from beneath his naval officer's cap, and, grudgingly, through misty eyes, she smiled back. It was as if he had been alive again tonight on the front steps, when she heard Harry tell Clarence Wiley that he would cope with the world by himself.

Her head turned towards the photograph of the first and second grades at Hadley School in New York, taken in 1934. There stood Harry in the back row, his head cocked to one side, his collar buttoned but his necktie sliding down, his inquisitive face sensitive and determined.

Constance lay back against the pillow, thinking of her sons. Bill deferred to Harry but competed hard with others. Harry preferred to go through life without direct confrontations, but when he was in a corner he could be a surprisingly tough customer.

Stubborn, Constance thought, looking again at her husband, who had left his teaching at Columbia at the age of thirty-nine to serve as a naval historian on a carrier which encountered a *kamikaze* in the last days of the war. Stubborn, both of you. She turned out the light, but still the faces remained in her mind. It had been Stephen's death that had sent Harry hurtling into uniform months before he would otherwise have been called. And now they were pulling him back in because he had enlisted instead of waiting to be drafted. And because he knew something about some kind of machines.

A pained, patient smile came finally onto her face as she slid into sleep. She knew her sons well. Under that indignation and genuine shock, she suspected that Harry was more than a bit fascinated with the situation. Five years before, they had trained him to fight, and brought him to a Germany where the fighting had just stopped. Now the locomotive had thundered forth again, fringed in fire, and many a young man was pausing thoughtfully, at work in his field, to hear the distant sound.

CHAPTER TWO

IT ISN'T HAPPENING to me, Harry thought. It isn't happening. The man ahead of him in the line, dressed in green fatigue trousers and a T-shirt, stepped up onto the wooden block under the hanging bright lights in the warehouse. There was a medic on a wooden platform on either side of the block, and as the man stepped up, the medic on either side grabbed an arm and thrust a hypodermic needle into it.

"This'll be a perfect fit," the young GI said, stepping back and looking at how the olive-drab trousers of the Class A uniform fit Harry.

Harry looked at him. "How long have you been in the Army?"

"A week."

"Were you a tailor on the outside?" Harry pulled down the trousers from where they were binding his crotch.

"Hell, no."

"That's swell." Harry moved off in the too-tight trousers, dragging his newly issued and rapidly filling barracks bag behind him.

*　　*　　*

Harry lay in his bunk, listening to the kid in the next bunk weeping in the dark. The soap-reeking barracks was packed with a mixture of men being recalled, and new draftees who had never spent a night away from home.

The kid sniffled again, and Harry turned restlessly in the hot night. The problem was that there seemed to be no one to whom he could explain his special situation. All afternoon he had moved from desk to desk, answering questions about who was his next of kin and who should his GI insurance be made out to, and what was his past employment experience. At each desk he would ask the bespectacled Pfc., "Say, where can I find somebody to talk to about the whole question of my being recalled in the first place?" and the Pfc. would say, "Not here, that's all I know," and pass him on to an identical-looking Pfc. who would ask about his religious affiliation, or whether he wanted to start a GI savings account.

"No!" Another kid was having a nightmare across the aisle. Harry buried his face in the lumpy pillow. At one of the desks they had told him that he was a corporal, and typed it in on half a dozen sheets, and then at the desks after that the Pfcs. had called him "Corporal."

Harry flopped over on his back and stared up at the dim wire netting of the upper bunk. That was the thing, he thought. You never knew when the Army was going to turn around and do something right. He had been a corporal when he had been in before, so they were recalling him with the rank he had held. It made sense. It was the only thing that made sense, and he had ducked out of a work detail after chow and taken his shiny khaki shirts and green fatigue shirts over to the tailor shop and waited while they sewed on the stripes. The stripes made him feel better, and when he had come back to the barracks one of the draftees had called him "Sir," and no one had said anything about his ducking the work detail. It was an improvement, but he had to find someone who would understand that he should never have been recalled in the first place.

Come on, Harry said to himself, staring up into the gloom. Get some sleep. He closed his eyes, and before them swam the lake in Maine, the happy summer place where they lived deliberately simple lives before the winter of schools and dances and the brumble-brumble of New York.

A slow smile spread on Harry's lips, and his eyes stayed closed.

Now he saw the granite-and-fir islands of Penobscot Bay, near the lake. He was back there again, he and Bill as very young boys playing around the little dark-shingled South Harbor Yacht Club. It was an afternoon lost in peaceful Maine mists before the Second World War. Bill was whacking away at the tennis backboard beside the rough brown clay court, and Harry was poking along the shore near the ramp leading to the float, waiting for his mother or father or someone to pick them up at the end of this afternoon. They were already late for supper at their house by the lake. All the boats were tied up, and sunset locked the harbor. The only sound was the tennis ball clanging on gut. It was getting cold. The yacht club's spaniel Mickey came shuffling down from the porch that overlooked the harbor, and Harry patted him behind his floppy ears.

Harry looked over the water, and then he blinked. The top of a sail was moving behind the island at the entrance to the harbor. He had never seen a sail so tall that it rose over the top of those trees. His mouth opened as he watched the white canvas moving in the last sunbeams, coming fast like a gull against the fading blue sky.

The boat slid from behind the island, her mast gold. The sail filled the sky. A winch whirred, the sails trimmed, and she was coming straight for the visitors' moorings a hundred yards offshore.

Harry gulped. He looked back in the direction of the tennis court, wanting to tell Bill about this, and then he was running down the ramp and onto the float.

"C'mon, Mickey," he called, untying the painter of the club's dinghy. The dog jumped in, tail wagging, and Harry had the oars in the locks and was on his way to look at the new arrival. He glanced over his shoulder as he rowed, his heart beating faster as he saw the beautiful green hull. She was the biggest yawl he had ever seen, almost as big as the lumber schooners from Camden. They had their main down now, gliding into the mooring just on the jib without using their engine. Mickey stood in the dinghy's bow, a canine figurehead, studying the yacht with the soft brown eyes of a moocher.

Harry heard the whine and rattle of the jib coming down, and then he pivoted the dinghy in the water and looked at the visitor as she lay at her mooring. He rowed facing forward, admiring the sleek side of the yacht, his eyes darting from the brass fittings to the crew furling the sails.

Harry paddled around to the stern. There was a little girl sitting there, her legs dangling over the water. She was dressed in a brown pinafore and a white blouse, and her bare feet swung back and forth in front of the gilt letters on the stern:

SPUME
HONOLULU

Mickey wagged his tail, and Harry stared at the little girl. She had a tan as deep as his own, and she looked as if she would rather be in a bathing suit.

"Hi," Harry said.

"Hello."

"Are you from Hawaii?" Harry asked, trying not to sound too impressed.

"No. The boat is. Some of the people are. They're rich."

"Oh." The dinghy was drifting, and Harry paddled it back even closer to the girl. With the evening breeze in her hair, her head high, she looked like something special from the sea.

"Do you live here?" the girl asked.

"Just in the summers. We live on Woodruff Pond. That's three miles from here."

"Woodruff Pond!" the girl exclaimed. "That's where we're going to stay!"

A woman came aft. "Anne, dear, I think we'd better — " She stopped, looking at this boy in blue jeans and wool shirt in the dinghy with the dog.

"We were just talking," the little girl said, swinging up and standing under the mizzen boom. "He lives here. In the summers."

"Oh." Across the few yards of water Harry saw the woman's expression become more friendly when the girl said, "In the summers." "What's your name?"

"Harry Purdick."

"Purdick?" The woman's expression really changed. "You must be one of Professor Purdick's sons."

"Uh huh."

"Well, isn't that nice! We've bought the house right next to yours! Harry, this is Anne Wiley, and I'm her mother."

"How do you do," Harry said.

II

Anne stood by the wall telephone in the Wiley's kitchen in Maine, and nodded at what Harry's disembodied voice was saying through the hissing wires from Camp Kilmer. She knew at least half a dozen people were listening in on the party line, and she wished they would get off.

"Well," she said loudly and slowly, "where is Fort Dix?"

"Just about forty miles from here," Harry's voice replied.

"Harry, when are they going to let you out?"

"I'm going to talk to them about it at Fort Dix," Harry said. "They're putting us on a bus for there early tomorrow morning, so I can't talk to anybody else about it here."

"Oh. Are you all right, Harry?"

"Sure, I'm all right. But some of these eighteen-year-old kids make me feel like an old man. Tell Mother I'll send you all an address down there as soon as I have one."

"Do you want me to send you anything?"

"Send yourself. As soon as I can have visitors I'll let you know."

III

Within minutes of their arrival at Fort Dix, they were standing in four ranks on a sandy area in front of four two-story barracks from which yellow paint was peeling. Under the blinding sun, a small mulatto captain, backed by three drill sergeants, was looking at them.

"You will have eight weeks of refresher infantry basic training here," the little man said. He picked his nose as he spoke. "Let me give you a piece of advice. During these next two months you'll see other basic training companies around here. Some of them will get orders for Europe, for Alaska, for Panama. They're gonna replace men in those areas whose time is up. Now you might get orders like that, but I wouldn't count on it. Don't go doping off on the firing range because you start thinking you're gonna end up guarding the Panama Canal. Most of you men are going to FECOM. That's Far East Command, and it's spelled K-O-R-E-A."

Oh no you don't, Harry thought, sweat stinging his eyes in the July sun.

IV

The administrative first sergeant smelled of beer. He sat behind his green metal desk in the Orderly Room and thumbed through a sheaf of mimeographed papers.

"That manual on counter-mortar radar is classified," he announced to Harry, who was standing at a sweaty At Ease in green fatigues. The sergeant's pig-like eyes narrowed further. "What do you want it for anyway?"

"That's what I'm supposed to be," Harry said. "That's what I was recalled for. When I was in before I had four months of counter-mortar radar, and I've forgotten everything about it.

I thought I ought to study up on it, in case they want to make me an instructor or something when I finish these eight weeks here."

The administrative first sergeant solemnly belched. "That instruction booklet is classified. I don't see any security clearance in your records. Anyway, we don't have any of them manuals anyway. Why don't you get your ass on out to Bayonet Training? You're already late."

CHAPTER THREE

Harry came walking up the hot tar road to the pale yellow Service Club building. Beside him was a Negro named Arch Jones, Junior, who had the bunk beneath his. They had been confined to the regimental area for this first three weeks of training, and this was the first Saturday that they had been allowed to have visitors. He and Arch were almost running as they strode to the building where their families were waiting for them.

Inside, it was a madhouse. Whole clans had appropriated tables, and Italian families were drinking red wine from paper cups, while their uniformed sons gnawed at long loaves of hard-crusted bread. In the corners men were kissing their wives passionately, and small children chased about the hardwood floor.

"Harry!" His mother was upon him, and they were embracing. Her silk dress felt strange under his roughened hands, like something from another world. Then Anne was in his arms. He kissed her for five seconds, the noise about him receding, and then he was holding her in his arms, looking at her, and her hand was touching the unfamiliar khaki shirt, feeling the brass button on his collar with the crossed Infantry rifles on it.

Bill slapped him on the back and said, "Boy, are they getting you in shape!"

Harry grinned and shook hands with his brother, who was wearing a seersucker suit. "I'd rather be out of shape, and out of here."

*　　*　　*

Later in the afternoon he and Anne were walking alone at the edge of one of the big rough-mown fields, before he had to take her back to the parking lot where his mother and Bill were waiting.

"We could get married in that five days' leave you get at the end of this," Anne said.

Harry nodded thoughtfully, keeping his arm about her as they moved slowly, occasionally kissing, in a half-staggering affectionate trance. "I think I still might be able to get out. Half a dozen guys in my barracks have gotten out of this thing in the past couple of weeks. They talked to the Red Cross and the chaplains and the personnel people."

A couple came the other way. The young soldier in light khaki shirt and trousers and overseas cap said, "Hi, Purdick," and they were alone again at the edge of the meadow.

"Anne, it's so damned confusing. Even if I have to stay in, a couple of the clerks in the Orderly Room say there's a good chance some of us might get sent to posts here to replace men in our specialties that are getting sent to Korea. See? Even this eight weeks may make us too late for what the Army needs out there right now." He looked at her, the soft thoughtful hazel eyes, the straight nose, the quick-to-smile mouth that was not smiling now. God, he thought, God, Anne, and if I do get sent out there and anything happens to me, what good is it going to do you to be married to me for five days?

She stopped walking and looked at him as if she had read his mind. "Harry, I've been reading the papers on this every day. We're really getting creamed over there in Korea."

"You probably know more about it than I do. We don't hear very much about it."

"The North Koreans have pushed the Americans right into a little pocket down at the end of the peninsula." Anne's voice faltered. "But Harry — just try to get out of the whole thing. Don't you want Daddy to try to — "

"Not yet." Harry kissed her. The smell of the warm hazy

meadow added to the tight sweetness in his throat. "Look, Anne. It'll work out. It has to work out. Suppose I do have to stay in for a few months, we'd still be getting married just about the time we were planning to, anyway."

Anne put her arms around him. "Harry, I don't care about school or anything else. Let's just get married."

"I love you." Harry's eyes were wet as he held her. He spoke into glowing brown hair. "I promise you we'll work it out the best way. It's just there're so damn many rumors here, I don't know what to think."

*　　*　　*

Anne sat in the back of the car as Bill drove it back to New York from their visit at Fort Dix. Her eyes were closed. She could hear Bill and his mother chatting, but it seemed at a great distance. She tried to think of Harry as she had seen him just forty-five minutes ago, wearing khakis and his face troubled, but instead she was remembering that first summer in Maine, when Harry and Bill had looked at her suspiciously for a week, and then suddenly they had been doing everything together, day after day. Her father had bought the catboat "Pine Cone" along with the house, and one day she and Harry and Bill had sailed the little boat for a picnic at the far end of the lake, chattering without stop.

Anne smiled. The voices in the front seat were a thousand miles away, and now they were sailing back up the lake. She was imitating Spencer Tracy in "Captains Courageous," which they had all seen.

"Cut it out, Anne!" Harry was lying on the floorboards in the catboat's cockpit, laughing so hard he hurt.

"And then he goes forward," Anne said, "with the boy in the bottom of the boat." She hopped onto the foredeck, clinging to the mast in the freshening breeze. She had taken the paper bag in which their sandwiches had been, and had cut and folded it so

that it looked like a watch cap. "And then he sees the big boat."
Anne's hand popped to the brim of her wild headgear and she
peered and scowled across the bright sunny waters. "And then
he says, 'Hey aboard the vessel!' "

"Be careful up there, Anne," Bill cried from the tiller.
"C'mon Harry, get off the deck."

"I can't, honest, Bill." Harry lay gasping, tears running down
his cheeks.

"And then he rows alongside," Anne went on, "and Spencer
Tracy yells about the boy being a new kind of fish." She put
both her hands to her mouth, leaning backwards, inhaling for a
supreme shout. A puff of wind struck. She grabbed for the
mast, and missed, and then she was crashing into dark water,
bubbles and choking, and she came up gasping and fighting. The
boat sizzled away from her with frightening speed. She saw
Harry come up from the floorboards where he had been laughing, and saw his frightened face look at her under the boom.
Then he was awkwardly putting his foot on the coaming, and
with a splash he was in the water, too. Her paper hat was floating halfway between them. Harry struck out for her. Beyond
Harry's soaked head coming through the water, she saw Bill's
white face looking over his shoulder as he swung the tiller and
jibed the boat around.

Harry came up to her in the water. "Hi, Anne."

"Hi," she managed through a mouthful of water.

Bill was running downwind of them, and now he came about
and luffed up alongside the two gasping, spluttering swimmers.
Anne felt his arms under her armpits, and she was scrambling
over the side. Then Bill was helping Harry over the stern.

"You're crazy!" Bill lashed out at Harry with his fist, and
Harry crashed to the deck, looking up at Bill with amazement.
"Supposing we *both* did that!" Bill yelled, his chest heaving as
much as Anne's and Harry's. "We'd all be swimming around in
the middle of the *lake!*"

Harry shook his head. There was no anger on his face. "I

knew you wouldn't jump in, Bill," he said. "Don't be mad with me."

CHAPTER FOUR

Harry lay in his top bunk, listening to the metallic boom of wall lockers being opened by soldiers who were getting back from New York on pass even later than he on this Sunday night.

"So she says, 'Oh, I love you,' " a voice said as two men in T-shirts walked to the latrine, "and I says, 'Honey, I can always take a later bus.' "

Harry grinned. His own week-end in New York had been terrific. Last night he had changed into civilian clothes at his mother's apartment, feeling the soft white button-down shirt and the gray tropical suit enfold him so gently after the uniform. The trousers had felt flowing, like something a pasha might wear for a turn around the harem.

And Anne. She had looked marvelous in a blue dress, with her tanned arms bare, and a gold clip near the round neckline. After dinner they had gone dancing, and wandered around the summer-night city streets, and then they had been in her family's empty apartment, lying on the couch, and it had been harder than ever to hold back. There was a strange soft sadness in their kisses, and he could not understand exactly what it was.

"Fourteen-ninety-five," a boy said, holding up a pair of boots in the light at the top of the latrine steps. "They *will* shine, buddy."

Harry shook his head, and stared from his bunk at the white-washed wooden ceiling above in the gloom. These were the same kids who had been crying in their bunks at Camp Kilmer those first nights. Now it was seven weeks later, and they were spending fourteen-ninety-five of their sixty dollars' monthly pay to buy combat boots in New York, specially-made boots that supposedly shined brighter than the regular ones the Army had issued them.

"*Sharp*, man," a Negro boy said, pausing to look admiringly at the boots the boy in the latrine doorway was holding up, like a prize catch of fish.

I don't know what it is, Harry thought, but it's happened. Now the men were inspecting each other's rifles every evening, whether there was a formal inspection or not. There was a run on Blitz cloths at the PX for shining up belt buckles, and men who had been physically timid seven weeks before were wrestling with each other just for fun.

I don't know how they do it, Harry thought, but it works. He found himself thinking of today in Central Park. He and Anne had walked out there after services at St. James's Episcopal Church, moving among the approving glances that passersby had given to the pretty girl and to his starched uniform, his gleaming low quarter shoes, his single red-white-and-black ribbon from the Occupation of Germany. It had been fun, walking along, feeling good, hoping those gray clouds would not turn to rain.

Harry shook his head in the night as he remembered something else. At one point Anne had asked him why he was looking so intently at a ridge above them in the Park, and he had realized that he was trying to figure out which route up it would give a rifleman the most cover.

II

The buzzer sounded right after chow, and they all trotted out of the barracks, wondering what this unscheduled formation was about.

The field first sergeant was standing there in the opening cool gusts of evening, wearing his red helmet liner, with a sheaf of papers in his hand.

"Parade Rest!" he yelled at the four green-clad platoons. A black piece of canvas flapped from the porch of a barracks across the way. "The following enlisted men will report to Fort Lewis, Washington, for immediate shipment to FECOM. Abbot, Accacio, Aguilar, Allen, Archer, Ascanio, Austin, Baker, Bernardo — "

Harry gasped. The sergeant was reading every name in the company. They were all being sent to the Far East.

III

It was a weekday afternoon near the end of August, and there were few people in Central Park. Harry had lunched with Bill and his mother on this last day, and now he and Anne were walking past the south end of the Metropolitan Museum. In two more hours he would go back to his mother's apartment, pick up his barracks bag, and head back to Fort Dix for the train that would take him to the West Coast.

"I was kind of interested in the special way you roll your socks up like that," Anne said. She had helped him repack the barracks bag this morning, with his mother bringing in the freshly laundered khakis and fatigues.

"They've got lots of little tricks," Harry said, looking at a fat pigeon scurrying across the asphalt path ahead of them. The idea that he was leaving this afternoon was so big that neither of them could take it in. These past five days there had been discussions about whether to get married now, about how long it would take to get blood tests, about forgetting a church wedding, about justices of the peace, about everything, and now it was too late for anything except this walk in the Park.

A baby carriage passed them, pushed by a white-clad nurse

wearing a shapeless brown hat. Anne looked at the Museum off to their right. "I was in the American Wing in there last week," she said. "Just walking around. You remember when we went there last Easter vacation?"

"Yes." Harry smiled. He was thinking of all the talks they had had about history. Anne was concentrating in European History at Radcliffe, and he had been getting more and more into American History at Harvard. Neither of them believed much in theories of history.

"You'll be a good instructor if that's what they make you, Harry," Anne said, somehow paralleling into his thoughts. She stepped out of the way of a man being pulled by a fox terrier on a leash. "You always were a good public speaker. Because you didn't beat a point to death. Remember that debate with the University of California?"

Harry nodded. He remembered Anne, up for a visit from her senior year at boarding school, sitting there in the Adams House Common Room. It had been the spring of his freshman year, and he and his friend Peter Barker had represented the Harvard Freshman Union team against two real hotshots from Berkeley. It had been the national question for the year, "Resolved, that the Chinese Communists are Agrarian Reformers." He and Peter had been assigned the negative, and they had let the boys from California talk themselves hoarse about Communist land reform. Bypassing all that, Peter and he had spent their entire time reciting the military feats of the Chinese Communists, and an amused three judges had given them the decision.

"That was a long time ago," Harry said.

"Why'd you sort of drop out of debating?"

"I guess I got tired of arguing."

Anne's hand slipped itself into his. They were passing through an old brick-lined tunnel under a road in the Park, and they turned to each other in the sudden sour-smelling coolness.

"Harry," Anne said, her voice throbbing, "I'll think of you every minute."

IV

Constance was working on her checkbooks in the apartment in New York, but the silence made her stop every few minutes.

All at once, she thought, putting down her pen and looking around the living room. It got quiet around here all at once. During Harry's leave the apartment had been a hive, with Anne dropping in and Harry on the telephone with old friends. Bill had charged in and out with things like a handwarmer from Abercrombie and Fitch. Harry had mentioned that he had heard that these lighter-fluid-burning handwarmer gadgets might be useful in Korea if he was there when winter came. Bill had bought one for him, and an olive-drab scarf from a war surplus store.

And now Harry was on the Pacific somewhere, and Bill had left for his first year at Harvard Law School, and Anne had gone back for her junior year at Radcliffe. The only sounds were the clock in the corner, and the stiff pages of her checkbook.

Most of the evening Harry's face had been before her, but now she looked at the framed picture of Anne that sat on the table against the wall. It was the one that had been in the *New York Times* last spring when their engagement was announced. It was a simple portrait of Anne in a dark dress, with a single strand of pearls about her neck. Her expression seemed to balance between suspicion and amusement.

Constance smiled at the picture. She knew that psychiatrists believed that a mother really wished to scar with nails the girl who would marry her son, but Anne was the daughter she had never had. Often she heard women discussing marriages, weighing them in terms of who had gained what, and who was not really getting what they deserved, but it had never occurred to her to apply the concept to Harry and Anne.

Her eyes softened. The checkbooks were still beneath her

hand, but the long memories of this apartment seemed to echo in the room.

It was a wartime Christmas. The boys were home from boarding school. Anne's father had been working in Washington, so Mabel had left Anne here for a few days while she joined Clarence for the few hours he could spare from his wartime job.

Constance cocked her head, as if listening for a special note which would set all to rights if it could be recaptured. Her husband had been in the Pacific, and she had been working for Censorship in New York, using the French she had learned at a finishing school in Paris when she was seventeen.

Anne was so nervous that one evening, Constance thought, and bit her lip as she remembered.

She was helping Anne to get ready for the dance. At the windows of the guest room were red-ribboned holly wreaths that she had bought on her way home from Censorship. The city hung white in snow, moonlight washing the darkest snow-flecked bricks.

"Is it really all right?" Anne asked, looking at the mirror's reflection of herself in her new dress.

"Darling, it's lovely," Constance said. She could see that Anne was trembling; it was her first big, evening dress dance. Down the hall Bill and Harry, home for the Christmas holidays, were calling back and forth as they wrestled their way into their dinner clothes.

"This tie's longer!" Harry yelled.

"I don't know how to tie it anyway!" Bill shot back. "What's the difference?" They both laughed, self-conscious, gay and nervous about the dance to which they were taking Anne.

Anne cleared her throat as she surveyed herself in the mirror. "I mean," she said, her hazel eyes looking beseechingly into Constance's blue ones, "you don't think my dress is too *young* or anything?"

Constance kissed her cheek, wishing for the thousandth time

that she had had a daughter to add to her two boys. "It's perfect, Anne dear."

Anne produced a black ribbon, and Constance helped her adjust the simple loop over her brown hair. For a moment tears came to Constance's eyes as she remembered her own fears and agonies and triumphs at dances. The awful sensation that no one was going to ask you to dance; the earthquake of relief when someone did; the horror that someone else might not cut in, that one would stumble on with the same partner hour after hour, with fixed smiles, on a Sahara of humiliation. Under her hand she felt that fresh young head of glowing brown hair.

As Anne was putting a few tentative drops of perfume behind her ears, Constance summoned Harry and Bill into her room and shut the door. "Now," she said with a firmness of tone that the boys had rarely heard matched, "I *hope* you both have a good time tonight. But Anne is your guest, and I expect you to *see to it* that she has a good time. I don't care what you have to do, ask your friends to dance with her, keep passing her back and forth between the two of you, do it."

"Yes, Mother," Bill murmured, and Harry, fresh-cheeked from the bath and a most unnecessary effort at shaving the down on his face, nodded in conscientious agreement.

"All right," Constance said, opening the door, and led the way out to the hall. "Flowers!" she hissed over her shoulder, and Harry dove off in the direction of the kitchen and the corsage that was in the refrigerator.

She was standing near the front door of the apartment when Harry came back into the hall, carrying the small white box of flowers. Bill was helping Anne on with her coat. Constance saw Harry falter in his stride as he looked at Anne in her first long evening dress, and then, as Harry walked towards Anne slowly, Constance's head turned. For a moment she saw Anne through Harry's eyes. She saw the blue tulle dress disappearing as Anne began buttoning the coat, the fair flushed skin of her collarbones and throat, the graceful neck, the touch of lipstick on her young lips. Bill had stepped back from her and was looking at his erstwhile summer wrestling companion as if she might break.

Anne's eyes watched Harry come towards her. Harry was looking at the black velvet collar of her coat, the thin white leather gloves on her hands, the little white pearl buttons on the insides of her wrists, and then he stopped before her.

"Here, Anne," he said, and shoved at her the paper box containing the corsage.

CHAPTER FIVE

Except for the oilskin sailors on watch, Harry was the only man above decks on the transport *Buckner*. A typhoon had turned the seas east of Japan into wind-lashed feathery gray dunes, and Harry preferred the screaming wind on deck to the vomit-covered passages below.

The *Buckner* groaned and dropped her head into a quick-opening gray boiling valley. Harry shivered as icy pellets of salt water broke on his face. The barracks bags of the two thousand soldiers aboard were locked in the hold, and the only clothes they had were green cotton fatigues, which had been considered adequate for a crossing to Korea in mid-September. No one had thought of typhoons.

II

Anne snatched the letter from her mailbox and ran with it to her room in Briggs Hall at Radcliffe. She tore it open, unable to focus on Harry's handwriting in her excitement. Finally the letters resolved themselves; the unfamiliar APO number at the upper right-hand corner of the page, and then, "Anne, Darling." She kissed the paper, her hands still trembling, and read it ravenously.

Well, I got here. I am in a port town called Pusan, and it is the living end. We got off the ship yesterday morning and since then it has been one long line for issuing equipment, and a lot of lectures and briefings on the situation here in Korea.

As far as I can make out, there have been American landings up north at Inchon, way behind the North Korean lines, and the North Koreans are pulling back up the Korean peninsula. Everybody around here is optimistic.

Right now it is about ten P.M. and I am lying in a newly-issued sleeping bag on the concrete floor of a rickety wooden warehouse where we will stay until they figure out what to do with us. I am writing this by the light of a candle stuck on this concrete floor. I still don't know where I am going. I haven't been able to find out which units have the machines in which I was trained in Germany. It's going to be pretty embarrassing when I can't remember the first thing about machines I last saw three years ago, but maybe some of it will come back to me.

The trip over was terrible. The transports over to Germany and back were no picnic, but as far as I can see the Army has forgotten all it ever knew about anything. Anyway, they had us in windowless compartments deep in the ship, no ventilation, not enough food, no laundry facilities, no nothing. The bunks, if you can call them that, were strips of canvas hung between steel pipes that were arranged in a kind of jungle gym effect from the ceiling to the floor. In my compartment there were two hundred men in one of these jungle gyms, sleeping on its six levels, so that if you were on the top level you had to climb up the outside of five other bunks to get there. I had a bunk in the middle of one of the jungle gyms, with a man sleeping on either side of me, so I had to climb up on the end of the thing and then hold onto a metal rafter on the ceiling and swing in feet first into my slot in this pigeon-hole arrangement. The men on either side of me spent the fourteen days throwing up. I spent every possible hour up on deck. You know how much I like the sea, but it was the worst two weeks of my life.

Pusan is the filthiest town I have ever seen. Thus far all the Koreans I have seen are dockhands. Their clothes are tattered and unwashed, and they stink from something they eat. They sit in circles on their haunches, doing nothing until eating time. Then they produce little metal boxes containing cold, gray, dirty-looking rice, and fish heads, which they eat with chop-sticks, in silence. I couldn't give less of a damn about defending them or their country. They don't seem too crazy about us either.

In the midst of this, I think of you every moment. This is sub-life, sub-human, and a million bright pictures of the United States keep coming in front of my eyes on an endless slide projector. Little things, just walking down the street with you, just going with you into that coffee shop on Madison Avenue near the Trans-Lux theatre, just the idea that you are beside me and everything is clean and we can finish the cup of coffee without anybody's yelling orders at us. All I am living for is to come back from this as fast as I can and marry you.

Write me at this address. I'll send you a new unit address when I get assigned. I hope everything is all right for you. You ask what you can do for me. Write me, Anne, write every chance you get. It doesn't have to be anything new or significant or chatty or anything. Just write.

With all my love,
Harry

Anne put the letter down. Her face was pale. I should have insisted that we get married, she thought. What use is it *not* being married? It's crazy not to be married to him now.

She closed her eyes, thinking of those few days' leave he had had at the end in New York. Her stomach twisted as she remembered how ready she had been for anything, everything, when they had embraced on those last nights. But he had acted almost as if he were already gone, as if any real sex had to wait until he got back. It seemed to her now that the days had been painful to him, as if he had already said good-bye to everything and hated to be reminded of how good it all was. And then there had been just that walk in the park, and his barracks bag in the taxi and neither of them able to speak as they rode through the city they had always known. And then she was walking away from the bus terminal on Eighth Avenue wondering if she would just topple into the gutter and die.

III

It was a clear, quiet, sunny morning. Harry stood at the back of the large crowd of replacements assembled in front of the big olive-drab administrative tent of the Second Division's replacement company. A corporal was calling out names, eighteen men at a time. The men would shuffle forward, the corporal would tell them which infantry company of the Second Division they were going to, and the eighteen men would plod off to the right, mount a truck, and be gone.

Harry had a carbine slung over his shoulder, and he gripped the wooden stock appreciatively. Most of the other men were carrying M-1 rifles, but they had issued him a carbine back in Pusan because he was a specialist. The light little carbine was the sign that he was not going to be thrown into a rifle company. It was his guarantee that he would not have to come to really close quarters with the North Koreans. Looking around at the goldish-red clay hills, covered with scrub, that formed this little valley twenty miles back from the front, Harry wondered if the Second Division had a mortar school around here somewhere. He had decided that he would end up in a regimental mortar company, or as an instructor at a mortar school.

"Following men for Charlie Company, Ninth Infantry," the corporal droned, not looking up from the mimeographed sheets in his hands. "Adams, Clarence H., Bruckmeister, Emil K., Carson, Jimmy D., De Luce, John, Encarnacion, Ignazio —" Harry pushed the front of his helmet back so that the morning sun could fall fully on his face, and shifted his pack on his back. It was a bore, waiting for these hundreds of riflemen to be sent forward before they got to the specialists. Of course, the riflemen had further forward to ride, so it was only fitting that they should start first.

" — Lorenz, Herman, Mason, Arthur M., Purdick, Harold, Raymond, Lewis J., Smith, Washington D. —" Harry blinked.

He could have sworn that someone had just called his name. Tentatively, not looking at anyone, he made his way around the edge of the green-clad crowd. The corporal was waiting while the group that had just been called moved off, making a clinking sound of rifle slings and entrenching shovels, towards the next truck.

" 'Scuse me, Corporal," Harry said. "Did you call Purdick? Harold Purdick?"

The corporal looked up, as if someone had asked him for a match when anybody could see he had both hands full. He ran a dirty forefinger down the line of names. "Yeah. Right here."

"Well, if it's for a rifle company, that's a mistake," Harry said politely, his tone inviting the corporal to share his amusement at the error. "I'm a counter-mortar radar technician. They don't have those in rifle companies. The only slot for me is in a regimental mortar company, or a mortar school or something like that."

The corporal stared at Harry, and then at the hundreds of men standing there waiting to be assigned. He jabbed his finger at Harry's name. "That's you, right? Purdick, Harold, Corporal?"

"Yes," Harry said pleasantly, "but I told you, it's a mistake. What's the use of sending me up to a line company where I don't belong? They'll just send me right back here."

One or two of the higher ranking replacements in the front of the crowd began to get the idea that Harry was arguing about being sent forward.

"C'mon, buddy," a sergeant first class said, "orders are orders." A few more men came out of their lethargy, and one called out, "What the hell, that's where we're all goin' — let's go!"

The man with the sheet of orders looked at the carbine on Harry's shoulder. "I can't straighten it out now," he said. "Tell them your story when you get up there. Maybe they'll let you come back on the same truck."

"Bye-byeee!" one of the men in the crowd shouted.

"Ah, screw you guys," Harry muttered, and strode off, his face red and angry, towards the truck.

The convoy of trucks carrying replacements for the Ninth Infantry Regiment stopped for a ten-minute break after an hour of weaving down the reddish clay road. They had driven slowly, honking aside water buffalo that were being prodded by Korean farmers wearing dirty flowing trousers and soft cloth shoes.

The green soldiers dropped stiffly from the open brown trucks, and made their way to the edge of the ditch beside the road. As if on command, two hundred fatigue trousers were opened, and two hundred men began to urinate.

Harry stood there relieving himself, the carbine slung over his shoulder, staring out over the empty harvested paddy fields. The still water in them stank. In the distance a girl in a pale lavender jacket and a full ground-length black skirt walked along the raised strip of earth separating two of the square watery expanses.

Then Harry heard the sound. It was like a heavy puff of air, like the sound of a man in the apartment above dropping a not-heavy shoe to the floor. Pumpf. Bumpf. Whump. The two hundred men all looked north as they buttoned up their trousers, and when they climbed back on the trucks no one looked at anyone else.

*   *   *

The truck pulled in at the bottom of a hill, and the first sergeant of Charlie Company came climbing out of a sandbagged hole that was the command post. Fresh trails led to the crest of the hill, where the company was dug in, facing north. An occasional shot banged out up there.

Harry was the first man off the truck. He got to the first sergeant just as the truck driver handed the squat little man the manila envelopes containing the records of the eighteen replacements.

"Sergeant," Harry said, "my name's Purdick. Please take a look at my records you've got there. You'll see I'm supposed to be a counter-battery mortar radar technician. I'm sure you don't have a slot for that in a line company. I'm supposed to go to the regimental mortar company." Harry held out his hand towards the driver, who was waiting to see if he could get out of here with his truck. "Just a second," Harry said. "I think I'll be going out of here with you."

The first sergeant rubbed a brown hand across his swarthy, mustachioed face. "Your name on this?" He held up the sheet of orders that the driver had handed him on top of the manila service record folders. Harry peered at it. His name was still there, just as it had been when the mineographed sheet started the trip up here.

"Yes, Sergeant."

"O.K." The dark brown eyes were expressionless. "Maybe you've been malassigned, but you haven't been misassigned. Now if you'll be quiet for a minute, buddy, I have a lot of things to do and I haven't much time to do it in." There was a short burst from a BAR on the crest. The sergeant waved at the truck driver that he could go, and the man took off for his truck on the run.

The square little sergeant looked at his new men. "All right," he said, "sit down over here by the CP. You don't have to worry about any rounds droppin' back in here. What you hear from up there is just some harassin' fire we're puttin' out. The party doesn't start until it gets dark." He ran his hand across his face again, while the men sat down, equipment clanking. "All right. Welcome to Charlie Company, Ninth Infantry. The general situation is that the gooks are hittin' us early every night with a sacrifice force while they hike their main force north. Then the next day we hike up the road until we start gettin' their sniper fire, and then we dig in. They wait until dark, hit us, and we go through the whole twenty-four-hour cycle again. Generally it's going very good. Very few casualties. We're making maybe eight miles a day. Maybe pretty soon the gooks — " he pointed his thumb over his shoulder, in the direction of the enemy, "really toss in the jock, and we can use trucks and go up maybe fifteen, twenty miles a day." He passed his hand across his face again, pointed up the hill, and said, "All right, go up that trail on the right. A sergeant will meet you up there and spot you into the platoons. If you hear a sound like a partridge breaking cover, hit the dirt."

Harry had just been put into a shoulder-high hole with a Pfc. named Quinn when there was a sound of loose dirt slipping over the rear edge. He turned and found a sunburned captain lowering himself into the hole.

"Sommers," the company commander said, holding out his hand. It was the first time an officer had proffered his hand to Harry. "I see they got an M-1 for you."

"Harry Purdick, sir." They shook hands.

"I guess you've met Quinn, here," the captain said, moving to the rear of the hole. "He'll show you the ropes. We're real glad to have you here, Purdick. We need every man we can get. This push is going real well, but we need every man we can get."

"Well, that's what I want to talk to you about, Captain." There was the snap of an enemy sniper bullet over their heads, and all three men ducked, though their heads had been well back of the parapet. "You see, sir, I'm a counter-mortar radar technician. I'm supposed to be with a regimental mortar company. I'm not supposed to be a rifleman." Another bullet whicked past.

"What kind of equipment are you talking about?" The captain's face was interested.

"Well, sir, you bring up two counter-mortar radar finders and set them up on either side of an area that's getting hit by enemy mortars. Then you turn them on and they start getting a side view of the trajectory of the enemy shells. Between the two of them you fix the position of the enemy mortars by triangulation, give the backward fix data to your own mortars and artillery, and that's it."

"Oh, yes." The captain nodded as he pulled out a pack of cigarettes and offered it around. Harry shook his head, and Quinn said in a stage whisper, "Take one for me." Harry did, and they all smiled. Quinn went back to digging a grenade sump in the corner of the hole.

"I know what you're talking about now," the company commander continued. "They don't work in Korea." He lit a cigarette. "I was talking to a forward observer about it the other day. They tried a couple of them on the perimeter at Pusan, but they could never get enough of an arc on the radar screen to figure out the position. With all these big hills, the gooks put their mortars on the reverse slope and by the time you pick it up on the screen it's too late."

"You mean they aren't using them in Korea at all?

The captain shook his head. "No." He exhaled smoke through his nose. "They packed up the ones they had and sent 'em back to the States."

Harry put his hand against the side of the foxhole farthest from the enemy. "Captain," he said, "I enlisted in the summer of 1945. I went over to Germany. I spent twenty-two months in the Army. The *only reason* they called me back in and sent me over here was to operate one of those machines."

The captain shrugged his shoulders. "I'm real sorry, Purdick. I don't doubt you've been screwed. But they've sent you to me as a rifleman, and I need riflemen. You'd better settle in. You want to get set good and tight on your side of this hole before they come tonight. Take it easy." He patted Harry's shoulder once, and slithered over the rear edge of the deep foxhole.

Harry stood watching the captain's bootsoles disappear. "What does he mean, 'before they come tonight'?"

The wiry pfc. stood up and looked around the hole like a

housewife looking for something in her kitchen. He took a rag that had a combination tool and three clips of ammunition spread out on it, and transferred it from the rear lip of the hole to a spot just to the right of where his rifle lay on the forward rim. "C'mere," he said. "Now go real easy." He waved Harry forward and they both raised their heads cautiously over the forward lip. Harry saw scrubby bushes, some barbed wire about seventy yards down the slope, a shallow valley, and a steep sandy hill on the opposite side of the valley. "They're over there," Quinn said as they lowered their heads. "On that hill."

"Right now?"

Quinn nodded. "Sometime after dark they're gonna try to get over here. Lots of 'em. They'll be running like ants, and screaming, but we've got trip flares out there, and machine guns all aimed in, and once we know they're coming, we've got parachute flares from our mortars." The freckled face smiled; he had a gold tooth, left center. "Once we got all that light on 'em, the artillery comes down on 'em, and our mortars, and then they run into the machine guns out there, and then at about three hundred yards we pick 'em up. We'll assign you a field of fire out there. All you've gotta do is keep putting in clips, aiming, firing, aiming, firing, and pretty soon the gooks are out of gas."

"Supposing it's not enough? Supposing they get right up here?"

Quinn shrugged his shoulders in a gesture that Harry found distressingly like that of the captain. Then he pointed at a row of grenades on a neat earthen shelf to the left of his rifle. "If you see me switch to grenades, you switch, too. If they get in close, those throw a lot more stuff around. We'll set you up with some on your side."

Harry bit his lip. "But look, supposing we heave a couple of those and they're still coming?"

Quinn shrugged his shoulders once more. "Purdick, then you just jump over the back and bug out to the bottom of the hill. And just don't get in my way when we're running down there."

*   *   *

"Knock that off!" A ghostly form moved in the darkness, and down the line there was the sound of a bolt snapping into place. Silence fell back on the line. Harry went through the motions of swallowing, but his throat felt like wool. It was a cold, clear night, and every pair of eyes in Charlie Company was probing the area of the barbed wire seventy yards out. Helmets would lift for a look at the grassy valley floor and the sandy slope less than a quarter of a mile away.

Harry's face twitched. He was sweating a sour scared sweat in the cold night, and the strange smell of it in his nostrils completed his fright. Beside him Quinn was chewing gum, the movement of his jaw the one motion in his helmeted silhouette.

Get me out of here, Harry thought. I'm not supposed to be here. I'm too good for this. He looked around in the night. All he saw was the man in the next hole checking to see that a grenade launcher was firmly on his rifle.

There was a wild yelling sound, many voices as if a mob of yammering madmen had turned into a quiet park, and then the American machine guns began firing into the valley, their tracers sailing out there red in the night. There was a pop-crack and Harry's head jerked up at the light that was sputtering from a silver parachute that was suddenly hanging over the scene. The flaming silver light grew. Harry looked down, and what he saw made his hands drop his rifle and clutch convulsively at the pebbles and earth on the forward rim of the foxhole. A huge gang of men was coming across the valley, shrieking.

They want to kill me, Harry thought. They want to kill me. He picked up the rifle, his breath coming in wild snorts, and got down into firing position.

"Not yet," Quinn said just as Harry started to squeeze the trigger. Harry blinked and put his eye behind the sight. He could see them bobbing uphill through the low bushes. Artillery was hitting them now, making big red blasts that faded from their outer rim back to the center. The earth was shaking like an animal.

Rifles started firing. Harry saw three heads coming up through the bushes under a flare, and fired. He picked up another target and fired again. Then again. All through his ribs and heart and head there was one choking instinct: to keep those screeching men away from him. He fired again, shifted his elbows slightly, fired again, and then squeezed off three shots at a bush that was waving from men jumping in and out and through it. His clip went tinging away, and he reached for the next clip that he had laid out to his right. It was there, and he slapped it down into his rifle, the bolt rode forward, and he thrust the rifle out again and fired at the first thing he picked up in his sights. Around him was a solid continuous tunnel of explosion, like an engine. He finished the clip, loaded again, put his cheek to the stock and his eye to the sight, and saw they were coming nearer.

You mustn't, he thought, you mustn't. He was cold now, moving in a controlled fury, wasting no motions, not thinking but moving his rifle, holding his breath, squeezing the trigger, reloading as if the rifle were part of himself. Three men were coming right up in front of their hole. He raised his rifle and as he did he heard Quinn's rifle go off like a machine gun and the three men went down kicking and clutching at the earth. Another one was coming up by himself, walking, holding his side and gasping. Harry looked at him in horror through the sights, at the way the man was holding his rifle as if it were a walking stick. He fired right below the center of the man's chest and the man straightened up with the impact, standing at attention on the slope, and then the rifles on either side of Harry went after the man and he backed down the slope, head pointing up as if looking at the stars, and disappeared still staggering backward behind a bush.

Silence. Quinn lit a cigarette. There was moaning and whimpering from the slope ahead.

Harry raised his head. The men in the next hole were stretching and moving around.

"Is that all?"

Quinn's cigarette was orange in the cold. "For tonight."

IV

Harry sat against a rock, his head down between his knees, gasping for breath in the chilly afternoon. He held his hands to his aching stomach, and felt the cramps twitching through his legs. They had just taken this hill in a series of sprints through low bushes and yellow loose earth, firing as they came. The other men had already recovered from the steep scramble. They had out their entrenching tools and were improving the holes from which the North Koreans had fled as they came over the crest.

He saw a pair of combat boots stop before him. Quinn was holding out Harry's rifle.

"Let's switch back," Quinn said.

"OK." He handed over the rifle beside him, and Quinn took it and walked off. Harry's sweaty face was a shocked, thoughtful mask as he watched the little Pfc. matter-of-factly starting to work on a hole that they would share. Halfway up the hill, Harry's rifle had jammed. The next thing he knew, Quinn had been beside him, handing him his own weapon that worked. Quinn had gone on up the hill like a rabbit, with enemy bullets spitting up dirt around him, armed only with Harry's weapon that would not fire back.

Harry forced himself to his feet. He checked his rifle. Somehow Quinn had fixed it. He moved towards where Quinn was in the waist-deep hole.

"You better get out your entrenching tool," Quinn said, heaving sandy earth over the edge of the hole with the little shovel. "They might be coming back."

"OK." Harry dropped stiff-legged into the hole, and began digging. He looked over at Quinn's impassive, freckled face. "I want to thank you for lending me your rifle."

Quinn looked at him, and then turned back to his shoveling. "Listen," he said, "you're new up here. You're doing OK. First day I got up here, a sergeant got hit, coming back to straighten me out."

Harry nodded. "Thanks, anyhow." They went on digging. Harry felt himself blushing. He remembered his thoughts the first night, I'm too good for this, get me out of here, it's all right for these peasants but not for me. Glancing about at the other green-clad men who were digging as the sun dropped behind the treeless steep hills, digging fast against the approach of night, he no longer felt among strangers.

V

They had spent most of the day probing the ridges of a valley off to the right of the main advance, and now they and the three South Korean soldiers attached to the squad were sitting in the hard-packed dirt barnyard of a Korean farmer. Harry lay with his back against the mud-and-straw wall of the house, listening to the ROK soldiers chatting with the farmer in this strange hook-sounding language.

"Here." A thin, olive boy named Interlicchio was leaning towards him from where he sat by one of the dark wood vertical beams set in the mud wall. "I got an extra Forever Yours. Ya want it?"

"Thanks." Harry took the candy bar, stripped the paper from it, and ate it mechanically. Staring at the Korean farmer in his loose-sleeved white shirt and heavy wool vest and long flowing trousers, he found himself wondering how the GIs appeared in this man's dark, shrewd, fathomless Oriental eyes.

I suppose we look like a bunch of men from Mars, Harry thought, feeling the stubble on his face and staring around at the helmets, the tall, whip-like radio antenna on the back of the man who was attached to them for these long reconnaissance patrols. The radio man was standing by a two-wheeled farm cart filled with straw, the black plastic telephone-like speaker in his hands and the green-metal radio slung on his back.

"Coach," he was saying into it, "this is Right Hand. Over." The long aerial waved above him in the late afternoon sun.

I wonder what the hell the farmer makes of that antenna, Harry thought. Probably thinks the guy is talking to himself.

"Ya always thinkin', uh, Purdick?" Interlicchio said.

"I don't know." Harry shrugged his shoulders. These days, moving forward in what was apparently a very successful offensive, he often thought of his father. A thought was trying to break through, a thought that his father had taken the attack almost to Japan before he was killed, and now for some reason it was necessary, five years later, to take the fight on past Japan.

But why? Harry thought. I mean, I know the North Koreans attacked this place, but is it just an eternal march to the west? The other day he had seen a man from the Ninth Cavalry Regiment. On his regimental insignia was a mounted Indian, because the Ninth Cavalry had fought Indians on the plains as America expanded West.

And the Indians are supposed to be related to the Japanese and the rest of them out here, Harry thought. The First Cavalry Division fought the Japanese all through the Second World War, and pushed 'em back to Tokyo, and now they're up here, pushing back Koreans. A hundred years of fighting Indians.

A picture of his father rose in his mind, his father in San Francisco at Christmas of 1944. His father had been a lieutenant commander then, a naval historian attached to the staff of Vice-Admiral Lincoln Schwimmer, on leave before the last big series of attacks in the Pacific.

Instead of the Korean barnyard with its few scrawny chickens running about, Harry saw again beautiful San Francisco, the city rising in pastel ridges of houses, golden slopes, and all of them together, walking around, chatting excitedly — his father, his mother, Bill and himself. Dinner, fumbling with chopsticks and laughing in Chinatown, and one night, New Year's Eve, when his mother and father had danced at the Mural Room in the St. Francis Hotel. They had all been staying at the St. Francis, and that was the first night he had tasted champagne. He was just eighteen, and he sipped champagne and asked Bill whether he liked it, and Bill said no, I don't, and Harry said, that's good, I don't either. But mostly he had watched his mother and father dancing. It was the first time he had seen them together since he was fourteen years old, and, watching them dancing, watching his mother's arm around his father's neck, watching her heels move obediently backwards as his dark uniform trousers moved forward on the dance floor, for the first time he had understood that they were not just Dad and Mother. They were a man and a woman, and once they had not even known each other, once, incredibly, they had even gone out with other people before they met. They were a man and a woman, and they had made him, and the thought had been like seeing a miracle, even though he understood it all in principle.

"C'mon," Interlicchio said. He shook Harry. "We're movin' out."

CHAPTER SIX

Bill Purdick sat in the back of the classroom in Langdell Hall, hoping that his name would not be called in this first-year law class in Torts.

"But my dear sir," the white-haired professor was saying to the student who was currently on the griddle, "suppose that we agree that the defendant was negligent in cutting down the tree so that it fell on his neighbor's car. How could he possibly be held responsible for the fact that his neighbor had the trunk of his car filled with blasting caps for a construction job, and that they went off and knocked down everything in sight?"

Bill smiled weakly. It was a game, it was a game that interested him and at which he wanted to do well, but this morning he did not feel very much like playing. He had found a letter from Harry in his mailbox on his way out of the dormitory to come to this class, and now he was trying to read it while attempting to maintain the same expression of cutthroat interest that came naturally to every other face in the hall. They were watching a tennis game in which at any moment a new student's name might be called to return the professor's serves.

Bill shook his head as he reread the brief paragraph in which Harry said that he was way behind the front working as a maintenance man on the same machines he had been with in Germany. There were no details, and somehow it was not like Harry to pass so quickly over the details of what he was doing. The return address, Company C, Ninth Infantry Regiment, did not sound much like a maintenance unit. Bill's lips pursed as he read the closing sentences. "You again make the wild suggestion that you should quit law school, enlist, and come over here and be in this thing too. If there is one thing I want you to do, it is *to stay out of this*. In the first place, it is a mess. In the second, it would drive Mother crazy if you got in it too. In the third place, some outfits are already in Seoul and the word is that we may have this thing wrapped up by Christmas. If we do, I might be able to get back by the time the new term starts in February. Now wouldn't you look like a chump lying on a rifle range down there at Fort Dix just about the time everybody else is getting out? And don't think they wouldn't keep you in for a couple of years to occupy this godforsaken Korea; that's just how I ended up in Germany. *Stay put*."

"Mister Purdick, *Palsgraf versus Long Island Railroad*. Please state the case."

Bill's face reddened. All the other students swiveled their heads towards him, many of the faces betraying a hope that he would mess it up.

"In this case," Bill said, his hands shaking as he grabbed the onion-skin paper on which he had briefed the case the night before, "plaintiff was carrying a paper sack containing fireworks, although these were invisible to the railway company's employee who helped push him aboard a crowded passenger car."

II

Harry came limping up the darkened street in Seoul, looking for his outfit, which he had been told was billeted near the railroad station. A sniper bullet had cut through his right buttock six days before when they had been cleaning out a town to the southwest, and now he was being returned to duty.

He turned the corner, and stopped at what he saw before him in the moonlight. Standing alone and apart from the shattered ugly little houses was a massive Oriental castle. Even in the silver night the red of its walls and the gold of its trim were visible.

The great roof ended in an elephant tusk sweep against the cold night clouds.

Harry advanced towards it, his helmeted head tilted back and a boyish expression of wonder and delight upon his newly thin face.

"Halt!"

Harry froze in mid-step. Two MPs coverged on him, one shining a light in his face. "OK," one of them said. Harry looked at the boy, whose horn-rimmed glasses emerged from a warm parka of the type that had not yet been issued to the infantry.

"What is this building?" Harry asked.

"It's the old South Gate of the city. They used to have a wall, now all they've got is the gate." The young MP peered at him through his glasses. "Why do you want to know?"

"I don't know," Harry said. "Beautiful, isn't it?"

Both MPs stared up at the wood and stone and brass, and Harry looked up at it again. Then he turned. "Where's the First of the Ninth?"

"Right down that street."

"Thanks." Harry walked away. About fifty yards further on across this open, crater-marked area, he turned and looked back at the beautiful proportions of the great structure. The MPs were gone, and Harry stood looking at it until his teeth began to chatter in the cold.

III

Constance Purdick had come up from New York to Cambridge for the week-end to see Bill. Anne had walked over from Radcliffe to join them, and they were sitting in a cafeteria just off Harvard Square. Each had brought a packet of letters from Harry, and they were reading excerpts to each other. Two days before, the United Nations Forces had entered the North Korean enemy capitol of Pyongyang, and Constance had also brought with her yesterday's *New York Times*, which was talking about the war in the past tense.

"Listen to this," Constance said across the plastic-topped table. "The Communists *had* used at some time during the war a total of twenty divisions. *Had*."

Bill nodded. "Looks like it's all over but the shouting."

Anne lifted a cup of coffee with a hand that was trembling from relief. "Today's what?"

"October twentieth," Bill said.

Anne smiled and looked from one of them to the other. "Wouldn't it be wonderful if he could be home for Christmas?"

IV

"I don't want you to make this patrol, Purdick," Quinn said. As he spoke, there was a clatter of small-arms fire up the valley. "That shot in the ass is still bothering you, and this is gonna be all night, and moving a lot."

"Look," Harry said, "I might as well — "

The tall, solemn boy named Interlicchio put his hand on Harry's arm. "Ya doin' ya share, Purdick."

Harry stood in a corner of the musky farmhouse, watching Tommy Quinn pull on a cigarette as he briefed his squad by lanternlight before they pushed off. It was just a month since he had spent that first night in the foxhole with Quinn, but Quinn had been jumped up to sergeant from pfc. in those weeks of the big push north. Now the Ninth Infantry was engaged in fighting a sideshow war with guerrillas that were harassing the supply lines of the American units which were pushing towards the Manchurian border.

"Now look," Quinn was saying, "we've got to get an SOP

about these gooks that come in to surrender with their rifles still slung on their shoulders. There's no use killing 'em if they want to surrender, and there's no use getting hurt if they just want to get close enough to take us out with 'em."

A thoughtful, tender expression filled Harry's face as he looked at these ten men who were going out into the night. At twenty-three, he was the oldest man in the squad. These boys were ordered to kill in the morning, and around the fire at night they shared with each other snapshots of their dogs and their girls, their high school buddies and their cars.

"Now for the ROKs," Quinn said, his gold tooth flashing in the shadows as he pointed to the three South Korean soldiers attached to the squad. They were nicknamed "Red," "White," and "Blue." "Now you, Red, you stick with me, uh?" Quinn's arms flapped towards his side expressively several times. "Right next to me, uh? Somebody try to surrender to us, you tell 'em drop their guns, *then* come in with hands up. Got that?"

The biggest of the Korean trio grunted that he understood, and Quinn looked at him dubiously.

Interlicchio shrugged his shoulders as he seated a clip in his BAR. "Whattaya gonna do, Sarge?"

"All right," Tommy Quinn said. "Saddle up. Purdick, you make sure nobody steals our sleeping bags, and we'll see you in the morning."

"Right, Sergeant," Harry said. They filed past him, each man giving him a brief encouraging nod or pat on the back as if it were he, rather than they, who had something to face.

V

Anne darling,

I had completely forgotten it was my birthday. Then that morning, Captain Sommers, the company commander, sent for me. I couldn't imagine what it would be about, and he handed me a cigar and told me that my records showed I had just turned twenty-four. Then the mail clerk gave me the packages from you and mother and Bill. The slippers you sent me are great, and soon I hope to be in a place where I can use them a little more.

Then by coincidence we had what was undoubtedly the most unusual birthday party of my life. That afternoon eleven of us were out walking around the hills outside of a town called Pugwon, and on our way back in we found a farmer who had some ducks in his yard. I think I told you about our three ROKs, Red, White and Blue (a ROK, the saying goes around here, is a gook who's pointed the other way), and, through Red, we opened negotiations with the farmer. The only thing he was willing to give us twelve ducks for was a pair of combat boots. Fortunately we had just been issued our shoepacs, a winter boot, which were back at the company, so one intrepid soul took off his lighter-weight boots. He was already wearing the super-heavy ski socks that were issued with the winter boots, so he made it back all right on the frozen ground. (The farmer, incidentally, killed the ducks by snapping their heads off in his hands — I don't mean just wringing their necks, but actually snapping the heads off.) Then our scrounging committee got to work with its usual resourcefulness, and we got some Army lard in five gallon square tin cans, dug a hole in the ground, got a fire going, skinned the ducks, rolled the ducks in flour, pepper, and salt, dropped them into the lard, and, when they were cooked, pulled the ducks out with bayonets and ate them. (More and more guys are throwing away their bayonets, incidentally. That should give you some idea of how close we all feel that this thing is to being over.)

The Second Division, to which my maintenance outfit is attached, has been securing the rear areas, more or less fighting a war behind the one that is in the news, but now we are being brought forward and the word is that we will all start off for a march up to the Yalu within a few days, just to nail the whole thing down. MacArthur says he hopes to have some troops back in Japan by Thanksgiving, and the great majority of us out of Korea by Christmas. That suits me fine. I've had every possible benefit, if there are any, that I could get out of this experience. I've seen how an army operates in a war, and I've learned an awful lot more respect than I ever had for the average American. My outfit has had a relatively easy time of it since I joined it, and now I want to get the hell out of here and marry you at our earliest convenience. Don't get the idea that cooking a lot of ducks in a hole in the ground is really my idea of a big time; it's just that it's a lot better than a lot of other things around here. You needn't save the recipe for the ducks. I don't think we'll have eleven children, and even if we do, I hope they're never outdoors so much that they get as hungry as we do here.

Thanks again for the slippers, darling. Write every chance you have.

With all my love,
Harry

VI

The morning light filtered through a cold gray mist on the hill, and Harry stretched in the hole in which he was on guard. A smell of C-ration soluble coffee drifted up from the platoon command post. In the next hole over he could see Interlicchio's long form, the olive skin and Florentine-coin profile lighting up with the quick Korean dawn.

Below, the valley was still.

"That's one thing I gotta say for you, Purdick," Interlicchio's sepulchral voice said into the coming sunrise.

"What's that?" Harry asked, pleased.

"You can do with very little sleep."

"Oh."

There was a rustle of canvas and Tommy Quinn came crawling out from under a shelter half that had been rigged over the far end of the hole. "Another day of hiking north," Quinn said.

"You think we're gonna stay on this hill? You're crazy." He grinned and waved his arm dramatically in the direction of the distant hills. "On to the Yalu! Everybody get your ass on up to the Yalu!"

Interlicchio looked thoughtfully at Quinn. "If you wasn't such a good sergeant, you'd make a real bad general. Right, Purdick?"

"Sure," Harry said, smiling.

"I was talking to a guy," Interlicchio said, staring accusingly at Quinn. "Guy said you had a soft job back at Pusan, you volunteered for this."

Quinn shrugged his shoulders. "I was in Graves Registration. Started getting to me. You know something? I don't like working with dead people."

Interlicchio snorted. "Just give me the chance, any day."

Quinn climbed out of the hole. "I mean it. They give you a mattress cover full of pieces, you're supposed to put it in a box and send it back to somebody in the States. Listen, you think a stiff looks bad out here — you know something? The way we got 'em, you couldn't be sure of who was who."

"How about dog tags?" Harry asked, checking to see that his own identification tags were around his neck.

"They get blown off the guy, or like a lot of guys he was carrying 'em in his pocket because they gave his chest a rash, and he loses 'em, or some damn thing." Quinn threw back his arms, and breathed deeply in the dawn. "A family back in the States, they've got maybe a seventy per cent chance of getting back who they think is in that box." He dismissed the topic with a wave of his arm. "On to the Yalu! Saddle up! Get ready to move out!" He disappeared down among the other holes that were his responsibility, cheerfully shouting in the dawn.

Harry gazed down the slope, watching helmeted heads popping up from holes as Quinn passed by. In the reddening light, men climbed stiffly from holes and began helping each other fold canvas shelter halves and roll up sleeping bags. Like a little family, they began visiting back and forth between holes, lending each other ammunition and tools, getting ready for the day's march. He stretched. The wound in his right buttock was aching, but he had never felt more alive than in this sharp sunrise. Glancing over at Interlicchio, he saw that the grave-faced boy was feeling this same strange well-being.

Interlicchio shrugged his shoulders happily and said, "Whattaya gonna do, uh?"

CHAPTER SEVEN

"G<small>ODDAMN</small>," Interlicchio said, "even cranberry sauce." He followed Quinn and Harry through the lightly falling snow. They had their weapons slung over their shoulders, and their mess kits held the Thanksgiving dinner they had just been served. Harry had his canteen cup full of hot coffee, and an apple in one pocket and an orange in the other. The smell of the hot turkey and sweet potatoes and mashed potatoes and giblet gravy was making his throat do painful things, and when Quinn set his connected metal dishes down on the fender of a truck he hastened to put his own beside them. Interlicchio stood his BAR against the truck and placed his mess kit on the flat hood.

"Wait a minute," Quinn said. Interlicchio looked over at him, his steel knife and fork poised to go at the food, and Harry's helmeted head turned and he looked at his squad leader in surprise. "This is Thanksgiving, isn't it?" Quinn said. "How about giving a little thanks? You want to say it, Purdick?"

"You go ahead, Sarge."

"All right. Take off your helmets. Bless us, O Lord, for these and all Thy gifts which we are about to receive from Thy Bounty. Through Christ Our Lord, Amen." He made the sign of the cross, as did Interlicchio, and Harry mumbled "Amen."

They began eating. After a minute Interlicchio turned his head, looking down the road to the rear. "Do you hear that?"

"No," Harry said firmly, popping a rapidly cooling biscuit into his mouth. He didn't care what was coming up or down the road; he was going to finish this miraculous meal.

"Sounds like a buzz saw," Quinn said between bites.

"Nah, it's a couple of cats, fighting," Interlicchio said, still staring into the gray veil of snow.

"Sounds as if there're some drums in there, somewhere," Harry said, and took a sip of the steaming coffee. Suddenly, out of the snow, came four men abreast, marching as if on parade, swinging their arms stiffly. Behind them came another four, and another, with strange spikes sticking up behind them. A great snarling filled the whirling snowy air, and drumbeats smashed against the trucks.

"It's bagpipes!" Harry said.

"Band and drums — !" a huge voice in a strange accent thundered as the lead men passed the Regimental Command Post, and the American colonel and his staff came skidding out into the snow, buckling on their pistol belts as they rushed to the side of the road to return the salute.

"Goddamn," Interlicchio whispered, "they're wearing skirts."

The kilted pipers passed the gaping GIs, and then the Scottish infantry came out of the snow, in baggy battle dress, a long line of men on either shoulder of the road, little different from an American unit trudging forward to the jump-off line.

"How about an orange, buddy?" Tommy Quinn said, and handed the one on his steel dish to a red-bearded sergeant.

"Thanks, lad," the man said, and disappeared in the snow.

Another Scot looked at the overflowing metal dishes, the turkey and mince pie and cashews and apples. "Bloody amazing," he called over his shoulder. "Eat like this all the time, do you?"

II

"I'll relieve you," Quinn said in normal conversational tones. "Go get some sleep." Harry jumped at hearing a man speak so loudly at night in a foxhole, but then he remembered that the fighting was over.

He stood beside Quinn for a minute as Tommy laid out his

weapon on the edge of the hole and felt with his hands in the darkness for the grenades. The company had dug in on this ridge above the Choktong River, south of the Yalu, but everyone was just going through the motions. Lighted cigarettes could be seen twinkling along the ridgeline. The rumor was hot and heavy that the ROK army would relieve, and that the Division would be heading south any day now, for Seoul and then home.

Harry looked once more at the big dim hills to the north into which the fleeing, shattered North Koreans had made their final retreat. Then he made his way to the part of the hole over which he and Quinn had stretched their shelter halves. The snow was not falling now, but the bitter blue winds tossed about the grainy white patches on the slope. Harry dropped to his knees, pushed his rifle in ahead of him, and crawled in under the closed-over part of the hole. Then, sitting on top of his sleeping bag, he took off his winter boots. He slid into the sleeping bag, arranged the blanket that was over it, and curled up one corner of the poncho below it to tuck his rifle in beside him. Harry looked out at the legs of Quinn, standing guard, and tried to calculate when he would have to come on again. The orders were that only one in six men had to be on guard, so he might be able to sleep through the night. He stretched, pulled his pile cap over his ears, and was asleep.

There was shouting, and bam bam, and Harry was out of his sleeping bag in his ski socks, out from under the covered half of the hole, his rifle in his right hand, no helmet on his head, flinging himself into firing position beside where Tommy Quinn was already blasting away. A flare went off, and the hair on Harry's hands froze at what he saw. It was impossible to see any water in the broad flat river, because it was filled with men wading across it. As far as the eye could see, to the left and the right, the river was filled with these men, and big additional columns were waiting patiently on the other side for their turn to get into the water and come across. The ones already across were coming up the slope at a slow jog. There were no open spaces; it was all just men, three or four hundred deep, coming on. There were bugles in the frozen air, and a high-pitched yipping sound from thousands of throats.

The artillery woke up and big bright blossoms began to explode in the carpet of men that were coming up the hill, but it made no difference. Tracer bullets went winging down the slope, but they made no difference. There was a clanging sound in the air, like cymbals, and the bugles kept sounding up and down the oncoming line. More columns were appearing across the river, trotting down to the edge.

Quinn had his squad leader carbine on full automatic, the brass cartridges spattering out as the weapon went off like a string of firecrackers. Harry kept aiming into the middle of that oncoming front rank, waist high, and squeezing as fast as he could. There was no possibility of missing.

"Better switch to grenades," Quinn gasped. Harry snatched one, pulled out the pin, and hurled it down the slope with everything he had. He did not wait for it to explode, but grabbed another, pulled the pin and threw, and then another.

"Let's go," Quinn's voice said, and Harry grabbed his rifle and was out the back of the hole, sprinting with only the heavy ski socks on his feet. There were other Americans ahead of him in the night, jerky-moving figures running on and beside a trail through the patches of snow. Then they were over the crest and down a trail, crashing through bushes, down into a valley, and there was the narrow road that served as the Main Supply Route. Other GIs were running down this road, ripping out onto it from bushes, gasping, panting, and then they were all running down the road almost like a column in formation, jogging down the snowy road, not looking back, gradually becoming calmer as the sounds of shooting ceased behind them, but not looking back, not stopping.

About two miles down the road there were trucks, lined up

and pointed in the same way the soldiers were running. The Transportation people were standing there, waving the men to the head of the convoy. Harry flung himself panting into a truck, and when it was full, the truck took off.

"Awright," a voice said as the trucks pulled into a frozen field by a crossroads at dawn. "Infantrymen get off here."

Harry climbed down. The six-week-old wound in his right buttock was aching from the run from the enemy. He had no boots, and the heavy ski socks were wet and stiffened from the snow. He had no helmet, and no cartridge belt. He had a rifle but no ammunition. Looking around him, he saw that almost no men had hung onto their weapons in their flight.

*   *   *

Harry came limping through the woods on this new ridgeline, peering down into one hole after another in the fading afternoon light. They had told him that what was left of his battalion was over here. So far he had seen everything else, men from the Twenty-Third Infantry, and men from the Twenty-Fourth Division which had been in another sector altogether.

"Hey, don't look any farther," a young lieutenant called. "I can use another rifleman right here."

Harry looked down at the helmetless lieutenant. "If you don't mind, sir, I'm supposed to report back to the First of the Ninth."

The lieutenant shook his head. "They're wiped out, soldier."

"Well, if you don't mind, sir, I'll just go on looking a little longer."

The lieutenant nodded. For a moment Harry was afraid the officer was going to cry. "Good luck."

Harry nodded and went on. He looked down at the winter boots that he had taken off a corpse three hours earlier. Coming through these woods, he had outfitted himself very well. He had a helmet now, and gloves, a cartridge belt, bandoleers of ammunition for his rifle, and even a .45 pistol. He had opened a can of C-ration corned beef hash that he found, licking the frozen cylinder of hash until it thawed, and now he walked on, a somewhat different man from the one he had been twenty-four hours before.

Tommy Quinn looked up from changing a dressing on the side of Interlicchio's throat. "You look a little bit like a guy named Purdick."

"Hello, Sarge."

"C'mon in. This hole's big enough for three."

Interlicchio's dark face lit with a smile, and he opened his mouth to say something.

"Talkin's no good for you now," Quinn said to him. "Interlicchio says he's glad to see you, Purdick."

"Me too," Harry said, lowering himself gingerly into the waist-deep hole. "Where's the rest of the squad?"

"I don't know, and believe me, I looked." Quinn shrugged his shoulders as he started to pack up a dead medic's musette bag after treating Interlicchio.

"Just what was that last night?" Harry asked.

Quinn looked startled. "Where the hell have you been? It was the Chinese."

"The *Chinese?* What are they doing in this war?" There was a sudden shush-shush-shush *braaam* and Harry was lying slammed against the front of the foxhole. His helmet was off, blood was coming from a point between his left shoulder and his neck, and he was alternately laughing and crying.

Quinn reopened the musette bag he had used to treat Interlicchio, and began pulling off Harry's clothes to get at the wound.

"It's not bad, Harry," he said quietly.

"I can feel it isn't so bad," Harry said, still alternately laughing and crying. "I just think this is a hell of a way to welcome a guy home."

*   *   *

They had beaten off some probing attacks during the night, and at noon a major came around.

"You look armed to the teeth in there," he said cheerfully, nodding approval at the newly deepened and camouflaged fox-hole, the way in which it commanded the slope, and the two light machine guns that Interlicchio and Quinn had taken from other, now silent, holes. "They're going to try to get the Division out to the south, and we have to hold the door open as long as we can." He noticed the makeshift sling on Harry's left arm. "What happened to you, soldier?"

"Mortar fragment got me between the shoulder and the neck, sir. My arm's sort of stiffened up."

The major nodded. "Soldier, get yourself back to the Division CP, if you can find it. They'll take you out with the walking wounded."

"Sir," Harry said, "I can still help — "

"You can't do much with one arm," the major said. "Get your ass out of here."

"Sir," Harry said, "these men and I — "

The major's light blue eyes passed over Harry as if he were not there, and fastened on Tommy Quinn. "Sergeant, I make you personally responsible for starting this man south."

"Yes, sir."

The major walked off. Harry looked down at the stock of one of the light machine guns.

"OK," Quinn said. "You better leave your rifle here. Just keep that .45 warm in your right-hand pocket."

Interlicchio gave a barking cough. "Wouldn't ya know it," he said, speaking for the first time since he had been hit in the throat. "Charlie Company gets the stick. Rearguard, for chris-sake."

"You better get moving before the major comes back," Quinn said to Harry. "You got enough food in case it takes you a while to hike down there?"

"Look," Harry said. "Don't worry about me. You guys are the ones — "

Interlicchio put his hand on Harry's arm. "Ya too sensitive, Purdick. Now get outta here, you heard the major."

Harry looked at both of them, and then away, into the snowy birch trees. He took his right glove off with his teeth and proffered his hand to Quinn.

"So long."

"So long."

Interlicchio waved Harry's hand away. "Purdick, all it needs now is violins. I'll see ya in a coupla days, for chrissake. Ya make me sick with this big good-bye."

"Sure." Harry suddenly understood. He patted Interlicchio on the shoulder, and worked his way up out of the snowy hole.

*   *   *

They had slapped the benches of the big truck up against its sides so that as many men as possible could be packed in to stand up in back. Harry's expression was a mixture of scorn and fear as he saw how the other walking wounded had managed to huddle into the center of the truck, leaving the less wary to be elbowed to the sides, where they would be the first to intercept anything flying through the air.

Everyone was yelling, and every kind of engine was turning over. Almost the entire Division had been ordered to retreat down this road, and vehicle after vehicle was pulling out of this assembly area.

There seemed to be no pattern to these convoys. Truck after truck, tank after tank, rolled out with men hanging all over it. Harry looked thoughtfully at the empty road leading off from this assembly point, at right angles, to the west. Nothing was moving west; everything was going down this road to the south. Harry sighed. He supposed they had their reasons.

The truck jolted across frozen ruts, passed an MP who was waving them on frantically, and started down the road. Harry looked back at the MP in his parka, catching a flash of the man's horn-rimmed glasses. It was the same MP who had stopped him in front of the castle-like South Gate that night in Seoul. It seemed a thousand years had passed.

The truck came skidding to a halt. Harry heard a machine gun hammering from the slope to one side of the road, and scattered American fire answering it.

"Get out get out hit the ditch!" The walking wounded piled off the tailgate of the truck, slipping and falling on the frozen ground and patches of ice, limping and hobbling as they rushed towards the ditch. Harry judged the distance to the ditch, saw two men lie twitching where they had been hit, and ducked instead under the rear axle of the truck. He lay there, his cheek pressed into the earth and his right hand covering his face. The Chinese gun was a .50 caliber, and the bullets came in with a great howling snap snap snap. Two bullets hacked into the truck body with a thank-bwonk, and Harry heard the truck's engine start. The truck rolled away from him and he was left lying flat in the center of the road.

"Hey the truck! The truck!" The walking wounded came scrambling back out of the ditch, chasing after the truck, but the driver had had it, he was not waiting for anyone. Harry lay in the road, his face that of a child realizing that he has been betrayed, and then the Chinese machine gun caught the men who were running after the truck and they became a group of broken faded green insects, lying in the road, feebly twisting an antenna here and there. He crawled off the road and into the ditch. There was a smell of gasoline and burnt powder and his own sour sweat of fear. Another, smaller truck came hurtling down the road, and the men who had not chased after their own truck when it pulled out now leapt to their feet and hailed this over-loaded truck. Harry stayed in the ditch. The truck slowed down, took three aboard, and then the men on it began kicking and pushing away the others crowding around. The truck gathered speed, breaking away from the men pursuing it, and then the Chinese machine gun found it. The truck stopped, paused as if taking a breath, and blew up in a column of rich yellow flame and silvery-black smoke. Burning figures leapt from it like flaming frogs, wriggled a few feet, and died.

Harry went on sitting with his back to the side of the ditch farthest from the road, hearing the Chinese gun firing over his head. He could see flames farther down the valley, and it occurred to him that what was happening here was happening all along this road. Another truck came past. As Harry watched from safety, the Chinese machine gun picked it up. The truck stopped, and the men in it piled out in a disorganized mob and came running for this ditch. The truck driver realized that he was better off driving on than standing in the road, and started up again. The men who had just thrown themselves into the ditch ran off in pursuit of the truck, and the Chinese machine gun cut them down as if they had all run over a rope tied across the road.

Darkness was beginning to fall. Harry sat there, oblivious to the cries for water, the cries for medics, the men leaping up to hitch rides with new vehicles coming down, sometimes getting a ride, sometimes getting shot down, sometimes getting back to the ditch to wait and try again. The idea of going out and finding that Chinese machine gun and killing it occurred to Harry, but he shook his head. There were grenades on the pack harnesses of some of the corpses around him, and he had an idea that he might just be able to silence that gun, even with one good arm and one stiff one, but he no longer cared.

With darkness there was a new and violent sound. The American artillery up by the rearguard was firing with an intensity that Harry had never heard before. A studious expression clamped his face. If they were still firing, it meant that there were still a few Americans, organized Americans, back where he had started this horrible ride.

Harry rose, keeping his head beneath the surface of the ditch. The night wind was like blue ice, and the wound in his left shoulder throbbed and the one in his right buttock ached. Slowly he walked along the ditch, standing more and more erect as the darkness fell. Sometimes his boot would step on a hand or an arm or a leg, and sometimes the thing beneath him would moan or twist. He kept moving north, ignoring the trucks still coming south in the darkness, not turning his head at any scream or skid or explosion or running or cursing or fighting in the darkness for places on the vehicles and their trailers. He did not know these men. They had never been introduced. He passed a flaming ambulance, the bodies of the men in the racks inside in bright black flaking-to-bits silhouette in the electric-white fire. Men wandered south in the darkness, calling the name of a buddy or a unit or for the Mother of God or Mama. Harry climbed onto the road, abandoning the ditch. As far as he could see, the Chinese were shooting at groups and vehicles moving south, not at one wounded corporal limping north.

A hand grabbed Harry. He saw the MP brassard, and found himself looking into the horn-rimmed glasses of the boy from that night in Seoul.

"You can't go that way," the boy said, as if explaining to a child. "The Chinks are coming that way. What do you think we're going this way for?"

Harry put his right hand into his pocket and slipped the safety catch off the .45. "I'm going to Charlie Company, Ninth Infantry," he lied. "They're in the rearguard and I have orders for them."

The MP's hand released Harry. "It's your funeral," he said, and hurried on.

It was absolutely still in the darkness at the assembly area from which he had started in the morning. At the snowy crossroads there were no MPs, no sentries, no vehicles. The American cannon had stopped firing half an hour before. The wind kicked bloody bandages and cardboard cartons across the rutted snow.

Harry paused under a waving pine, looking at the road leading west. The silence was the final chilling thing. He knew that it was the vacuum between the departure of one army and the arrival of another. Not even one straggler from the Americans; not yet the first scout sliding through the woods for the Chinese. But he could feel them coming in the forest, in the hills.

He had gambled and lost. Harry shook his head and stepped out from the concealment of the tree. He had to keep moving or he would freeze to death. He had to walk west down the empty road, down the center of the road, in plain sight, until those light tan dots slid out of the woods and took him prisoner on the road.

Harry took the .45 out of his pocket. That's all, brother, he thought, and threw it into a snowbank. He walked on, down the ghostly empty gray road, his face twisting. At one moment he was just hurting, flame in his shoulder and aching ice in his right buttock and stiff stinging where the wind lashed his face. Then he was hurting in a different way, humiliated and angry and impotent at all that he had seen, crying angry like a man who has just enough strength to rise again and again before a bully's attacks, only to be knocked flat each time he does. He could still hear echoing in his head the whimpering of those men on the road and in the ditch; he could see the lashing winter boots as the men on the trucks fended off the ones running to try to catch a ride. His face settled into a final tragic mask.

He heard a purring noise behind him; it became a metal heartbeat echoing off the snowy pines on either side of the road. He turned. Almost on top of him was an American half-track with quadruple .50 caliber machine guns mounted on it. There were men walking along in front of it with mine detectors, and others with rifles, their eyes scanning the forest. Behind the half-track came more men on foot in open formation, with rifles and carbines, and then a column of great dark cannon, all spaced and ordered and moving with less sound than one motorcycle.

Harry put up his hand, and a rifleman stepped up to him, covering him until he could see that this human being, whatever he was, was in no condition to hurt anyone.

"Get him on the Quad Fifty," a voice said. Harry was being lifted into the warm cab of the vehicle and someone was handing him a canteen cup that was warm, he could feel the warmth right through his frozen stiff fingers, he pulled the edge of the cup towards him, the curving metal lip was at his mouth, he tilted it, it was coffee, hot and sweet and good.

"What's it like down the other road?" the driver said to Harry.

"You made the right turn," Harry said. "Stick with this."

"Don't worry."

Harry took another deep swallow of the coffee. "Were you the guys laying down that barrage?"

"Right. That really buttoned the Chinks up. I think we got out just in time. They told us earlier not to use this road because it had refugees on it and we wouldn't get through, but they must've cleared out by now."

Harry tilted the cup up. "What happened to the First of the Ninth?"

"They didn't get out. They were right in front of us. They saved our ass."

Harry let the empty metal cup sit in his lap. "You don't mind if I get some sleep, do you?"

"Help yourself."

CHAPTER EIGHT

Harry sat at a small desk in what had been a dispatcher's office in the railroad freight yards at Seoul. It was night, and the December wind rattled the shelter halves that had been rigged over the window frames from which the glass had been blasted. The ten new men for whom he was responsible were sleeping on the wooden floor.

Harry looked down at the letters that had been delivered to him earlier today. There they sat, like communications from another world: Anne, frantic about the newspaper accounts of what had happened to the Second Division; his mother, saying she hoped his maintenance unit had been well behind the lines when the Chinese wiped out all those poor boys; his future father-in-law, saying that now this was an entirely new war. Clarence Wiley's letter said that surely the Army had had time to train up men in Harry's specialty, and that he thought it was time he went to Washington and looked up some of his World War II friends in the Pentagon with an eye towards getting him released "from a tour of duty you shouldn't have had to serve in the first place."

Harry had finished his reassuring replies to Anne and his mother, and now he looked down at the sheet of paper on which he was writing to Clarence Wiley. He pushed back the small round wooden stool on which he was sitting, and walked over to the pot-bellied stove in the corner. There was a bale of sand-colored summer uniforms sitting beside the stove. Earlier today Harry had seen the Quartermaster people burning ten-foot-high piles of summer uniforms before evacuating to the south, and he had told two of the new replacements to get hold of as many as they could, for fuel.

He picked the lid off the stove with the bayonet that was kept beside it. With his left arm, which was gradually becoming less stiff, he picked up a shirt and threw it into the fire. He had had no idea that cloth would burn so well, or smell so much like a garbage dump.

Harry put the lid back on the stove and walked towards the door. Pulling back the canvas that had been pinned over the shattered window frames, he looked out at the eerie lights in the cloudy night sky. All over the soon-to-be-abandoned city, piles of equipment were being burned, and from time to time there was a dull boom as something was dynamited. Occasionally there were even more distant sounds of the rearguard divisions, holding off the Chinese, as they fell back.

Harry returned to the desk in the corner. The new men were sleeping restlessly. He put his elbows on the table, and folded his hands, raising them to his chin. The thing that surprised him was that he still seemed able to function. For a couple of days, when he had first arrived here on that retreating artillery convoy, this one room had housed, very comfortably, all that was left of Charlie Company. Of the one hundred and forty men who had been on line when the Chinese hit, only three had been sitting in this room when he came wandering in. For two days Harry, as a corporal, had been acting company commander in this room, as they sat and waited for the other survivors. Three more men, including a sergeant, had come in during the next days, and that had been all. Then new men had started appearing; a new company commander, who had promptly made Harry a sergeant; new lieutenants; and finally these brand-new privates, fresh from the States and understandably scared stiff. There was no more Quinn, no more Interlicchio, no more Captain Sommers with his weather-burned face.

"No!" a boy said in his sleep, and Harry turned and looked at the young faces in the weak light of the lantern by which he was writing Clarence Wiley. The word was that they would go out by truck tomorrow to Chungju, a city sixty miles to the southeast, to stay in reserve and rebuild the Division. These ten men were his; he was their squad leader, their Quinn. He smiled as he thought of the awe in which they held him. He was their twice-wounded combat-experienced squad leader sergeant. They had even found out that he had been in Germany five years before; in their eyes he was an Old Soldier, and by the current standards of Charlie Company, he certainly was.

Harry picked up the ball-point pen, blew on his hands, and finished writing Clarence Wiley. "I appreciate the offer about the Pentagon people, but unfortunately there are not, after all, many men around here right now with my specialty. I will be breaking some new ones in, and after that perhaps we can reconsider."

II

"Anne," Mabel Wiley said, "all I'm saying is that I don't think you ought to look at articles like that. It just upsets you."

Anne threw down the copy of *Life* with the photos of the Marines fighting their way south out of the Changjin reservoir. She looked at her mother, and then she looked around the living room in New York, the scores of Christmas cards on tables and stuck in between the books on the shelves, the Christmas tree in the corner.

"What am I supposed to do?" she asked her mother, her voice trembling. "Pretend it isn't happening?"

"Anne, dear, I'm sure Harry wouldn't want you to get upset this way. He's not one of those Marines, dear. He's perfectly safe, he says so himself."

"How do I know he's safe?" Anne asked, her lip trembling. "If he's so safe, why do I have those dreams?"

Mabel picked up the magazine that Anne had flung to the floor. "Darling, it's perfectly *understandable* that you have those dreams. You're worried about him. I'm worried about him. We're all worried about him. But we can't just stop and do that and nothing else, and *neither should you.*"

"Give me the magazine," Anne said. She opened it and looked into the stubbled faces under the frost-covered helmets, as if they had something to tell her, as if she had something to tell them.

III

Harry breathed a sigh of relief as he led the patrol back in through an outpost on a slope outside of Chungju. Somebody from Charlie Company had had to make a patrol today, even though it was Christmas. The company commander had made the unassailable point that Harry's squad could use every bit of practice it could get while they were in this quiet sector, and off they had gone for a six-mile prowl paralleling ridgelines.

Harry stopped and let his squad pass by him single file, counting noses to make sure no one was floundering around in the thicketed deep snow through which they had just come. He smiled as he saw the happy expressions on their faces. They had opened their Christmas presents before they went out, and most of them had spent the six miles looking for the enemy, but thinking of home. Now they were headed for their Christmas dinner.

"Hi, Sarge." It was Carmichael, the youngest of his ten new boys, coming along second from the end of the line. Carmichael's mother had sent him a pair of ice skates for Christmas, and he had begged Harry to let him take them on this patrol. So pink-cheeked Private Carmichael had the blade of an ice skate sticking out of the big pocket on each side of his field jacket.

"How're you doing, Carmichael?" Harry said as the boy passed, and then he fell in at the tail of the line. Looking at them strung out ahead of him as they moved down the slope towards the dirty gray cluster of houses that was Chungju, Harry's face was thoughtful. He winced as Carmichael slipped on a patch of ice, righted himself, and strode on, trying to do his best. Carmichael reminded him of himself as he had been five years before, looking hopefully at a mirror in his *kasserne* in Germany, ready to annihilate each whisker as it appeared.

His glance moved to the backs of other young soldiers along the line, thinking of that moment this morning when they had opened their presents. One boy had received exactly one present, two worn one-dollar bills in an envelope from his mother.

"That's *real* nice of Ma," the boy had said in a Kentucky accent, meaning it. A boy from North Dakota had opened up a package containing a new pocket Bible. One young Negro soldier from the Virgin Islands had received nothing, but three of the other boys had gotten him into a card game before patrol briefing and deliberately let him win.

Suddenly, within a few hundred yards of a warm-enough billet and a turkey dinner, Harry was angry. As far as he could see from letters from his friends, everyone was going right on through college and graduate school as if nothing was wrong. He did not like the way in which this nightmare was reserved exclusively for the young uneducated poor. Fifty nations stood up there in the United Nations General Assembly and condemned aggression in Korea, and how did they implement it? They went down to a street corner and grabbed Interlicchio and gave him eight weeks of basic training and bye-bye baby.

Harry's mouth tightened. He was thinking of all the bull sessions late at night at Harvard. His college generation had believed that if ever there was another war, it would be over in five minutes.

"Clear the weapons, Sarge?" the boy in front of him asked.

"Right," Harry snapped, and went down the line, checking to see that the raw new boys had successfully unloaded their weapons before re-entering their billets on this Christmas afternoon.

CHAPTER NINE

"WHEN I want your advice," Harry whispered to Carmichael, "I'll ask for it." The pink-cheeked boy looked away, hurt, and the other members of the squad lay silent under the snowy bushes on the ridgeline, watching this suspicious-looking force that was bivouacked across the ravine. Harry looked again through the binoculars he had drawn at Battalion before they had started this reconnaissance patrol. The men under the trees three hundred yards away were wearing American uniforms, some with the big black shield of the Second Division on their left shoulders, but there was something about the way they moved, about the way they had laid out their simple camp under the low trees, that did not look right.

Harry marked the map that he had partly unfolded in his upended helmet, which lay before him in the snow. Then he motioned to the radio man who had accompanied them, and the man came crawling towards him, the big oblong olive box wiggling on his back. Harry took the black radio telephone that the man extended towards him, blew into the speaker, and said softly, "Lonely Heart, this is Valentine, over."

Battalion acknowledged.

Harry continued in low tones. "I am at co-ordinate Charlie-three, on the crest of the west ridge, facing east. Got it, over."

The telephone breathed metallically, "Roger, over."

"On the east ridge, I say again, east ridge, are approximately three to four hundred unidentified troops. They are wearing GI uniforms with Second Division patches. They are bivouacked under the trees from the east ridge down to the bottom of the ravine, over."

"Roger, wait one." There was a pause, and then the machine said, "We are checking this force out now. If Division says they aren't ours, we'll ask for air strike. Just hold there and observe. Stay off the air unless they move, over."

"Wilco, out."

Harry returned the hand-set to the radio man, and the squad lay hidden, staring at the men under the bushes across the way. They appeared to be sitting over there waiting for something, and Harry knew what it was: darkness. When it was dark they would come in, bypassing the forward outposts, their uniforms creating no suspicion when they were dimly seen along the roads leading into the Division's heart. Looking at these captured uniforms, Harry's eyes narrowed. These uniforms and M-1s and BARs had come from the bodies of men he had known.

"How long's it gonna be, Sarge?" Carmichael was whispering again.

"I don't know." If you want to do something useful, Carmichael, he thought, you better pray the Air Force hits the right ridge.

When the planes came, Harry did not see them any sooner than the Chinese did. The jets were just there, dropping out of a leaden sky way ahead of their sound, then the sharp pop of their machine guns, objects falling from the lead plane, and the Chinese camp suddenly exploded in a sheet of yellow flame that splashed uphill.

"Napalm," one of the boys beside Harry gasped. Harry had his binoculars to his eyes. The planes had rockets, too, and these were bursting and splintering trees. The Chinese were running wildly within their area, starting out on one side and dashing back as flaming gasoline jelly chased them with long bright fingers. Human torches ran screaming downhill through snowy bushes.

Harry put his glasses down. In between the howl of the jets

there was a rising crescendo of ground noise, the roar of flame and the shrieking of men.

"Battalion, Sarge."

Harry took the phone.

"Valentine, this is Lonely Heart. Strike is in progress, over."

"This is Valentine, I see it very clearly, over."

"Air Force liaison wants to know if you have any corrections before they make last passes, over."

Harry looked at the blackened hillside, the little roasted ants twisting on their backs. In a slow, dry voice, he said, "You are right on target. That force is at least seventy-five per cent casualty. Request permission to return, over."

There was a pause. "Everybody is very happy about this one. Congratulations and come on in, over."

"Roger, out." Harry handed back the phone to the radio man and looked at his squad. "Battalion thinks you're the greatest. Let's go back in." He had just decided to write Clarence Wiley and tell him to go ahead and talk to his Pentagon friends.

II

Bill sat in the cafeteria off Harvard Square, sipping a cup of hot chocolate and looking through the big plate-glass window at the people in the snowy street. Anne had called and said she had a particularly interesting letter from Harry, and here he sat, waiting for her to show up.

He grimaced as the bitter dregs of the hot chocolate touched his tongue, and stared again at the wind-bent boys and girls hustling through the snow. He knew better than to think that Anne had bad news for him about Harry, if there were any really bad news his mother would have heard it first and called him, but he could not rid himself of apprehension.

She just had a letter from him, Bill thought. That's all. There was a tap on the glass. Anne had come from the opposite direction, and was standing before the window, smiling her quick, shy smile, her hair snow-wet where it swept forward from under a scarf. Thick white crystals crusted the shoulders of her camel's hair coat.

"Hi," she said, coming through the door. "Terrific news." She divested herself of coat and scarf in quick, graceful motions, and was sitting beside him at the plastic-topped table, putting a letter before him. "Harry's going to let my father try to spring him out of there."

Bill let out his breath. The apprehensions were shadows, only shadows. "Great!"

"I know how Dad'll do it," Anne said. "He'll go on a real campaign. He'll go to Washington and perch on the corners of people's desks."

"I'll bet he will," Bill said happily. "What would you like? Coffee? Tea? Hot chocolate?"

III

"Don't bother me, Carmichael," Harry said to his fuzz-faced problem child as he motioned his men to climb into the back of the truck. "We can't stop now to look for your dog tags. Maybe somebody'll find them around the area while we're gone." He swung up on the truck, and stood looking at the Battalion Orderly Room tent while another squad climbed into the truck with them. Charlie Company was being detached to act as protection for the Fifteenth Field Artillery in something called Task Force Oscar. The artillery's mission was to support the Eighth Regiment of the Eighth ROK Division on a push north; Charlie Company's mission was to protect the American artillery in case the Koreans decided to retreat without letting them in on the secret.

A clerk came out of the Orderly Room tent, and Harry's heart missed a beat. The man was looking for somebody; in a moment it was clear that it was not for any of the lowly rifle-men on this truck. The clerk shrugged his shoulders, and went back into the warm tent. Harry shook his head. Ever since he had sent that letter off to Clarence Wiley, he had found plenty of excuses to hang around Battalion headquarters. Now they were being detached from the Battalion for this Oscar business, and if anything came through, a transfer, or orders to return to the States for a discharge, or even just a form asking him to give supplementary information, he would be miles from here. So far the only thing that had come out of that Orderly Room for him was that they had made him a sergeant first class, a reward for the air strike.

"You set there, Sergeant?" one of the new lieutenants said as he strode past in the snow, trying not to indicate that he was looking for his jeep and could not find it.

"Yes, sir," Harry said. What do you think we're standing here for, you meathead? He stared at the lieutenant's back. We'll always be ready twenty minutes ahead of you.

"Move out!" somebody was yelling. Harry sat down on the icy bench in the truck and watched the dark olive tents of Battalion recede in their white setting.

CHAPTER TEN

Harry grinned as he sat in a corner of the Korean farmhouse listening to the Belgian machine gunners chatting in French. Task Force Oscar was turning out to be a good deal. For a week now they had been in the same reserve positions in front of the American artillery, hearing their shells whooshing overhead as they supported the slow ROK advance. At the rate the ROKs were going, it would be another week before the artillery would have to shift forward.

But the best part of it was this every-other-day trip up to this farmhouse, nearer the front, which was the command post of the Belgian machine gun company in direct support of the ROK infantry. "Sergeant," Harry's new company commander would say, "I'm taking the jeep up the road to coordinate with the Belgians, and I want you to ride shotgun. Don't forget your mess gear." They would tear up the snowy road in the falling blue darkness, and arrive at just about the time the Belgians were ladling out a twenty-gallon kettle of the most delicious soup Harry had ever tasted. The Belgian mess sergeant was a huge red-faced man with blue eyes and a gold handle-bar mustache, who laughed uproariously in the same way that other men breathed. The Belgians were cheerful, professional, fatalistic, and hospitable, and, gnawing on a piece of fresh French bread and wolfing down steaming onion soup or pea soup or potato soup, it was easy to put a lot of things out of mind.

"Merci bien, monsieur," Harry said in his prep school French as the Belgian mess sergeant forced half a long loaf of bread on him for the return trip. The Belgian giant thought Harry's

French was the cream of the jest, and produced a jug of red wine and forced that on him as well.

Goddamn, Harry thought, this is more like it.

"I'll have to inspect that wine there, Purdick," Harry's captain said, and so they departed down the road in the jeep, passing the jug back and forth in the fifteen-below-zero cold. Harry kept thinking of how stunned his men would be when he came in with enough wine left to give them a taste. He could see Carmichael's boyish face breaking into a brilliant smile, and hear him saying, "Hey, Sarge, what next?"

Harry heard the pop of a flare, and came out of his sleeping bag with his boots on. He slapped his helmet on his head, buckled on his cartridge belt, tucked some C-ration cans in his pocket, and then, and only then, equipped to retreat, did he stride to the front of his covered-over foxhole and peer out.

The hills were white and silent under the silver flare, but up the road he heard the Belgian machine guns hammering into the night.

"Sarge, that means the Chinks already got through the ROK front, huh?" Carmichael asked as he studied the fireworks to the north.

"Yes, if you want to call it a front," Harry said, but even as he stepped out of this hole and checked the other holes, he could sense that the boys were steady. "Tie your bootlaces!" Harry called into the night, and dropped on one knee to do the same. Then he stood on the packed-down snow between two holes, his hands to the brim of his helmet, shading his eyes from the light of the flares overhead as he tried to see what was coming off. The Belgian machine guns were going all out.

There was sudden small-arms fire from the rear, right from the middle of the artillery positions which Harry's company was supposed to protect.

"People on the hill to the left! People on the hill to the left!"

Harry looked. Right across the up-slanting snowfield, a

long column of sand-colored men were jogging diagonally down the hill, deliberately giving the guns of this company a wide berth, heading to hook into the artillery positions from the rear.

Harry's new platoon leader lieutenant came skidding through the snow. "Take up positions to the left along the road!"

"Yes, sir," Harry said. As he got his men out of their holes and following him through the knee-deep snow to take up a position to block any further Chinese columns trying to out-flank them, he saw out of the corner of his eye that some vehicles were coming down the road from the holocaust up forward, coming fast in their retreat. Just as he got his men into position under the snowy bushes beside the road, another Chinese column five times their number came over the hill, not two hundred yards away, heading right towards them.

"All right," Harry said. "Fire when I fire, keep it up until you hear me yell to bug out, and then bug out right with me."

"Hey, Sarge," Carmichael muttered as he put his M-1 to his shoulder, "what next?"

II

"We're going to stay here until evening," Harry said. "Then we'll try to move again." It was a strangely beautiful sunrise in these snowy hills, with a lavender light rolling down the slopes. It was silent now after a night of confusion, of Korean refugees climbing out of this country through snowy trails, of ROK soldiers matter-of-factly wading south through the snow, of gun-fire suddenly exploding from exactly the direction in which everyone was fleeing. In the thrashing slippery darkness Harry had lost his men, and now he and Carmichael and two artillery-men were huddled in the lee of a big rock atop a snow-covered hill. In the distance, on other hills, there were tiny knots of GIs and ROKs trying to make their way out. From time to time a group of fifty or sixty or eighty Chinese would appear in the dawn, methodically combing the hills to find them. It was a panorama of large groups hunting small groups.

Harry closed his eyes and leaned his helmeted head against the side of the big rock. It was that surprise November Chinese offensive all over again.

If I get out of this, Harry said to himself, I am going to shoot off my big toe and see what they do about that.

"Sarge!" The whisper was electric, and Harry came awake from dozing against the side of the rock. It was mid-morning. Fifty yards away, two Chinese in their vertically quilted sand-colored uniforms were standing on the edge of the ridge. As Harry watched, his finger moving to the trigger of his weapon, the Chinese moved towards the rock, motioning up and down with their burp guns.

"Maybe they want to surrender," Carmichael whispered.

"Don't be ridiculous," Harry said.

"Hell," one of the two artillerymen said, "I'm not going to surrender to just two Chinese."

Just then a lone ROK soldier appeared, wandering up over the ridge at a different angle. The Chinese did not see him. The ROK cut loose full automatic with his carbine. One Chinese went down, the other swung and fired his burp gun at the ROK, and then both the ROK and the second Chinese went down. All lay still.

"That does it," Harry said after a stunned silence. "There'll be more of them coming up right behind where those two came from." The four of them half-stood, half-knelt, crouching behind the rock, their weapons leveled over its top. Harry rested his weapon on the cold dark-gray surface, and rubbed his hands. He looked down at his raw, bruised whitish-reddish hands. Good-bye, he said.

A long line of Chinese appeared from left to right over the ridge, running, fanned out, the flaps of their winter caps swinging back and forth against their cheeks. They started firing, and the four Americans blasted back. The Chinese came on at a steady jog, firing, some dropping, but coming on.

"Ark!" Carmichael spun and slid into the snow. Another American went down. Harry fired and then squeezed again. His weapon was empty. He threw it down and leapt back from the rock with his hands up. The Chinese stopped firing and formed a semicircle in front of the rock. Something slammed into him; it was the other surviving American, lurching with his hands up.

A Chinese stepped to within five feet of Harry. He had a pistol with a big wooden handle. With his other hand, he motioned Harry and the other man to come out from behind the rock. The Chinese opened his mouth slightly, making a noise like "chr, chr." Now other Chinese were behind them, keeping them covered.

The Chinese lieutenant turned, giving rapid instructions to his men. The sand-clad men started moving around, shooting in the head everyone who was still down, Chinese, the lone Korean, and Carmichael and the other American.

Harry looked up at the sky. The morning was turning sunny and warm. The lieutenant, who had pivoted half away from Harry while giving more instructions, turned. His face was expressionless. Then he looked into Harry's eyes and made a sweeping gesture with his pistol, including the dead khaki sacks in the snow, the lightly wounded Chinese who were hobbling off supported between their comrades, and screamed at Harry. It was in Chinese, but it was, "See what you did!" Then he advanced on the American next to Harry and kicked him in the groin. The man fell to the ground and vomited. He kicked for Harry's groin. Harry twisted away, and saw the boot clearly, a light canvas boot with a heavy brown leather toe. The kick hit Harry's hip bone. The Chinese shrieked with rage and then another kick hit just beneath it as Harry fell, and another kick hit his ear. Harry lay there feeling his ear both numb and stinging, and blood coming down the side of his face. Then the Chinese kicked him in the stomach and Harry doubled up, the wind knocked out of him, gasping and crying for breath.

The lieutenant turned and said something more to his men. His voice was calm again, his face without expression. Several Chinese gathered about the lieutenant, and they nodded as he gave them orders. Then the lieutenant motioned to the Americans to get up. Harry rose, holding his stomach. The other man could not get up, and they pulled him to his feet, where he hung between two of the Chinese, still doubled over.

They're bigger than I realized, Harry thought numbly.

There was a sound of cannon to the south. All the Chinese turned their heads and listened thoughtfully.

Don't tell me we're counter-attacking so soon, Harry said to himself.

The lieutenant motioned for Harry and the other man to take off their boots and field jackets. As Harry did, he watched them working over the two American corpses. They took their jackets, pile caps, helmets, weapons, boots, and then took everything in their pockets.

A Chinese soldier came up to Harry and began taking everything out of his pockets. Harry stood still, scarcely noticing. He was watching them take Carmichael's wallet from his pocket as he lay in the snow, and then the letters that Harry knew were from Carmichael's mother. The dead boy's helmet had fallen off when they had shot him in the face. His hair moved in the breeze.

The lieutenant stepped up to Harry, and reached for his throat. Harry leaned away, but the lieutenant grabbed at his dog tags and indicated that he should take them off. He stood looking at them for a moment, curious, and called over one of his men. They studied the dog tags, laughed, shrugged their shoulders, and then the lieutenant let the small metal identification plates drop onto the rock beside Carmichael's body. He motioned to Harry and the surviving artilleryman to follow him, and the entire party moved off.

Harry looked back just before he took the first step over the ridge. The rock stood silent in the sunny morning. A Chinese prodded Harry with a burp gun, and he moved over the edge, his heavy ski socks sinking deep in the snow. Ahead of him, the lieutenant still had his pistol in one hand, and Harry's winter boots dangling from the other.

Five steps further down the slope, Harry stopped as if lightning had struck the sunny hilltop. He had just remembered that Carmichael was the one who had lost his dog tags, and that his own identification tags were now lying next to Carmichael's empty-pocketed body.

There was a blast of gunfire, coming nearer, and a Chinese pushed Harry with the flat of his hand, hustling him down the slope. Harry's head twisted backwards as he moved reluctantly downhill.

Wait a minute, he thought, his mouth working soundlessly. When our counter-attack gets up here they're going to think that's *me*. He half-raised his hand towards the back of the lieutenant who had his boots.

Wait a minute. Just give me a minute, just let me go back and get those dog tags. You've got to let me explain, got to let me write a letter to Anne and let me explain.

The Chinese behind him pushed him again with the flat of his hand.

*　　*　　*

Harry sat in the snow under pine trees, shivering as he massaged his bare feet. He had wrung out the heavy socks and now he had one under each armpit, trying to warm and dry them before he put them back on. They had been sitting here for hours on this bank of a frozen creek. Every few minutes the Chinese would bring in another group of prisoners, and there were now about two hundred officers and enlisted men in various stages of undress, sitting silent and dazed as the light left the sky. Some still had their wallets and watches and wedding rings;

others had been picked clean. Harry had seen a few men from
his company, and, a few yards away, the big Belgian mess sergeant was propped against the base of a tree. He was not laughing now.

Harry saw sand-clad legs approaching him. One Chinese was
carrying a burp gun, and the other, wearing sand-colored riding-
breeches but otherwise indistinguishable in uniform from the
enlisted men, had a sheet of paper in his hand. He thrust it in
front of Harry. On it were pictures of the insignia of every rank
in the United States Army, from five-star general to pfc. The
man pointed at Harry, and Harry pointed at the stripes of sergeant first class. The man nodded, and the two pairs of legs
moved on to the next man. Harry felt like asking them to give
him back his boots and field jacket.

A man near Harry stood up to try to move around to keep
himself warm in the cold, and promptly a Chinese carrying a
rifle with a long bayonet on it appeared and indicated unmistakably that he should sit back down in the snow. Harry looked
around the area. Under a tree fifty yards away, three older Chinese officers, without insignia but with those padded riding
breeches, were huddled over a map. From time to time an officer would come up to them, report, and stand at attention as he
received further orders. Large bodies of Chinese passed north
through the woods just beyond, silent faded tan ghosts coming
to life now that night was falling. The sound of guns seemed to
be coming closer.

I'll bet he's a general, Harry thought, looking at the oldest
of the three senior officers. He has the look. I'll bet this is a division command post. Harry put his socks back on, shaking his
head as he thought of an American division command post, complete with sandbags and olive tents and radio vans and vehicles
of every description racing in and out. Here it was just three
men under a tree.

"May I have your attention." The prisoners looked up. On

the opposite bank of the frozen creek a Chinese officer was standing, trim and erect.

My God, Harry thought, that's just the phrase American officers use.

"I am Comrade Liu," the officer said in perfectly accented English. "Let me congratulate you on being liberated from this dreadful and unfortunate war. You have fought bravely and we respect your courage. Let me assure you that you are safe now and will be cared for by the Chinese People's Volunteer Army. Soon you will return to your homeland and loved ones."

The men on the bank stirred and sat up straighter.

"I realize that you are aware that you have been used as cannon fodder by the Wall Street warmongers. You are innocent. We have no bad feelings against you. You are members of the working class in the United States. The Chinese People's Volunteer Army is friends of the working class of the United States. We have a lenient policy towards you, and your personal possessions and valuables will not be touched." Harry thought about his boots and field jacket, and the men going through Carmichael's pockets, taking the letters from his mother.

"Unfortunately you have been presented to date with only one side of the story. My superiors are happy that you have been captured, so that they have an opportunity to present their side of the story. For this reason we are going to march you to places where we have educational facilities established. We have no desire to keep you separated from your loved ones, but until we can arrange for your exchange we want to present you with our side of the story."

Harry saw a movement out of the corner of his eye. To one side of the group, two squads of Chinese soldiers were moving into place. They had horseshoe bedrolls slung over one shoulder and tied at the waist on the other side, and they looked ready to move out on this march.

"When you arrive at these schools, you will be kept there long enough to learn that Wall Street was the true aggressor in this dreadful and unfortunate war. We will prove to you conclusively that the North Koreans were not the aggressors, as I know you have been taught, but that South Korea attacked North Korea, aided and abetted by the ruling circles in the United States." The light was fading now, but the khaki uniform glowed bright on the snowy bank. "This school will last only a very few months. At that time, you will be sent back to your families who are waiting for you." Harry looked at a young boy who was sitting near him. The boy's mouth was open, and he was nodding.

"In conclusion," the officer said, "I ask for your cooperation on the march north. You must cooperate with your guards in staying off the trails in daytime. The United States Air Force has no further use for you prisoners, and will kill you if they see you on the trails. When you get to the schools, there will be warm buildings, warm clothing, and good food, but unfortunately there is not much food here because the capitalist airplanes have destroyed the crops and warehouses here in the south. Now, we need twenty volunteers to drive trucks we have captured."

Hands went up everywhere. Goddamit, Harry thought, we don't have to help them that much.

"Very well." Guards had selected twenty men to drive trucks and were leading them off. "Now we must organize for the march north. I want to see you form in squads of fourteen men, leading man facing me." Everyone scrambled from the snow, and there was a rush forward to be leading men. The boys in front stood at attention, looking across at the officer above them on the opposite bank, standing tall and wanting the approval of this sharp officer who was going to get them home.

"Very good," the officer said. "One of our soldiers will be between every two of your squads." There was some movement at the right forward corner of the square of shivering Americans, and then, squad by squad, they filed off on a trail uphill through the dark woods.

III

Clarence Wiley sat in the Pentagon office of a brigadier general whom he had first met here in Washington during the Second World War. The general was in the Judge Advocate's office and normally had nothing to do with the recall of inactive reservists or the duty assignments of soldiers, but Clarence had been in here so often recently that wheels were beginning to turn. Clarence had learned during the war that the way to get something hard done was to keep coming back until it was less onerous for the people to do the favor you wanted than to see your face once more. On this theory, he was coming to Washington once a week, taking a room at the Mayflower, and had begun a campaign to get Harry transferred or discharged. Thus far the campaign had taken him into the offices of one senator, two congressmen, three generals, and five colonels. This particular general, however, seemed to know some telephone number that could, in a matter of minutes, tell him exactly where Harry was and whether his status had yet been changed. When he had been in here yesterday the report was that orders were being cut that would transfer Harry back to Japan, and that a further disposition of his case would be made there. Now, ten minutes after he had arrived this morning, the general had stepped out of the room to make the daily, confidential, out-of-channels call.

Clarence sighed. In the past ten days he had learned that Harry had been in the thick of it, not in any maintenance outfit as his letters had claimed, and while he thought it was good of Harry not to want to worry anybody, it made it all the more imperative to get him out of there.

The general came back into the room. Usually when Clarence made a motion to rise the general gestured for him to stay put, but this time the man's hands remained at his sides. Clarence rose, and then he saw that the man's face looked quite different.

"No," the general said. "Sit down, please, Mister Wiley." The general backed up against his desk and sat against its edge.

"What's happened to Harry?" Clarence snapped.

"He's reported killed in action. Just came in."

"It can't be," Clarence said. "You sent out the orders — "

The general cleared his throat as he looked down at the green carpet on the floor. "There's no mistake. I'm terribly sorry."

Clarence rose. "Are you absolutely certain?"

The general nodded. "We have the body. I'm terribly sorry."

Clarence nodded. "I'll have to get back to New York."

"Yes." The general picked up Clarence's overcoat and helped him into it. "I don't know if — we can expedite this. If you want the funeral in New York."

Clarence turned, uncomprehending. "What?"

"If you want him brought back, I think we can fly it here."

"Oh." Clarence nodded again. He looked down at the hat in his hand. "Yes. Thank you."

IV

I don't know how long they think we're going to be able to do this without any food, Harry thought slowly as he rose to his feet. For three nights they had marched in single file on narrow trails up and down snowy hills, and during the days they had slept, curled in the snow like animals, under trees and bushes. Now, shivering and wincing at how his stiff heavy wool socks rubbed the raw red skin of his feet, he came shuffling through the trees, ready to move out at about three in the darkening afternoon for the fourth night's march without boots.

The guards were taking up their places between each squad

of fourteen men on the trail. Harry brushed past one of the Chinese, looking at that bedroll tied around the man's body. He knew that in that bedroll the guards carried a bag of meal that the GIs called "bug powder." The word was that it tasted like bad peanut butter, but right now the thought of bad peanut butter was enough to make Harry's stomach flail demandingly against his sides like a pile of snakes. He had had no idea that the stomach could make such active protestations, like a separate human being down there, churning and twisting and growling and knifing pain inwards. Until he had been without food for four days, he had never known his stomach. Faint, his head aching, his eyes dull and the corners of his mouth puckered, he stepped into his file of fourteen faded-green men. He felt like crying, but no tears came.

Something twinkled above the hill in the afternoon air. Harry looked up and saw a silver plane dropping on him as if it were being thrown. He dove off the trail on the downhill side, rolled through the snow, found himself on his feet again and smashing downhill through frozen thickets. He tripped, felt an icicle-covered branch whip his left eyeball, and went down just as there was a great hollow boom. Heat smacked the back of his neck. He turned. A huge yellow yo-yo of flame was rolling down the hill, leaving a string of fire behind it. Heat hit his face in a sudden slap, and he threw his hands before his face. Another plane trapezed in from another direction. Harry leapt behind the trunk of a small tree. Looking up, he saw the Air Force star on the side of the propeller-driven plane, and flame along its wings as its machine guns strafed. Suddenly another plane was coming in yet another direction. Harry rotated around the tree trunk, huddling against it. He heard the snap of bullets and saw geysers of snow leap everywhere. There was another boom, heat falling on him, and screaming. Looking up towards the trail, Harry saw Americans running, their clothes afire. There was cursing, another hot boom and brilliant flame everywhere, sweat pouring from him, more bullets, thick black smoke wiggling through the snowy bushes. A man came sprinting downhill, on fire, great gobs of the napalm jelly hanging on his head and shoulders, turning into fire. With one despairing shriek the man dove into snow, hoping the snow would stop it. The snow withdrew instantly in every direction and he was left, a burning long pile of ashes, lying in the center of a circle of last autumn's leaves. Harry kept rotating crouching around the tree trunk as the glaring silver planes came in from every different direction, bullets chipping frozen bark that hummed like daggers. Then it stopped.

Harry climbed uphill through smoke, past burning remnants of men. A smell of gasoline and roast meat hung in the air. On the trail, some of the Chinese guards were trying to grab the surviving Americans, who were wandering around in circles, to make them stand still. Other guards were tending to their own wounded, under a tree.

Harry stood on the trail, his hands at his sides and his face twitching as the Chinese herded more and more men into position to continue the march.

"Right through," a man said. Harry turned and looked behind him. Two GIs were supporting a man between them. The man's trousers were down, and yet another man was tearing off part of the wounded man's long winter underwear to bind up a big, bloody bullet hole in his thigh.

"You bet your ass I'm gonna continue the march," the man's ashy-blue face was saying. "You see any field hospital around here?"

A Chinese officer came down the line, one he had not seen before, and Harry blinked. The man was wearing an American officer's dress green blouse thrown over his shoulders like a cape. On it were four or five rows of American ribbons. In the Chinese officer's hand was a fifth of whiskey. The man came up to Harry and offered him a drink from the bottle. Harry stared at it. It was Seagram's 7 Crown. Then he stared at the officer. The man was sober.

"Are you a hallucination?" Harry asked.

"Yes," the man said, and vanished.

V

Harry coughed, a harsh bark that twisted him as he lay in the snow. His left eye was swollen shut from the ice-covered branch that had lashed it when he had been running from the American planes the day before.

The Chinese guards were moving about now, ready to get them going again in the darkening afternoon. Harry's one good eye looked down at his hands. He could see clearly the outline of the bones in his hand between his wrist and his fingers. The skin between them was sinking down every day. It had been five days without food. The headaches and constant craving pains had passed, and what he was seeing now was only a dim, flickering, black-and-white approximation of life.

A Chinese came along the path, stopped in front of where Harry and the others were sitting or lying in the snow, and put down two pails. The buckets were fifteen yards from Harry, but he smelled food instantly, was on his feet, and running towards the pails. He fell to his knees before one of the pails, drove both hands into the soupy grain, and clapped a handful in his mouth. Just then an elbow knocked him aside, and a new man was bent over it. Then everyone was there, tripping each other, shoving, kicking, green-clad arms striking like snakes for the two pails.

Harry crawled back on his knees among the fighting men. Staying low, ignoring a kick in the ribs and another on the thigh, he slipped in under them, rose with all his strength, jammed both hands into the bucket and then let himself be pushed away, looking only down at the purple, white-streaked grain in his hands and eating one waxy handful, standing at the edge of the fighting, grunting, cursing mob, then the other handful. Licking his frozen dirty hands, with a springier stride, he turned and waded back into the fight again.

They moved out twenty minutes later. Harry could see better, even though the afternoon was steadily darkening. The knives of hunger were back again. The handfuls of food had revived him enough to be hungry.

CHAPTER ELEVEN

The coffin, draped in an American flag, was coming down the aisle at the end of the service on the shoulders of Harry's friends from college. Ahead of them marched seven soldiers from Governor's Island. Behind the casket came Constance Purdick, leaning heavily on Bill's arm, her face a shadow under the dark veil. Behind them was Anne, walking between her mother and father. She had only a light veil from a black hat, and her head was tilted slightly backwards. Her shocked mask of a face stared over the red-and-white stripes running towards her from the flag over the casket, and her eyes fixed on the throbbing impulses of daylight at the Gothic arch of the church door.

Constance looked at the boys and girls standing in the pews, friends of Harry's and Bill's. Everyone in the church was young. She saw the shining heads of hair, and her eyes came back to the slowly swinging end of the flag as it bridged the two rows of gray-suited young pallbearers.

It was bitterly cold at the cemetery overlooking the Hudson; the minister kept on his overcoat as he gave the final benediction. Anne stared at the flag-draped coffin poised above the sharp-cut hole in the frozen ground. She kept breathing deeply, afraid that something was choking her. All she could think of was that she and Harry were in a car somewhere, and that he was driving around turns, up and down, his arms moving, hands on the wheel, and she was beside him.

The soldiers who had accompanied the casket were folding the flag; one stepped forward to Harry's mother, saluted, and handed her the folded banner. Constance Purdick gave the boy a smile, and said quite audibly, "Thank you for everything you've done." Then the soldiers were at salute. There was an oily whirring noise and the casket sank into the grave.

II

"Man, I don't like that one bit," the deep, tired, hoarse voice beside him said.

"It's awful." Harry was standing at the doorway of the ten-by-fifteen-foot hut into which the Chinese had herded them for the daylight hours, and he and this huge Negro from Philadelphia named Pete Murphy were looking at something. The Korean villagers were tossing pebbles at two GIs who had been put into a pig pen for the day. This morning, when they had arrived in this village, the two boys had seen two honeycombs on a ledge by a farmhouse kitchen, and had grabbed them. The Chinese guards had retrieved the honeycombs and, considering that they spoke no English, had done a remarkable job of sign language. Pointing to a bag of grain that had been acquired in yesterday's village and which the prisoners had taken turns carrying all night, they had indicated that the people of Korea were already sharing their food with the prisoners, and that this barbaric act of theft had to be punished. Then they had put the prisoners in the pig pen and left them to the mercies of the villagers, while taking away the bag of grain, which could be cooked later in the day and dished out, as usual, before they began the night march.

"I don't think those pebbles are hurting them much," Harry said, "but goddamit." The Koreans, adults and children, were tossing the pebbles through the slats of the pig pen, which had been emptied of pigs for the occasion.

"We still in South Korea, aren't we?" Pete Murphy asked.

"Sure." Harry looked at the villagers. Some of the children appeared to be really enjoying it, but the older ones were doing it mainly to show the Chinese that their hearts were in the right place. At night when they passed through a village, the villagers would turn out and taunt them, but sometimes an old man would stop his jeering and slip some tobacco leaves to a GI.

"I don't like it one bit," Pete Murphy rasped. Harry shrugged his shoulders and turned back into the crowded hut and the stench of his comrades. The overcast that marked the end of a Korean winter afternoon was hanging over the village, and he knew that soon they would get their handful of cracked corn or sorghum or soya beans, and move out again on the march. It was time to put together his footgear.

Harry sat down among the men lying on the dirt floor. A Chinese guard passed the hut and motioned to Pete Murphy to get back from the doorway. Watching the long slung rifle on the guard's back recede, Harry thought about how the sign language did not seem to work both ways. Time after time they had held their hands to their stomachs and pointed to their mouths, trying to explain that one handful of soggy boiled grain was not enough to last them twenty-four hours. The Chinese did not even shrug their shoulders. They looked blank.

"How them elegant boots doing for you?" a boy from Kentucky asked, propping himself on one elbow.

"Fine," Harry said, and managed a smile. He had lost track of the date, but he counted the nights. They were just about to start Night Eighteen. Six days before, with the soles worn from his ski socks, wearing the ankle part of his socks around his bleeding feet in the snow, he had found a pair of straw sandals in a root cellar where they had been kept for the day. The next evening, in an old shed, he had found a ski mitten that someone in the group had left behind. The discoveries had sent him into an orgy of ripping and binding. Now he had socks, made by tearing up parts of his long winter underwear. Over them were the straw sandals. He had split the top of the ski mitten, and it sloshed along as a precarious overshoe to his right foot, the outside of which no longer had a sense of touch.

A sudden pain in the pubic hairs made Harry wince and curse. He pulled open his trousers, found the louse with his crab-like body just turning red from the blood he was sucking, and killed it.

There was a sudden limping rush to and through the doorway. Harry got to his feet and followed, taking off his winter pile cap with the canvas outside and wool lining. Advancing to the pot of lukewarm water with pellets of grain sitting at its bottom, he turned his cap inside out. Using it as a bowl, he plunged it down among the thin grains of millet, scooping as many of them from the bottom as he could. Then he made his way back inside the hut and sat down against the wall. Looking down into the soggy hatful, he saw the bodies of maggots, milk-colored little worms an inch long and big around as a pencil.

Harry stared to one side. The other men were systematically picking the maggots out of their food. Harry looked down again. The floating maggots were bigger and richer than the few grains of millet. He closed his eyes and began eating it all with his fingers. The millet tasted like sand, and the maggots tasted like glue. Harry did not stop until he had turned the cap back right side out and licked even the taste of food from the dirty canvas.

III

"Well, I'm sorry you don't think it looks like him," the president of his undergraduate club at Harvard said to Bill.

"I'd know who it was, I guess," Bill answered. Several of them were standing looking at the hastily commissioned portrait done from a photograph of Harry. It had just been hung above the fireplace in the club's living room. Beneath it in a glassed-over velvet box were Harry's decorations. There was the blue enamel Combat Infantry Badge with the silver rifle on it and wreath around it, and then the ribbon and medallion for being in service during the Second World War, just at the close before going to Germany; the medal for the Occupation of Germany, the medal for Korea, the United Nations medal for those serving in Korea. And the Purple Heart, with two little twists of metal on it, one for his second wound and one for dying.

"Sure," Bill said. "I guess it looks like him." He turned, nodding politely, and went out into the snowy Cambridge afternoon.

IV

The cramp hit Harry, and he stepped off the trail, just managing to get his trousers down as the twentieth dysentery spasm of the night hit him. He lay gasping in the snow, twisted to one side, dripping mucus and blood into the white cold powder. After a minute he rose, dizzy, and pulled up his trousers with a great effort. Men were passing, their heads down against the wind. Harry stepped back on the trail and began an odd, hobbling double-time to try to get back up to his place in the line.

V

Anne sat in the class at Radcliffe, her hand holding the pen and taking notes. She had always been good at being able to take lecture notes while thinking of something else, but now she was absolutely spectacular at it.

She tried quite consciously to bring herself back to the class, to these references to Gladstone's views on education. You must keep busy, her mother had said. You must stay at Radcliffe. You must keep busy.

I am busy, Anne said, watching her hand hold the pen and write. Look at me. See? I am busy.

VI

They got to their feet at the end of the ten-minute break they took every two hours. Harry bent down to check that everything around his feet was bound as firmly as possible, and then he noticed that the captain who had been ahead of him in line was not getting up.

"C'mon," Harry said, shaking the man's shoulder. "Let's go."

"I'll catch up to you," the man said.

"No, no," Harry said. "Come on with us now." He looked at the man's bearded filthy face in the moonlight.

"You go ahead," the man said in a weak voice.

"C'mon. You can walk. You walked this far. I just saw you walk right to here."

"Go ahead. I'll be all right."

Harry bent and tried to lift the captain, but he was far too weak. His hands slipped from the man's snow-wet jacket. Forms were beginning to move past them now, their feet soft hisses in the snow. "Listen," Harry said urgently, "you can make it."

"No, I can't." The captain shook his head. "My insides are gone. Too sick. Too sick."

"Listen. Do you have a girl? Don't you want to get back and see her?"

"I've got a wife and two kids."

"Well, God," Harry said, grabbing the man's shoulders and shaking them, "you've *got* to make it!"

The man lay back in the snow and looked up at Harry, an almost baby-like expression on his face. "I think about them all the time."

Harry looked down at the captain, measuring his size, knowing that he did not have the strength to drag him fifty yards. Shapes pushed past him in the snow. Harry gazed down at the man's boots, and then he knelt and began to fumble at the frozen laces.

"No." The man looked away from him like a virgin afraid, turning his head against the snow.

"Then get up."

"I can't."

Harry pulled off the man's boots and walked on, one dangling from either hand as he hobbled back to his place in the line.

VII

"You're kidding," Bill said slowly.

The doctor at the recruiting station shook his head. "You have flat feet."

"I *can't* have flat feet," Bill said. "My feet have never given me the slightest trouble. I've played football and basketball and baseball — I've never had any trouble with my feet."

The doctor smiled. "Ever done much hiking?"

Bill's face was red. "No," he said angrily.

The doctor slapped a rubber stamp on Bill's enlistment forms. Reading it upside down, Bill could see the "NOT," and he knew the other word was "Accepted."

It was snowing as he came out into the slushy March streets of downtown Boston. He felt an urge to laugh. Here he was, unable to concentrate on anything at law school, wanting to enlist, wanting to kill the people who had killed Harry, and they would not let him do it. Life would not let him do something hard; it would only let him do something like sit over books that had lost meaning for him.

There was a bar on the corner.

CHAPTER TWELVE

THEY WERE PASSING through a North Korean village in the middle of the night, and the villagers were standing laughing as these bearded scarecrows filed through. Heavy wet snowflakes were falling.

A young man approached the GI who was limping through the snow ahead of the big Negro, Pete Murphy. As Harry, coming along behind Pete, watched, the young Korean held out a handful of tobacco leaves to the struggling American, saying "tombi, tombi," which they had learned was the word for tobacco. The woozy GI limped out of line, extending his hand, and the Korean spat in his face. The young Korean turned towards the less venturesome villagers who were hanging back nearer their houses, wanting them to appreciate what he had done to show off for them. Pete Murphy stepped out of line, and hit him so hard with what was left of his two hundred and fifty pounds that the man went skidding on his back through the wet snow until he came to rest against the mud wall of a cottage. The big Negro stepped back into line and moved on without a sound.

*　　*　　*

"Look," the boy from Georgia who was in the Signal Corps whispered during a break. He produced a length of rubber-coated wire from his pocket. "Watch careful, hear?" Harry and Pete huddled close to him in the moonlight, both turning their heads to see if one of the guards stationed between groups was coming along the line. "When you fin' these commo wires along the trail, the best way is to cut it if you kin, then just keep

reelin' it up 'till you got as much as you kin carry, then cut it
again, and heave the coil to hell and gone downhill in the snow.
But if you can't cut it, if you can't get through it with
what you're usin', then strip this outer coatin' off one side — see?
Then you'll see these two inner wires, both wrapped in rubber,
right? Strip the rubber off both those, git the two copper wires
tweaked together, and you'll short circuit the line."

"Smooth, man," Pete Murphy said.

"When you tweak it," Harry asked, "supposing you
touch — " A cramp hit him, and he was down beside the trail,
spots before his eyes, pulling his pants down. He no longer had
to worry about getting his long underwear off in these dysentery convulsions. The crotch had rotted away.

II

Anne worked her way back up the wet snowy slope on the
grounds of the observatory near Radcliffe, using the herring-
bone as she climbed on her skies. She was trying to tire herself
out, alone on this slope, before going back to the dormitory for
supper.

At the top she paused, panting. It was cold, but she felt warm.
She had debated about whether to buy this new pair of ski pants
and the quilted parka, but finally she had decided that her old
ones really looked disgraceful.

The sun was setting behind a tree-covered hill, etching the
trunks in fire as a thick blue-gray sky closed in behind her.

It's so beautiful, she thought. Quiet. A picture rose as if she
were standing away from it, of Harry and her walking through
Central Park laughing in the snow, one day a year before. That
day they had ended up at the Metropolitan Museum. Among
the Egyptian mummies, they had talked for a while and decided
to make a formal announcement of their engagement.

Anne closed her eyes. She thrust viciously into the snow with her ski poles, and shot downhill.

III

Harry fell and groggily got back on his feet. You've got to stay awake, he told himself. Got to. Don't try sleeping when you're walking. He looked down at the winter boots that he had taken from that captain. For a few days he had thought the new boots would get him through, all by themselves, but then they had crossed a wild upland plateau, with no villages and no food for three days. His dysentery had stopped, but the men were dropping out fast now. It was Night Thirty-Two, and even though they were getting their daily handfuls of grain again, man after man was toppling into the snow.

There was a sound coming down the trail as they crossed a frozen stream. Another of the frequent groups of Chinese replacements going south was coming along, laughing and chattering and raising hell. As Harry started up the steep slope on the right-hand side of the trail, down they came, in their padded jackets, none of them carrying weapons but every man carrying some type of supplies. In addition to his own bedroll, each man had a box of ammunition or a couple of mortar rounds, and frequently two men would come along, carrying something heavier suspended on a pole.

Harry looked at them, feeling the difference between the two sides of the trail as if it were a canyon. They were alive, and he was almost dead. Some nights he could feel life leaving him as if he were a sponge going dry. One night he had slipped and fallen on a rock and gouged the side of his head, and if Pete Murphy had not half-carried him through the rest of the night, his anvil arm around him, he knew that would have been the end.

The trail was becoming steeper. He gasped as he leaned forward, slowly placing one foot before the other, feeling a stitch in his side and the ache from the old wound in his buttock and the newer one in his shoulder, and always, always, the hunger like steel traps snapping on his flesh in his stomach. To fall was not just unpleasant; it was a loss of the energy that had to be used as carefully as water on a desert.

The slope had turned so steep that it was necessary to go almost on hands and feet. The Chinese kept coming past the other way, cheerful, their rise-and-fall voices cushioned in the snowy bushes. As Harry lifted a foot to go forward, hunched over, one of the Chinese reached over from his side of the trail and punched his shoulder. To Harry it was like being hit with a shovel. His feet gave way, and he rolled backwards for twenty yards down the trail, directly between the Americans crawling up and the Chinese taking long strides down.

Harry rose, reaching for his face to try to get the snow out of his eyes. The same man had now come down the trail to this point, and reached out, flat-handed, and struck the center of Harry's chest. Harry went over backwards, and skidded like a top on his back, spinning as he went downhill, seeing the night sky and men passing like tree trunks overhead, and a jab on his back and then his head as he hit frozen roots across the trail, and then, thirty yards farther down, where he had been fifteen minutes before, he came to rest against a tree trunk with a crash that knocked the wind out of him and sent a flashing pain through his shoulder.

Harry rose, stepped back into line, his dizzy head down. Holding his stomach and trying to help it pull the air back inside, he began going up the slope again.

He was in a panic. Three or four days' worth of energy was suddenly gone from him in that shattering cascade of falls and bruises. Despite what he had seen happen to other men, now, for the first time, he realized that he might die any hour now on this march. Until now it had been something that happened to other men, but here it was, a gray paper wall and he was walking right into it.

Harry looked off to the snowy bushes on his right. That was what he wanted, a warm little house of his own in the bushes, where he could eat bread and drink milk. Anne would be in there, and his mother, and Bill, and they would all be happy in the little house in the bushes.

Harry felt a strange tingling in his scalp. It was as if someone were walking beside him, walking easily and gently as he forced one slipping-down foot above the other on the icy trail. The tingling went down the back of his head, down his neck, and spread across his shoulders. He kept his eyes forward, but he knew that his dead father was walking with him.

"I'm glad you're here," Harry said in a low voice. The wind rustled the acres of snowy low bushes on the slope. Harry smiled. He was remembering the last time he had seen his father, when they had gone out to join him in San Francisco in 1944 when his father's carrier was in from the Pacific at Christmas. He remembered their walks around the beautiful hilly city, and his father in the dark naval uniform.

"You'll help me," Harry said in a grunt as he grabbed at the bottom of a frozen bush to pull him around a bend in the trail.

We have to get you out of here, his father said to him in the wind.

"Yes, sir," Harry whispered, and for the first time he began to look at the bushes and trees and wildness not as something holding him to the trail, but as a great gray screen through which he could swim away. To go on like this was death. There was no chance that it was not. The line of men on the trail grew shorter every night. The other way, to take some food and hide in the woods and sleep when you wanted to sleep and walk only when you wanted to walk, that was a chance of living.

Go south. Harry's eyes were wild. Go south for the winter. Every day he went on this way he was going farther from where he wanted to be. He had gone on like a blind little pony, taking his turns carrying the grain bag. If he could go back those thirty-two nights, if he could slip through what everyone called a front but what he knew were just outposts of one army that dwindled until they became outposts of the other army — and if he could not, if these hills starved him out, then all he had to do was come back down to the trails, the roads, and surrender again. His eyes narrowed, and he nodded.

CHAPTER THIRTEEN

Constance sat at her little writing desk in the apartment in New York, changing her will so that there was no reference in it to Harry. She hated to see the document before her, but Clarence Wiley had offered to do it, and she had said she preferred to do it herself.

As she struck out Harry's name, as she changed the proportions that Bill was to receive, she found herself thinking of one afternoon when she had taken Harry and Bill, as little boys, to the Zoo. They had wanted to stay in the Lion House, so she had told them to join her by the seals. Eventually they had come out of the brick building into the spring sunlight, both wearing double-breasted navy blue coats with brass buttons. Bill's school cap had been on straight, and Harry's had been pushed back from his forehead.

"Mother," Harry said in great excitement, running towards her, "the mother lion has two kittens."

Constance held out her arms to slow down this steam engine and said, "Cubs, dear, not kittens."

A tear fell on the typed document. Constance brushed it away and kept on striking out Harry's name.

II

Tonight was the night. There was a quarter moon in the sky. Harry was marching in the center of the seven men who remained of the fourteen in his squad who had started this march thirty-four nights before. Keeping as much distance as possible between the guard ahead and the guard behind, Harry had been very generous tonight about carrying the grain bag. At each ten-minute stop in the darkness he had filled another of his pockets with the cracked corn. Even his gloves were stuffed with it, and tied together at his belt. With the amount he had taken, some men would go hungry tomorrow, and he knew it. Missing one meal might make the difference between life and death to one of these men and he knew that too.

The long file came to a halt in the snow. Harry stepped off the path, as many men did, and took down his trousers, squatting as if he were relieving himself. After three minutes he began backing up slowly, still squatting, watching the guards to the left and to the right as they sat at the side of the trail, their backs towards him. By the time the men rose again and began shuffling back to the trail, Harry had worked his way about twenty-five feet from the trail. Harry squatted there as they moved out, hoping that no one would notice him, but knowing that in any case it was not unusual for a man to be seen this way beside the trail before pulling up his pants and rushing to catch up to his place in the line. His squad moved off, big Pete Murphy's shoulders like a pillar in the darkness, then the guard with his long rifle slung over his shoulder and his springy, well-fed step, then another squad shuffling and limping past, another guard, fed on different food and better cooked and more of it, another squad, another blank-faced guard looking straight ahead, and then the trail was empty. Harry remained in the same position for about five minutes. He pulled up his pants and started south.

III

Constance stared at the clothes spread out on Harry's bed at the apartment. For five weeks she had avoided going near that closet, but this afternoon she had decided to get it over with.

Harry's sweaters and sneakers and khaki slacks and sport shirts were in the house in Maine, left there when he had been recalled the past July, but she had put his suits and dinner clothes in bags here, so that he would have them when he got out of the Army and married Anne. Now they were on the bed, and she stood looking down at them.

She looked at the two tuxedos, the one Harry had worn when he was in prep school and home for vacations, and the one from Harvard days, after he had outgrown the first. She touched the lapel of the smaller one, remembering the night Anne had been here at Christmas before her first big dance. She heard the voices of the boys, coming from this room they had shared while she was helping Anne get ready, the laughter about tieing their bow ties. She saw Harry handing Anne the box with the corsage in it, Anne in her long white gloves, her gray coat with her velvet collar, Harry's pink face, all of them so young with glowing hair and skins that seemed to cast energy into the soft air.

I'm sure some charity can use these clothes, she thought, and then she pulled the black dinner jacket towards her and gripped it against her face.

IV

A scream woke Harry. He had gone to sleep in a dry patch under some bushes after his third night working his way south across country.

The sun was shining, and in its light a long-skirted Korean woman was running from this hilltop, a baby strapped to her back and another child running beside her. She threw one more frightened glance over her shoulder, and disappeared in the direction of the village he had sneaked past before dawn.

Harry sat up. That does it, he thought. They'll find me anywhere I go around here. With an effort, he rose to his feet. The sunlight felt good on his face, and the sky was blue. If that woman keeps her mouth shut about what she saw up here, if nobody comes, I'll move on after a while. He took a few steps through the thicket, wincing at the effort it cost to move his stiff, frozen legs. He felt a sharp sting in his armpit, and reached in under his clothes, found the louse, and killed it. Then he reached into the left breast pocket of his fatigues and brought out a handful of cracked corn. He put a few of the kernels in his mouth and stood in the sunlight, letting them soften before he chewed. He knew that he should be worrying about what was going to happen next, but he did not have the strength to worry. His legs folded under him and he collapsed sitting to the ground.

When they came, they were hostile. Six or seven of the village farmers came onto the hill, carrying grub axes and hoes. Harry stepped out of the thicket, patting his sides and then holding his hands open so that they could see he was not armed. The youngest of the men prodded him with a grub axe, and then they were all going downhill.

The village had about a dozen houses. Harry sat on the ground with his back resting against the mud and straw wall of one of them, while thirty or forty people of all ages stood looking at him. Harry stared back. He was looking at the long, full black skirts of the women, and the pale pastel shades of their bolero jackets. The colors pleased him. In this thin cold air, against these windswept treeless dun-colored hills, the colors looked just right.

After a time two North Korean soldiers appeared. They pulled him to his feet and searched him. The bigger of the two pulled his hand out of Harry's trousers pocket and turned to the crowd, showing them this raw pig food that the strange bearded filthy man carried with him. He wafted the corn aside contemptuously, letting it fall to the frozen earth, and then hit Harry, not hard, but Harry went down. Then the other kicked him.

Harry looked up at them. Including that air strike, he said to them with his red eyes, I killed about three or four hundred of you people before you got me. I wish it could have been more. Now go ahead and get this show for the local yokels over with. They kicked him a few more times, not hard, and then lifted him to his feet, took him to an empty hut, and threw him inside.

*   *   *

Harry lay on the floor of the cold hut, trying to pull some straw bags he had found over himself. It was night, and he could hear the two North Koreans chatting as they stood guard by the door. On the floor beside him was a gourd of water they had brought him, and a bowl that had contained boiled sorghum. When they had brought the meal to him, the gourdful of water had been hot, and Harry had been surprised at how good hot water tasted by itself. Immediately after eating he had needed to relieve himself, and he had knocked on the door and explained in sign language that he wanted to be allowed outside for that purpose. Permission denied. He had relieved himself squatting in the corner, and buried the feces in the dirt floor.

There seemed to be a party going on somewhere. In the crack under the door he could see the lights of a fire blazing across the hard earth courtyard. People were laughing and talking and coming and going.

Suddenly there was the worst shriek that Harry had ever heard. It did not sound human and it kept going while Harry, unstrung, leapt to his feet and moved distractedly about the darkened, mud-walled interior. The scream faded and the sounds of laughter and conversation continued. Harry slumped to the floor, trying to arrange his bed of straw sacks under him and pulling the other sacks over him.

For an hour he looked straight up into the darkness. Ideas tumbled through his head, but he could not grasp them. For the first time since he was captured, he saw pictures of the fighting. He saw Tommy Quinn and Interlicchio in that hole in the snow, each one with a light machine gun, dug in for the last stand, buying time while the rest of the Division tried to get out to the south.

Harry twisted on the cold earth. The bowl of sorghum had brought his hunger back full force.

The door opened. An old Korean woman came towards him in the flickering shadows of the fire outside, and put two more bowls beside him. Harry stared down at them, his nostrils twitching. There were chopsticks across a bowl of steaming rice, and in the other bowl there was a kind of meat stew. Outside, the sounds of the party went on.

I wonder if the war is over, Harry thought wildly, and began eating, not with the chopsticks, but with his hands. He grabbed the small chunks of hot meat out of the gravy, and then pushed some of the rice into the gravy to sop it up, eating with both hands, hand over hand. He licked his fingers, he licked the bowls, drank some of the water from the gourd, and lay back on his straw sacks in a pleasant haze. Then he felt himself starting to vomit the rich food. He turned on his side, his face a pained sweating mask of determination, and forced himself to keep it down. Bile came into his mouth, and he spat that out, but he kept the food down, and, his face still taut, fell asleep.

*　　*　　*

"Stand up." A foot was pushing at Harry; he opened his eyes and daylight rushed into them through the door. A man in Chinese uniform was standing over him. After a moment Harry realized that he had been addressed in English.

"All right." Harry rose, taking stock of himself, noticing how well he felt after the meal and the deep sleep. The Chinese motioned to him to come outside. Before the door there was a wounded Chinese lying on a low wide pair of boards that were supported by four things that looked like baby-carriage wheels. The boy lying on the makeshift wagon had his legs bandaged from the feet to the knees.

Probably stepped on an anti-personnel mine, Harry thought.

"Why are you here?" the Chinese who had awakened him asked.

"I'll be goddamned if I know," Harry said slowly, and then he realized that that was not what the man was asking him. He looked at him. The man was about thirty, small, and had big ears that stuck out on either side of his moon face. "I fell asleep during a rest stop," Harry lied. "The column moved off without me."

"Not true," the man said. "You try escape."

"Escape not possible," Harry said, simplifying his speech. He kept looking at the man. He had an instant instinct that he should be nice to this man.

"You not grateful," the man said. "Try escape. I have orders take you north for school."

"OK," Harry said. "All right. I'm ready to go."

"This school very good for you."

"I'm sure it will be," Harry replied. "This is the guy who's going to get me food."

The Chinese bent over the wounded man on the low flat wagon. Harry noticed that the Chinese had his bedroll slung over his shoulder, ready to move out. The man picked up a rope made of straw, attached to the axle of the two baby-carriage wheels under the wounded man's head, and handed the end of the rope to Harry. "We take this man north. You pull."

"We pull together?" Harry asked.

"You only pull."

Harry laughed. "I couldn't pull this man half a mile. Can't you see I'm sick?"

The Chinese dropped the rope, hit Harry in the middle of the chest, and Harry went down. "You prisoner, you pull."

Harry sat on the ground, looking up at the man. The man handed him the end of the rope, where he was sitting.

"Got it," Harry said, and stood up with the rope in his hands. "But I have to have something to eat. I need strength to pull. Need food to pull."

"You *have* food," the Chinese said angrily. "Korean people share good food with you last night. You not grateful."

"Forget it," Harry said. He moved around to the front of the wagon, the rope in his hands, and started pulling the wounded man across the hard-packed earth of the farmyard, the Chinese beside him. A few yards on, in the center of the village, they passed the remains of a fire. Beside the fire was a pile of fur and a dog's head.

"The scream and the meat," Harry muttered.

"What?"

"Nothing."

"Pull."

"I *am* pulling," Harry said, and they moved out of the village on a trail heading north.

*   *   *

By late afternoon Harry was in agony. Being a tiny group, they could move in daylight without fear that an American plane would waste a bomb on them, but the baby-carriage wheels had never been designed with a slushy trail in mind. When their thin rims were not sinking into the melting snow, they were sliding off muddy patches into the bushes. When he kept his gloves on, the wet straw rope slid through them, and when he took his gloves off the rough strands put fibrous splinters in the palms of his hands. At every bump the wounded man moaned, and the other Chinese remained stolid, only saying, "You be careful!" in chorus with each bump and moan.

Harry gritted his teeth as he pulled the wagon around a bend in the trail. Hatred and frustration were closing on him like fog. The other Chinese would not lift a hand to help, even on the steepest inclines. At times they were going forward only inches at a time. In this slipping, aching haze, his only way of striking back was to yank the wagon across every bump as hard as he could. Harry would yank, the man would groan, and Harry would start looking for another bump.

They came downhill, the trail becoming steeper.

"Go slow you be careful."

Screw you, Harry thought. Ahead of him he saw a sharp turn in the trail. He was letting the patient down feet first, holding the wagon back from going downhill as fast as it wanted to go, and now he let the wagon take him faster and faster, until he was chasing after it holding onto the end of the rope.

"You be careful!" the voice behind him shouted. Harry was smiling. The wagon hit the turn, did not make it, and the patient was off it and rolling downhill. The boy came to rest in the leaves under a bush, screaming deliriously. Putting a solicitous expression on his face, Harry bent over the wounded man. He could see that leaves and burrs had gotten into the dressings on the man's legs.

"You be careful! You not grateful!" The other Chinese was in a rage.

Harry turned. "How about helping me put him back on the wagon?"

The man helped him do that. "Now," Harry said, "how about helping me slow down this wagon so that doesn't happen again?"

The Chinese looked at him. There was a trace of amusement and respect on his face. "A'right."

CHAPTER FOURTEEN

His NAME was Lee, and he was turning out to be a pretty decent guy. Three days ago they had left the patient and the cart in a village where there had been a doctor. Since the question of who was to pull, and how much, had evaporated, Harry and the English-speaking Chinese had walked north in an entirely different spirit. They talked during the breaks they took on the trail, and Lee had taught him some Chinese words. When they came to the village where they were to spend the night, Lee would act coldly towards Harry, and Harry played along. But every night and every morning there was a bowl of boiled sorghum and a bowl of hot water thrust at Harry by the local militiamen who guarded him in whatever hut he was put, and he knew there was Lee to thank for that.

They were coming to a place in the trail where there were some flat rocks, and Harry knew that Lee would stop there for a rest and a smoke. He had something that he wanted to talk to Lee about, and each mile they went farther north would make it just that more difficult.

"OK," Lee said, using the slang he had learned in these past days from Harry. "We stop here ten minutes."

"Hao," Harry said wearily, using the Chinese for "good" that Lee had taught him.

They chatted aimlessly for a few minutes, with Lee checking the meanings and usage of a few words as they came up. Lee had been educated for five years at a mission school in Szechuan, and, Harry thought, there were two ways of looking at it. Either those missionaries had been the worst English teachers in the world, or Lee had been one of their worst students.

"Listen, Lee," Harry said in a new tone, "you want a lot of gold? A lot of money?"

The two sticking-out ears swiveled towards Harry. "What do?" Lee asked, exhaling hot-stinking dry smoke from the crude leaf-tobacco cigarette he had rolled.

"Look," Harry said, accompanying his words with careful, definite gestures. "You take me south instead of north. We go by night. In the day I hide in the woods, you get food in villages and bring to me. We go through your army, go through outposts, come to my army. My army very happy to see me. I tell them you my friend. I tell them you help me escape. They give you a lot of money. You can come live in the United States. My family take care of you. Good life in the United States."

"I see movie," Lee said. "You make me servant. You make me bring breakfast on little table to you bed."

Harry was about to nod agreement at any idea, when he saw the look in Lee's eye.

"No, Lee," he said quickly. "You can do anything you want to. My family give you money. Good life, Lee. You can have a car, and — "

"Automobile?"

"Hell yes, automobile. Big roads, no war, no dirty little villages, big city, good clothes. Lots of Chinese people in the United States, Lee. They make friends with you."

"You family live in San Frisco?"

"No, but you can go and live in San Francisco if you want to."

"American can go any city live he want to?"

Harry nodded vigorously. "Hell yes, Lee. Good job, good clothes, good house, good food, good friends. You're single, aren't you? All right, we'll get a beautiful Chinese girl for you in San Francisco."

"San Frisco good city, but Chinese there from Canton not Szechuan."

Harry clenched his fist. "For chrissake, Lee, I can't help that."

"We talk more other time." Lee rose from the flat rock on which they were sitting. "You father live?"

"No." Harry scratched at his beard. "My father was killed by the Japanese during the war."

Lee took a long look at Harry.

The bastard thinks I don't have any money to give him because my father's dead, Harry thought, and shrugged his shoulders.

"That interesting," Lee said. "Japanese kill my father too."

II

"I don't *know* what I want to do this summer," Anne said as she sat with her parents after dinner in their living room in New York. She had come down from Radcliffe for Easter vacation.

"Europe, dear," Mabel Wiley cooed. "When school finishes in June, go on over to Europe with those two girls who asked you to."

"I don't know," Anne said. "It seems so crazy, some people dying in Korea and me thinking about a summer vacation in Europe."

Clarence's lips compressed in agreement.

Mabel glanced stonily at Clarence, though he had not said a word. "I've always wanted you to travel, dear, and particularly now, it's going to do you a world of good. I don't see why you should have any hesitation about going. I was reading the other day, they're expecting a quarter of a million American tourists in Europe this summer. Why shouldn't you be one of them?"

Clarence stood and went into his study. Believe me, Anne, he thought as he sat down to a little after-dinner work, you're on that ship right now.

III

Lee had said nothing, but Harry sensed that at some point to-day they were arriving at their destination. Last night had been Night Fifty-Four. During the days of his escape he had stopped counting, but recently he had reconstructed it all carefully, his mind eagerly accepting the exercise of remembering which days had been spent in root cellars, which in huts, which in caves, until he felt that he had accounted for every stop of the journey.

As they walked along this soggy April trail, Harry gazed at the electric blue flowers that grew in the thickets on a nearby hill. Today his mind seemed to spin. Half the time he was worried about making one final appeal to Lee, and the other half of the time some instinct was telling him to enjoy this move-ment, this changing countryside with these first spring flowers clinging to them like patches of light blue mist.

They sat beside each other on a slender fallen birch trunk be-side the trail.

"No," Lee said when he grasped that Harry was bringing the subject up again.

"Why not, Lee?" Harry could feel his throat going soft, and tears starting in his eyes.

"Too much chance," Lee said. His voice was gentle. "Life better now in China." He looked at Harry. "How 'bout Amer-ica stay one side Pacific Ocean, China stay other side?"

"How about North Korea not attack South Korea?" Harry shot back. He at last believed that Lee was going to deliver him wherever he had to go.

"Korean people our cousin," Lee said. "Not you cousin."

"The Japanese your cousins too?" Harry asked, looking down and stripping a sliver of bark from the fallen birch.

Lee smiled. "No. They you cousin. You keep."

"Thanks."

Lee rose, tossing the stub of his leaf cigarette into a remaining patch of snow. "Pu'dick, pretty soon we come school for you. We say good-bye now. Say no good-bye at school."

"Sure," Harry said, getting up from the birch trunk.

Lee extended his hand. "Good luck, Pu'dick. I hope you live." For a moment he looked embarrassed as he stared at the condition Harry was in. "Pu'dick, Chinese People Volunteer Army not expect catch so many American prisoner. No food, no house, no medicine for you."

Harry took the proffered small hand. "Tsai cheeyen," he said, using the words for farewell he had learned from Lee.

*   *   *

Harry sniffed the air. There was a strong rotting sweet odor coming from ahead of them. They had just passed through a town, but the smell was coming from ahead, rather than behind.

Maybe it's some kind of factory, Harry thought, his bearded face wrinkling with the impact of the stench.

"Town people say we go this road," Lee said. They turned left onto a road perhaps twelve feet wide, moving gently uphill. The rains had cut rivulets across it, but Harry saw not the slightest sign of either footprints or vehicle tracks.

"You sure this is the right place?" Harry asked. The smell was increasing.

"Sure. This you school. Be good for you."

"Smells like a chemical warfare school," Harry muttered.

Twenty minutes up this shallow valley, the ground leveled and their destination came to view. Looking ahead, Harry could see that the road ended by turning into the main street of a small encampment. On either side of the dirt thoroughfare was a single spaced row of huts with corrugated tin roofs. On the small hills forming the horseshoe in which the camp lay, there was no vegetation.

A Chinese sentry stepped from behind a small guard shack down the road from where the twin rows of shacks faced each other. He was carrying a rifle slung on his back, and he nodded matter-of-factly at the sight of another prisoner being brought in. He asked Lee a question, and then there seemed to be some problem, because both of them stopped talking and each in turn used the palm of his left hand as a blackboard upon which he quickly drew combinations of vari-angled lines with his right index finger. After sixty seconds of this the guard grunted "hao," and disappeared back into his guard shack.

"Why can't you talk to each other?" Harry asked.

"Come from different part China," Lee said out of the side of his mouth, watching to see when the guard would reappear.

"You mean you can't speak the same language?"

"Writing all the same everywhere in China. He speak only Canton dialect."

The guard reappeared, and Lee made his face look disapprovingly at Harry. The guard handed Harry a small steel bowl, and gave Lee a piece of paper on which he had written something.

"Doesn't he need my name?" Harry asked.

"You name not important," Lee said. "This piece of paper tell I bring one more man here." Lee put the piece of paper into a pocket, and without nodding walked off down the road up which they had come. The guard motioned to Harry to enter the camp by himself.

Gripping the small steel bowl he had been handed, Harry walked slowly up the slight incline. The smell was so bad that it seemed to burn his lungs. As he came closer, he saw that there were two concrete wells spaced along this dirt street between the two lines of huts. The huts themselves were long, with five doorways in each. As he came within fifty yards of the nearest, the first American he had seen since his escape came crawling over the threshold. The man crawled a few more yards and then pitched forward into the soft April earth, trying to get his trousers down as he writhed in an attack of dysentery. Harry

changed course to move and help him, and as he did he began to
see human feces on the ground. They were everywhere, increasing in frequency as he neared the huts.

Harry bent over the bearded, ragged boy, his eyes narrowing
in disgust as he saw the lice in the beard and the filth on the torn
remains of faded green fatigue pants.

I suppose I look like this, too, Harry thought with horror. But
at least I can walk. Lee fed me two bowls a day. Harry looked
over his shoulder, down the road up which he had come. Lee
was out of sight. Then he turned his attention back to the
wracked, gasping body before him. "What can I do to help you,
buddy?"

The boy looked up at him through dull yellowed eyes. "Jus'
leave me alone."

"OK." Harry straightened up and walked to the doorway
through which the GI had crawled. He peered into the stinking
gloom, and his mouth opened and his eyes widened at what he
saw. Under the low soot-blackened ceiling, in a space about
thirteen by fifteen feet, there were twenty Americans. Some sat
propped with their backs to the mud-and-rush walls, and others
lay on their sides. Two stared at him with fever-bright eyes that
were enormous in their shrunken faces. Emaciation had pulled
their lips back from their teeth; they looked like foxes.

Harry stepped back from the doorway as if he had been
struck. He moved dazedly past other doorways, seeing the dim
forms inside. Retreating towards the center of the dirt road,
glancing down to avoid stepping in the feces that were everywhere, he saw six men coming out of a hut across the way, staggering as they carried something on empty rice sacks slung between two poles. They moved past him without an indication
that he was there; he saw a dead red-headed boy on his side on
the rice sacks, his skin like green stone and the April breeze tugging at his shaggy hair.

From a corner of his eye he saw smoke coming from a big
square hut beyond the row of smaller structures. Instantly he

headed towards it, drawn by the promise of the smoke, the promise that a house that could make smoke had life, had food, had energy.

He poked his head through the wide door. Before him was an unpillared expanse of dirty floor, perhaps thirty by forty feet wide, rising from the flat center area to a dirt bank against each wall. Along these dirt banks at intervals were big holes, and on two of them sat kettles.

The kitchen, Harry thought, the kitchen, the kitchen. As his eyes grew accustomed to the darkness, he saw a small knot of GIs sitting on bags of grain in the corner.

Food, Harry thought, this is where they keep the food. You've got to stay here where they keep the food.

He advanced hesitantly across the dim big room. One of the men in the corner rose to his feet and strode towards Harry, yelling, "How many times do I have to tell you guys to stay out of here!"

When Harry did not slink away, the man stood blocking him, his hands on his hips, eying him curiously. "You new here?"

"I just got here," Harry said. "I'm a cook."

The man laughed soundlessly. "Sure you're a cook. You're the chef at the Waldorf-Astoria."

"Hold it." Another form appeared from the darkness and eyes above a beard stared at Harry. "Don't I know you? What was your outfit?"

"Charlie Company, Ninth Infantry," Harry said.

"You look less and less like a guy named Purdick," the beard said, a gold tooth shining through it, and Tommy Quinn and Harry slowly raised their hands towards each other.

"I thought you were dead in that rearguard," Harry said.

"I sort of was." Quinn motioned the other man away. "I was out like a light for three days. When I woke up they had me."

"What happened to Interlicchio?"

"Him getting killed was the last thing I saw before I went out."

Harry looked around. "I didn't know you were a cook."

"Sure I'm a cook. I was the chef at the Waldorf-Astoria." Tommy gestured with his head in the direction of the men in the corner, and Harry followed him over. "Fellas," Quinn said, "I want you to meet an old buddy of mine. This is Purdick, got it? He's a cook."

"O.K.," one of the men sitting on a bag of grain said, "so he's a cook."

*　　*　　*

"We have to do it," Tommy Quinn whispered in the darkness, "because the cooks are the only ones left with the strength to do it. Wouldn't you know I'd end up back in Graves Registration?" He and Harry were standing knee deep in a mass grave they were digging in the soft earth on the hillside just beyond the camp. There were lanterns at the edge, and the two Chinese guards moved along opposite sides of the long shallow trench in which the cooks were digging.

"How many guys are dying here?" Harry whispered back.

"About ten a day. It's getting worse. One time there, we were up around four hundred, now we've got about two hundred and fifty left."

"I thought this was supposed to be a school." Harry saw a guard coming slowly down his side, and dug harder.

"I think they've got some schools somewhere. They moved some guys out of here and took them somewhere. I wish they'd move us all out."

"God, yes. At least they ought to clean this place up."

"Who's going to clean it up?" Quinn rested on his shovel, his gold tooth sparkling in the dull light. "The guys can't do it. Most of them don't have the strength to make it all the way to those latrine trenches off there behind the huts. You shovel all that shit up one day, it's back there the next."

Harry looked down at the loam on his shovel. "What do they call this place?"

"The Bean Camp."

"Why?"

Quinn resumed digging. "Because we eat beans. Period." He shook his head. "Imagine giving guys with dysentery a diet of beans."

One of the guards said something and gestured, and the men began climbing out of the trench.

"Now," Quinn said, "we go over and fill in the one we dug last night that got filled up today."

Harry walked behind him, carrying his shovel. The guards were ahead, the cones of light from the lanterns bobbing from one shredded GI fatigue uniform to another. "Hold it here," Quinn whispered, grabbing Harry's elbow. Harry looked down and saw that he had been about to walk across a tangle of bodies that lay in a shallow ditch. "Just take the earth from this side and shovel it out over them." Everyone was working quickly. Harry aimed a shovelful and cast it out over the corpses. He saw the clods strike a stiff upsticking hand, and he kept pitching dirt at it until the hand disappeared.

IV

Clarence Wiley had finished lunch at his club, and was smoking a cigar in its reading room before going back to the office. He sat back in the leather armchair, looking at the *Herald Tribune* in his lap. President Truman had just summarily relieved General MacArthur of his commands in the Far East, and the general was coming home.

God almighty, Clarence thought, there's a haberdasher who really doesn't take any lip from the help. His forehead knit as he looked at the résumé of MacArthur's career. Commander of the Rainbow Division in France when Truman was a captain in the same division. Superintendent of West Point when Truman failed in the haberdashery. Chief of Staff of the United

States Army when Truman was Presiding Judge of Jackson County, Missouri.

He shook his head. Truman was right in relieving him for shooting his mouth off, but it was possible that MacArthur knew what he was talking about.

Clarence stubbed out his cigar, and his mouth tightened. This was the United States, the *United States*, getting kicked around out there. During the war he had seen what this country could do when it put its mind to it. You need ten thousand planes, all right, when do you need them? You need three hundred and fifty cities of ten thousand men each, all right, we'll build them. And here we were, nowhere, quietly burying Harry Purdicks and turning to the sports page.

I know there are reasons, Clarence thought, putting the paper aside and standing up. We have to think about the Russians and their bombs, but I don't think Joe Stalin is going to start throwing bombs about a place called Korea. I really don't. And in the meantime we tell the Chinese, OK, you bring your team over to the field you like best, over in Korea where we can't use our tanks, and we'll play it out there and nowhere else. He shrugged his shoulders and walked out of the club.

V

Four of the camp's twelve remaining buildings were blasted and burning as the P-51s pulled out of their last strafing runs. The American planes formed up and flew south in the May afternoon. It was the fourth raid this week.

Harry's head rose cautiously from the slit trench up the slope behind the cookhouse.

I wonder what they think this place is, he thought, looking after the V of planes flying south. Then his eyes lowered to the scene in the two square acres of filth below. Men were gathering around one of the buildings, going in under its smoking riddled tin roof and emerging with men who had been too weak to move when the sound of the propeller engines announced the planes two minutes before they attacked. Others were digging in the rear end of a hut, pulling men from the wreckage of what had been a small individual kitchen when miners lived here with their families.

Harry climbed from the slit trench and moved downhill. The planes were almost out of sight in the silver Korean sky. They looked so detached now, not at all like the flame-spitting sharks that had slashed through this valley.

"Haw! Gee! C'mon theyah you Lester!" Harry turned his head. A GI who had gone insane was driving an imaginary team of two mules past the upper well in the camp's center street. He had somewhere acquired an oversize Chinese winter quilted cap; its ear flaps swung fiercely as he strode stiff-legged amidst smoke and flames and shock-staggering men, his arms outstretched by invisible reins and his voice bellowing at his team.

VI

Despite Bill's urging that it was too much trouble, Constance had come up to Cambridge to hear him argue the second and last of his moot court Ames Competition cases near the end of his first Law School year. Anne had come over from Radcliffe to hear him, too. Now the competition was over, and they were walking across Cambridge Common in the May evening, Anne on one side of Bill and Constance on the other.

"I don't see how you could possibly win that case, the way you describe the laws on it," Anne mused as Constance and Bill matched their strides to hers.

Bill nodded. He and his partner had won as far as their presentation of the case was concerned, and everyone was agreed that this particular case about the duty of a brickyard owner to keep children from playing among brickstacks was an impossible one for the appellant.

"I want to take a look at the Yard," Constance said softly as they came out of the park, and Bill and Anne nodded as they moved through the velvet evening.

Ten minutes later they had made their way to the center of Harvard Yard, and were standing between Widener Library and the chapel, in the expanse that had served as an outdoor theater for Bill's graduation the previous year.

Constance's voice said in flat tones, "Harry would have been graduating here in a few weeks."

They looked at each other in the dim lights under the newly green elms, and involuntarily reached for each other's sleeves.

VII

"I know the endings are a little different," Tommy Quinn said, "but how about saying the Our Father with me?"

Harry nodded. It was sunset, and he and Tommy had just finished covering over the bodies of seven men who had been torn apart as they lay in this slit trench dug in a hut's dirt floor. This air-raid shelter for men too weak to make it to the hillside had taken a direct hit from a P-51's rocket.

" — and lead us not into temptation," Tommy was murmuring, and Harry joined in, "but deliver us from evil." Tommy said, "Amen," and Harry went on, "For Thine is the Kingdom, and the Power, and the Glory, for ever and ever. Amen."

Tommy Quinn made the sign of the cross, and they stepped out through the blasted-open back wall of the flimsy structure. They headed wearily towards their own hut.

Tommy looked at the rapidly falling night. "What do you think? Maybe two hours' sleep before Bedcheck Charlie comes?"

"Maybe." Harry stepped over some decomposing flesh around

which flies were buzzing. "Bedcheck Charlie" was the nick-name the boys had given to the B-26 that was hitting them now every evening, after the daytime shift were finished with their .50 caliber bullets and rockets. He and Tommy tried to be in that slit trench on the slope before the bomber came, but most of the men lay in their huts, dizzy-sick and resigned to their fate.

"How many guys do we have left?" Harry asked.

"Well, let's see. The Chinks moved about a hundred out of here the other day, don't you figure?"

"Right."

"I guess that left about forty. Now these seven guys we just fixed are gone, and we're still losing five, six a day from all the other stuff, before the planes even come." Quinn spat. "Pretty soon it's gonna be you and me alone in the Fun House."

"I'm scared, Tommy." Harry looked at the lower of the two wells as they passed it. Yesterday someone had thrown down the bucket on the end of a rope, as usual, and when he heard no splash, looked in and saw a corpse down there. No one knew how it got there.

"Well," Tommy offered, "we could say the Our Father again."

"Let's say it hard."

VIII

Bill sat back in his seat in the examination room, and grimaced at the questions on the examination in Property. He had been writing for two hours, and the exam was scheduled to last two hours more. Bill pulled his seersucker jacket over to him from the seat beside him, and took a Nestle's Chocolate Crunch bar from its pocket. Slipping off the paper wrapper and then peeling back the silver foil, he bit into it, staring at the men around him leaning forward over their papers, the pens moving, the rapt expressions.

He looked at the windows set high in the white-washed walls of this room, and at the fresh green leaves waltzing in the breeze of the first of June. Then he stared at a young man near him who was sweating, and not from heat.

Brother, Bill silently addressed the sweating, worried student, nothing in the world is that important. Nothing.

I don't know, Bill said to himself. If that's the most important thing in the world to this guy, then it is. He shook his head.

What do I think is important? I don't know. He looked down at the exam paper. There were lots of little games to play. Little questions about who owned the oil under the ground, and who would get Aunt Minerva's money if her will said this instead of that.

A great desire swept over Bill. He wanted to rise and shout, "Come *on*, this is too goddamn undignified! We're *men*, not mice running through a maze!"

He finished the chocolate bar and went back to work on the exam.

IX

Harry was sitting in the morning sunshine in front of the one remaining unbombed hut, when he heard feet coming. A Chinese he had never seen before was standing above him, unarmed. Harry saw that the man had his bedroll across his shoulder.

"Hubba, hubba!" the Chinese shouted. "We go new camp now!"

"Just a minute." Harry rose slowly and stiffly. "I have to pack my suitcase." He went inside, scooped his steel bowl from where it sat on the floor, and came back outside.

"That all you possession?" the interpreter asked.

"That's right," Harry answered. The four other survivors came out into the June sunlight, and for an instant Harry saw them as if he had never seen them before. Since his capture in February, he had not had a shave or a bath, a haircut or a tooth-brush, and the others were in like case.

"Make line," the interpreter said, pointing at the ground before him. Harry and the four others, all that were left, shuffled into a rank. Two of them were supporting a buddy whose head hung forward on his chest.

"Count!" the Chinese shouted.

"One!" a hoarse voice cried. Tommy Quinn said "Two!", another man shouted once for himself and once for the sick buddy he was supporting, and when Harry growled "Five," the interpreter seemed satisfied. He turned and they followed him past the well in which the corpse lay, past huts in which the last of two hundred men who had died here still lay, past wreckage from which earlier bomb-torn corpses could not be extricated. They moved slowly past burned timbers, picking their way across feces, and then the sugary stink of rotting flesh receded as they moved down the road.

Three miles had been covered in slow, tottering stages when the two men who were supporting their friend looked at each other across his hanging-forward shaggy neck. They put him down beside the road, and one knelt and put his ear to the man's bone-cage of a chest. He rose, shaking his head, and then there were four men walking down the silent June road, with the Chinese in front looking over his shoulder at them and yelling "hubba hubba!" The sound sank into soft green trees.

CHAPTER FIFTEEN

Aɴɴᴇ sᴛᴏᴏᴅ ᴀʟᴏɴᴇ at the rail of the Cunard liner *Georgic* as the ship left the Statue of Liberty behind. Over her shoulder came the sounds of college boys and girls chattering excitedly as they made their first impromptu tours of the ship; beneath her, gulls cried as they slid alongside the great black cliff of the ship's side. The sun was breaking through a haze that had hung over the harbor, and even this ponderous old ship began to take on speed as she headed down the bay towards the open ocean and Europe.

Anne shook her head. She was not quite sure how she had gotten here. Her mother had packed her bags, and she remembered having a passport photo taken. Her two traveling companions had made up the itinerary, and her father had given her what she was sure was too much money in travelers' checks, and now she was standing here thinking about how Harry went on a ship in one direction, and now you're going on a ship in another.

Anne looked at the Jersey shore, thinking of butterfly evenings spent there when she was a debutante, champagne and violins and the headlights of whatever car you were in lighting up the country roads in the night. Out there on this June Saturday afternoon there were wedding receptions going on, green-and-white striped tents and young men in gray suits and the bridesmaids in rich blue satin and the groom red and sweating in his cutaway.

We would have been getting married just about now, Anne thought, her eyes closing. Just about now. She could see Harry in his cutaway, laughing and chatting and relieved now that the church part was over. She saw the champagne glass in his hand, saw him bending over to kiss old friends of his mother's on the cheek.

Her head slipped forward, and she clutched the rail.

"You all right, Miss?" A little cockney deck steward in white jacket and black cap was bending forward over the rail, his sharp-featured face turned towards hers. "If you're feeling seasick, Miss, it's better not to look down at the waves. Just look up at the sky."

"Thank you," Anne said.

II

"Why should I carry water up those steps for somebody else?" Harry asked indignantly. He and an American captain who was a doctor were arguing as they stood before the Korean school building to which the four survivors of the Bean Camp had been brought. "There must be three hundred GIs in there," Harry said, nodding towards the big low dark wooden structure. "They've all been here for months. What am I supposed to do, be Gunga Din for this outfit?"

"Look, Sergeant," the doctor said, "you are one of the few men who could get up and down those steps. There's just enough water up here for cooking, but not enough to get all the people here cleaned up."

They both looked for a moment at the steep, two-hundred-yard flight of stone steps that led from this hilltop schoolhouse to the muddy little village below.

"Those steps are steep," Harry said, glaring resentfully at the little bald man who still had silver bars preserved on the collar of clean green fatigues. "I know damn well I'd collapse if I start carrying buckets of water up that thing. You can't do it on this slop they feed us here."

An American major had drifted up and was standing by, listening. The doctor held out his hands towards Harry. "Look.

I have a little hut down in the village. That's where the Chinese let me live and keep what few medicines I have. I've got two medics down there with me. You can move in too. I'll get you enough food so you can make it up these steps with the water, and then you can help me get these men on their feet. If we can get some extra wood and water up here, we can make fires and hot water and get them cleaned up, and — "

"You look," Harry said. "There are three hundred guys in there." He jabbed his finger in the direction of the large empty window frames in the aged, unpainted wooden building. "If those three hundred guys in there haven't carried any extra water up here in four months, I'm not going to start doing it for them." Harry turned and walked away. The major who had been watching shrugged his shoulders and went on pacing along the outside of the building.

The bald-headed little doctor looked at Harry's back. "All right," he whispered, "the hell with it."

III

They had arrived in Paris on the boat train from Le Havre three hours before, and now, at sunset, Anne and the two girls with whom she was traveling had emerged from their hotel. None of them had been in Paris before, and they had no idea of which way to walk in order to find a place to eat dinner. They wandered across the Rue de Rivoli, onto the wide graveled area before the open-mouthed dark stone wings of the Louvre, the silver Paris sky turning pink above them. To their right the formal trees and hedges and walks of the Tuileries stretched into dusk. Above those trees, in the distance, the Eiffel Tower stood in dark lavender haze.

The lights went on in the ornate street lamps. Anne stopped, staring at the lights twinkling in the trees, avenues of light leading away into this beautiful new place. Motor bicycles puttered past, the sounds of their engines bouncing from ancient walls. A couple passed them, the young Frenchman wearing a dark double-breasted worn blue serge suit, the stockingless girl in a skirt and light short-sleeved sweater, their arms about each other, the man's mouth close to her ear, saying things she wanted to hear.

IV

Harry and Tommy Quinn walked down the long unlit hall of the Korean hilltop schoolhouse, on either side of a West Point first lieutenant named Swann who was from Cheyenne, Wyoming. Swann had been wounded in the leg, but he kept up his pace to that of Harry and Tommy as they came to the end, turned, and walked back its length.

The July night was warm; the only sound was the sudden patter when a man bolted from one of the big stripped classrooms where the men slept, across the hall to the big concrete latrine with its troughs in the floor. Then there were the wracking, explosive sounds of a man with dysentery relieving himself; later the man would come walking slowly, sometimes crawling, back to where he had begun.

"That's ten laps," the West Pointer said as he came to the doorway of their schoolroom in which one hundred prisoners of all ranks lay in sick, sometimes delirious sleep. His leathery snub-nosed face smiled. "Think I'll go back and get in the horizontal parade rest position for a while."

"See you later, sir," Harry said, and Tommy echoed him. Swann was the first officer whom Harry had called "Sir" since he was captured. Harry and Tommy walked on, past the two other big rooms each holding a hundred men. There was a lantern in the room at the far end of the hall, and Harry and Tommy stopped, looking at the bald-headed little doctor. Leaning on the wooden sill that partitioned the room from the hall, Harry watched the doctor opening a cyst on a man's neck, using a razor blade to do it. One of the doctor's two well-fed medics knelt beside him as he operated on the man who was lying on the wooden floor.

Tommy moved on, and Harry caught up with him. Often they walked for half an hour without exchanging a word. One would go and lie down for a while, and Swann would come back out and fall into step. They walked this way because they saw what was happening to the men who did not get up and move around. Everyone was hungry, but when you lay still you were not hungry. When you lay still you felt warm and comfortable and not hungry, but if a man stayed off his feet for a day, he died within forty-eight hours. Harry did not know why, but he saw it happening, and he walked, and Tommy walked, and Swann walked.

V

Constance sat in one of the wicker chairs on the porch of the little brown-shingled South Harbor Yacht Club on Penobscot Bay near the lake in Maine, watching the Seventeens coming into the harbor at the end of this race. She wished that her eyes were still good enough to make out the numbers on the distant sails, so that she could tell which boat Bill was in, but it was enough to know that he was out there.

Two flaxen-haired little girls rushed past, chasing a dog, and Constance smiled. There had been some discussion about whether to come to Maine this summer, but she was glad they had come. There were memories everywhere, of Harry on those same sailboats, of Harry and Anne and Bill, but it was the Maine that he had loved, and she loved it still. The salt breeze touched her cheeks; her chin lifted as she saw the tilted sails on the water.

VI

"What?" Harry could not believe his ears.

The English-speaking Chinese repeated it. "Come, we play basketball now." He passed on. The guards were rounding up the hundred men who were still able to walk.

Harry shrugged his shoulders and looked at Tommy Quinn. "That's what I thought he said."

"Well," Tommy replied, "maybe they've got a different way of playing."

Harry stood with his elbows on the partition, waiting while the guards pulled some of the men to their feet and herded them out. The doctor had finished working on some of his patients, and, as Harry watched, a GI surreptitiously handed the doctor his wrist watch, and the doctor handed him two ears of corn. The doctor was selling the men's possessions down in the village for food and tobacco. Some of the prisoners still had their wallets, and, amazingly, there was even a market for American dollars in that dingy little cluster of houses at the bottom of the hill.

Harry looked at the expression on the face of the bald-headed man. The doctor was still working on his patients, but each day his face seemed to grow colder, more withdrawn.

At the end of a mile's walk, during which they had stopped three times in order to let the weaker men catch up, they came to a hard-packed dirt area between two wooden schoolhouses. Fixed to the wall of each schoolhouse was a metal hoop, and there were a dozen Chinese in brown shorts, stripped to the waist, racing up and down the court and shooting baskets from every conceivable angle. Korean children were packed along the far side of the court to watch.

"Come play now," the English-speaking Chinese said to the crowd of filth-encrusted GIs who were standing beside the court, some of their chests heaving with the exertion of walking the mile to get here.

No one moved. Finally Tommy Quinn said, "For chrissake," and took off his torn fatigue shirt and walked onto the court. The children howled with laughter at the beard and long hair and skeleton white ribs.

"How about you, Purdick?" a boy named Flattley from Detroit asked.

"Me?" Harry said. "I'm the least coordinated guy in the Army."

"But you've got some strength," Flattley said. "I'll do it if you will."

"OK." Harry walked onto the court. He had an idea that he was going to be knocked down on that dirt, and he kept his fatigue shirt on.

Finally five GIs were on their half of the court, taking up the conventional forward and guard positions. As soon as they were in place the dozen Chinese came tearing down the court in a flying wedge, pushing them aside, and the one man who had been dribbling the ball behind them went up for an easy lay-up shot and made it. The school children applauded.

"Chinese People Volunteer Army two points, United States Army zero," the interpreter cried, and repeated it in Korean, and then in Chinese.

Lieutenant Swann came limping out onto the court and up to the interpreter, who was apparently also referee.

"This game is played with five men on a side," he said politely.

"We have twelve men, all like to play," the interpreter said.

"All right," Swann said. "I'm number six for my side." He limped over to join the two guards in the back court. Three other GIs came out from the sidelines. The Chinese came sweeping down again, past two men in the front line who could barely reach out to make an ineffectual swipe at them as they went by, and scored again. The children went wild.

*

"Chinese People Volunteer Army one hundred points, United States Army no points!" the interpreter cried jubilantly. "We stop now." A guard came out with an armful of ears of corn, and each American who had played was given one. Three of the players had to be carried on the return trip.

VII

As she moved around this marble dance floor on the roof of the hotel in Venice, Anne could feel her two friends staring at her and the tall young man with her. This afternoon, when they had run into these three boys from Yale that one of the girls knew, it had begun with a drink in the Piazza San Marco, and then dinner in a place down one of the side streets, and now dancing beside a low rooftop ledge overlooking the Grand Canal. Venice was cool this evening. There were stars in the sky, and the lights below cast the canal in luminous green water between shadowless light stone housefront arches and pillars.

"But I mean, those prices in Paris — " the young man was saying, and Anne smiled brightly and nodded. The orchestra was playing from *Call Me Madam*, "I Only Know What's the Best Thing for You." She saw her two friends still staring at her as they danced past in the arms of their identically dressed, seersucker-jacketed Yale men. The girls' faces reflected curiosity, and a touch of disapproval. They had been telling her she ought to go out more in the evenings on this trip. At last she had, and now they looked at her like that.

You don't understand, Anne thought. You don't get it. It doesn't make the slightest difference whether I'm here or whether I left you after dinner and went back to the hotel. This boy wanted me to come, so I came. He wants me to dance with him and smile at him and laugh at his jokes, and he's a nice boy and that's that. I don't care how it looks. The only place I care how it looks is in my heart, and if you saw that, it would ruin the evening for all of you.

"— get to Carcassonne?"

"No," Anne said. "We didn't get there."

VIII

Harry and a dozen other men had been working on a burial detail when an interpreter had appeared and told the guards to get them back to the big schoolhouse. As they arrived, walking quickly, Harry saw that every man who could move had been assembled on the flagstones between the front steps of the building and the steep stone staircase down into the village.

Tommy Quinn snorted. "Maybe they want to take a group picture," he said. Harry smiled thinly. As each day passed, he wanted less and less to do with the Chinese, and it looked as if they had something pretty definite in mind.

Flattley from Detroit whispered, "Maybe those truce talks we hear about got something. Maybe the war's over."

Quinn shook his head. "Cut it out, will you, Flattley? Don't even think about it."

"What else have I got to think about?"

Lieutenant Swann suddenly barked, "All right, men, let's hold it till we see what these birds have going here!"

Everyone, majors on down, became still at the sound of the West Pointer's voice. Harry straightened up and tried to look like something.

After a minute there was a sudden turning of heads, and then men moved forward to the edge of the steep stone steps leading the two hundred yards down to the village. What looked like a small Chinese military formation was coming solemnly up the steps. In the center of the first three men was the bald-headed American doctor in his crisp fatigues with the captain's bars on the collar. Behind them came two rows of guards, bayonets fixed on their rifles. The small formation poured over the edge of the top step. The GIs fell back as the Chinese kept on marching until they were almost halfway across the flagstone area in front of the school. An interpreter whom they had never seen before, marching on the American doctor's right, gave a curt order, and the contingent stopped as one man. Then one of the Chinese from the rear rank came trotting around to the front of the column, carrying a wooden box which he placed at the American doctor's feet.

Don't tell me they've decided to give him something besides Chinese aspirin to work with, Harry thought.

"May I have your attention," the new interpreter said. Harry blinked. He was not sure that it was the same man who had promised them so many things the night he was captured, but it was the same sort of super-interpreter, erect, vibrant, fluent, totally different from the other English-speaking Chinese, and the peasant guards. "You are all familiar with this doctor," the man said, stepping three yards off and pointing at the bald-headed captain. "Step forward," he said sharply, and the doctor stepped forward two paces, beside the wooden box. He folded his hands in front of him and hung his head.

Harry glanced at Lieutenant Swann. The West Pointer's eyes were narrowed.

"We have discovered that many of you have given your possessions to this doctor in return for food and tobacco," the interpreter said. "For a wristwatch you have received two ears of corn. What you do not know is that for your wristwatches he has been receiving ten ears of corn, and for your capitalistic dollar bills the misguided Korean people have given him five times what he has given you."

There was a strange sigh among the assembled men, as if something they had all known but not recognized was now in view.

"He has enriched himself at your expense," the political officer continued. "He no longer eats any of the food you eat. On his table in the village there are chickens and meat and vegetables.

This from a doctor who has sworn to take every possible care of his patients." The officer nodded to the doctor.

The little clean-shaven man nodded in return, and took yet another step forward. He cleared his throat. "As you know — " his eyes raised, saw the cold scores of eyes above beards gazing at him, and fell again. "As you know, for some time I tried to interest you men in bringing extra water and wood up here so that we could have made fires and boiled water and cleaned you up." There was a wistful tone in his voice. "If we could have cleaned you up — "

"The self-criticism!" the officer shouted. "The self-criticism!"

The doctor nodded. "I became discouraged, and I decided that I would try to heal you, but to make really sure that my medics and I were in the best of health so that I could go on taking care of you. I see now that I took advantage of the situation. I realize that I was a capitalist exploiting you. I criticize myself for stealing from helpless men. I attribute this crime to my bourgeois background and lack of knowledge of true socialist values."

Harry looked at Swann again. Swann's eyes were shut as he listened to this man who was technically a brother officer.

The interpreter stepped up to the wooden box. "We have retrieved your possessions from the Korean people who misguidedly bought them," he said.

Quinn whispered from the side of his mouth, "Getting it back must have been a pisser," and Harry choked back a laugh.

"If each man who has dealt with the doctor will step forward and identify his possessions or the number of capitalistic dollars, this return of possessions to you will be complete." The officer smiled encouragingly and made a graceful, open-handed gesture towards the box.

No one moved. From the back of the crowd, there came a loud imitation of a fart.

The Chinese officer flushed. "In any case," he said, "this miserable capitalist will now do himself what he asked others to do. He will carry wood and water from the village to here. He will do it every day. He will do it all day. No one is to assist this enemy of the people." The Chinese gave another command. The military formation about-faced and marched out of sight over the edge of the stone steps, leaving the box on the flagstones behind them. Men rushed for the box, fighting and snatching and knocking each other down.

Harry looked at Swann. He was slowly shaking his head.

IX

Bill sat in the cottage in Maine. It was a cold, foggy evening, and the fire was not burning well. He had a glass of scotch in one hand, and in the other was a post card from Anne.

Dear Bill,

Hope you're getting good and rested before your second round with law school.

We're in Zermatt after a terrific jaunt via South of France, Rome, Florence and Venice in a rented car. All the clichés are true, and I'm delighted that they are — the Leaning Tower really leans, and the gondolas in Venice are real, not props.

Hope everything is all right with you.

Best,
Anne

Bill stared at the post card. He was drinking a lot in these quiet evenings, after his mother went upstairs to bed.

I hope you're having a ball, Anne, he thought. It sounds that way. Harry's dead and you're in a gondola and I'm out there racing Seventeens. Swell.

A loon cried on the far side of the lake, the wildest cry. Bill listened to the lonely haunting sound, and raised his glass again.

X

"You're going to have to help me up, Tommy," Harry said in a rasping voice.

"You're OK, buddy," Quinn's voice said, and he lifted Harry to his feet.

"Thanks." Harry put out his hand against the schoolroom wall to steady himself. He had come down with dry beri-beri, and his thighs were no bigger than his ankles. "Swann out there?"

"Right in formation," Quinn said, and lay down for a rest on the wooden floor.

Harry made his way out to the hall. Swann turned in his endless pacing and came towards him in the filtered noon light. "How are you making it, Sergeant?"

"Fine, thank you, sir." Harry fell in beside him and they walked together down the hall. Now it was Harry who had to keep up to the limping West Pointer. The sweet stink of death was everywhere. Since the doctor had been put to carrying wood and water, his visits had ceased. The dysentery was worse than ever, and now most of the survivors had either the dry beri-beri that made you a skeleton, or the wet beri-beri that made the scrotum enlarge to the size of a football. Each day more men were staying down, not making that one necessary effort to stand and keep moving. Some, too weak to make it to the latrine, defecated where they lay. The flies came and hovered over them in these late August days, laying the eggs that hatched into maggots. When a man awoke and found himself alive in small white worms, he would turn to the wall and pray for death, and death would oblige.

Swann had taken out his wallet, and was looking at the snapshot of his young wife. He gazed at it for three laps up and down the hall.

"Your turn, Sergeant," he said, and handed the small photo to Harry. He knew that Harry liked looking at it.

Harry took it. Swann's wife was lovely. The picture showed her in a beaver coat, standing in front of her white frame house in Cheyenne. Harry knew that his eyes were playing tricks on him, but when he stared at the snapshot the beaver coat would remain the same, but Anne's face looked out at him from above the collar. It was Anne. Staring at it, he could not think that there was anything else in the world but Anne. He could not remember a time when he had not known her. He could not remember a time when he had not loved her.

After ten minutes of holding the snapshot before him as he made his plodding, dizzy way up and down the corridor, Anne's face faded, and it was again Mrs. Swann.

"Thank you, sir," Harry said, and handed the snapshot back. He noticed the blue-stoned big gold ring on Swann's hand as he took it back.

"Is that a West Point ring, sir?"

"Yes. Want to look at it?"

"Yes, sir." Harry took it from him, noticing how easily it had come off the emaciated finger. On its sides were, in relief, a gladiator's helm and a sword. Above them was an eagle, wings outstretched, and to one side the words

DUTY HONOR COUNTRY

Harry handed it back. They paced up and down the corridor for another ten laps. Harry saw a thoughtful expression wrinkling Swann's leathery brow. Twice the West Pointer started to speak.

"Sergeant," Lieutenant Swann finally said, his snub-nosed cowboy face grave, "if I don't get out of this, I want you to take this ring. Leave this gold wedding band on my left hand, but get this back to them in Cheyenne."

"Who's 'them,' sir?"

Swann smiled. "Well, my father and my wife." His eyes looked eight thousand miles away. "I married the girl next door. My father went to the Academy, too. I want my wife to have this ring."

"I'm sure it won't be necessary, sir," Harry croaked from his dry, feverish throat.

"Look at the poor son of a bitch," Swann said, and they paused halfway down the hall. The doctor had just appeared over the edge of the stone steps from the village below. He had a bucket of water in his hands, and he was panting from the exertion of carrying it up the hill. The noon sunlight seemed to shine right through his bald skull and sunken cheeks. A guard motioned to him to leave the bucket there and stagger back down and get another.

CHAPTER SIXTEEN

Anne's white-gloved hand shot up in greeting as she caught sight of her mother and father waving to her from the pier. The engines had stopped, and there was a strange vacuum, filling with gray water swirling about massive wooden pilings. More and more voices called back from the ship to shore.

Anne brought her gloved hand to her mouth and blew her parents a kiss.

I hope you like my sun tan, she thought. I lay out there all those hours on the way back, just so you'd feel I was in perfect shape.

Better. That's the word, Anne thought. I'm better. Sure. She gazed down fondly at her father as he raised his Panama hat to her in the warm September afternoon. Mabel Wiley was wearing a beige cotton suit.

They look fine, Anne thought, nodding to them. And from here on I'm going to do my best. I really am. I'm going to keep busy, and try to be useful to other people. I'm going to study hard and maybe sneak through with a *cum laude*, and hope that I'll be all right.

II

"I'd hate to have to hit you, sir," Tommy Quinn said, "but you've got to get on your feet, no matter what I have to do."

Swann stared at him from suddenly sunken eyes. "I'd be happy to, Sergeant Quinn," he whispered, "but I can't."

Harry moved over to them. Tommy had just helped him to his own feet, and now he bent and the two of them pulled Swann up from the floor. The lieutenant just hung between them, his knees buckling.

"One foot ahead of the other, sir," Quinn said. It seemed an eternity as they waited, breathing hard from the exertion of holding him up between them. Slowly Swann stiffened one leg, and then, groaning as a weight-lifter groans, he straightened the other.

"All right," he gasped from his hunger-shriveled mouth. "Let's try a step." He moved forward and both legs buckled.

"Sir," Harry said, "we'll walk you up and down the hall between us. Just this way." And so they dragged Lieutenant Swann back and forth down the hall, the West Pointer's legs occasionally moving, as a cold engine turns over for a few revolutions.

III

Bill stood on the sidewalk outside his old undergraduate club in Cambridge. With great drunken dignity, he looked from the face of his friend Peedy Adams to the face of his friend Ward Smith.

"Are you suggesting," he asked, "that I can't get back over to the Law School by my*self?*"

"Why don't we just walk with you?"

The door to the club opened again, and Bill had a flashing glimpse of the entrance hall, the living room, and Harry's portrait and medals above the fireplace.

"All right," Bill said. "Let's walk to the Law School together, and — " he leaned forward solemnly " — and stop for a drink at Cronin's on the way."

IV

"I don't know where they're taking us, Lieutenant," Harry said, "but we're taking you with us." The afternoon was drawing to a close; the sixty survivors of the past months in the schoolhouse sat on the front steps, feeling silent and strange because of what had been happening in the past twenty-four hours. The afternoon before they had been herded down to a stream, with Harry and Tommy Quinn dragging Lieutenant Swann. The Chinese had given each man half a bar of laundry soap, and told them to bathe. They had passed out scissors, and the men had cut each other's hair, and trimmed beards, while standing waist-deep in the stream. When they had come ashore they had been given thin brown gingham trousers and a Russian-style collarless shirt, made to hang outside the trousers, and a pair of cloth sandals with canvas soles. Then this morning the guards had brought in a thick soup with little chunks of duck floating in it, plus a side dish of rice. This fantastic delicacy had started as many peace rumors as there were men.

Someone came over and sat down familiarly beside Harry.

"The doctor died," he said.

Quinn said, "Oh." Harry just kept gazing into the distance, hearing the every-afternoon rumble of anti-aircraft fire to the east.

"Yeah. I just saw him in there now." The man looked at Harry. "Don't you say hello to your old friends any more?"

Harry stared at him. "Who are you?"

"I'm Flattley."

Harry grinned. "I'm sorry, Flattley. I didn't recognize you without your beard. It's like meeting new people."

"Say," Flattley said, "what do you think? You think all this stuff means the war's over?"

"If the war's over," Harry said, "those planes of ours ought to stop bombing that valley over to the east of here."

"Anyway," Tommy Quinn said, "thank God they never thought this place was worth a bomb."

There was the sound of feet, and then a formation of Chinese guards, bedrolls on their shoulders, appeared over the top of the steps. They motioned to the men to head down the long flight of stone steps which had been off limits to everyone but the doctor and his two medics.

Harry looked around in the dusk. The men were helping each other to their feet in front of this schoolhouse in which no classes had been given. Two hundred and forty men had died here of starvation combined with disease; the last to die still lay on the filth-covered floors.

"OK, Lieutenant," Tommy Quinn said, "here we go." He and Harry pulled Swann to his feet and placed his paper-thin arms around their shoulders.

At the bottom of the steps there were three big two-and-a-half-ton captured American trucks, still with the white stars on their cab doors. Lounging beside them were three well-fed GIs.

Harry stared at them, remembering his contempt for the men who had rushed forward to volunteer as truck drivers the night he was captured.

Brother, Harry said to himself, if I'd known what I was in for, I would have been the first guy in line.

"I must be dreaming," Tommy Quinn said, looking at the trucks. "We're Chinese infantry. We only walk." The guards were moving among the sixty survivors, prodding them aboard, twenty to a truck.

"C'mon, Flattley," Harry croaked. "Help us get the lieutenant up here."

Just as they pulled the lieutenant aboard and placed him on the flat metal floor of the stripped-down open truck, there was an excited murmur among the men. Harry turned and saw that the schoolhouse on the hilltop was aflame. Silhouetted against the fire, two Chinese guards were running down the steps, fuel cans swinging in their hands. For a moment he thought of the doctor and the other bodies in there, and then the truck started with a slight jolt that knocked them all from their shaky legs.

V

Anne strode furiously across her small room in Briggs Hall and stopped just short of punching the window pane. Then she went back to her textbook and read it again to make sure that it said what she thought it said. This autumn she had decided to take a course in the history of the Far East, to try to make some sense out of the mess out there, and she was reading far ahead of the lectures.

There it was. Korea, 1592. Not 1950. The Japanese, bent upon the conquest of Korea, had approached the Yalu River via the same valleys the Americans had taken a bit less than a year before now, after the Inchon landings. The Chinese had let the Japanese get right up to the Yalu, and then poured across. 1592.

"No," Anne said thickly. "Didn't we have *anybody* who'd read this even once? Did we really have to go string ourselves out up there so they cut through us like paper?"

Not paper, Anne thought. Like flesh. She swallowed, bit her lip, and went on reading.

VI

The nighttime road was knocking them apart. During the days they slept in mud huts in villages while the trucks were camouflaged under nearby trees, but from dusk to dawn they moved north on these rutted rocky roads, the steel floor plates hammering at men who were swollen with wet beri-beri or wracked with dysentery.

"Not again," Tommy Quinn said, and Harry put his arms before his face and flattened out on the metal plates. A big man named Leboeuf from New Hampshire was rising groggily and making his way to the side of the truck. His bare legs were puffed up like fat marble columns from wet beri-beri, and he wore only the Russian-style shirt because he could not fit into any trousers. He had uncontrollable dysentery. Somewhere he had acquired a big metal frying pan with a wooden handle, and when he felt an attack coming he placed it beneath him. Then he tried to make his shaky way to the side of the truck to throw the contents of the frying pan over the side, but invariably the air rushing past the truck caught it and sprayed the wet yellow material over the other occupants, as well as the windshield of the truck behind, which would promptly switch on its window wipers.

"How's Swann making it?" Tommy asked as they both lay face downwards on the steel floor plates, trying to avoid Leboeuf's barrage.

"Very damn badly," Harry replied.

*   *   *

The guard came to the door of the mud hut. It was four o'clock in the late September afternoon, time to mount the trucks for the night ride.

Tommy Quinn was already on his feet. Harry crawled over to wake up Lieutenant Swann, who was lying on his side, knees doubled up, his face to the wall.

"Come on, sir," Harry said, shaking his shoulder gently. "Time to move out." He withdrew his hand suddenly. Under the thin gingham shirt, Swann's shoulder felt like a dead stick.

Tommy Quinn saw the look in Harry's eye, and dropped to his knees beside him. Together, they turned the lieutenant over and tried to put him on his back, but the body was stiff; it rolled

into the sideways position on its other side, knees still doubled
up.

"That's all," Tommy said. He made the sign of the cross, and
rose. The guards were shouting at them to get out of the hut
and onto the trucks.

Harry looked down at the lieutenant's hand, and then drew
the gold West Point ring from a stiffened, emaciated finger.

Anne's picture, he thought, I've got to get Anne's picture. He
reached into the breast pocket of the new brown shirt. Pulling
out Lieutenant Swann's wallet, he put it and the West Point ring
in the pocket of his shirt.

Harry stood up. A Chinese guard was standing by the door,
giving him a knowing smile as Harry looked into his breast
pocket to make sure that the ring and the wallet were safe.

He thinks I'm stealing from Swann, Harry thought, and suddenly he was shouting at the guard.

"You don't understand!" Harry yelled. "You don't *understand!*"

The guard smiled and motioned to Harry to come outside and
get on the truck.

CHAPTER SEVENTEEN

"I F PYOKTONG looks good to you, buddy," the Marine sergeant said, "I hate to think where you've been till now."

Harry shrugged his shoulders and went on eating his bowl of turnip soup. It was nine in the morning; he and Tommy and some of the other survivors of the truck trip north were sitting on the ground before the thatch-roofed mud hut to which they had been assigned when they arrived four days before.

"I'll tell you," Harry said, finishing the turnip soup and picking up the small bowl of sorghum, "if all along we could have had a meal like this twice a day the way we get it here, I think ninety per cent of the guys would have made it through the march and everything."

"Maybe." The Marine sergeant looked in disgust at his bowl of soup and bowl of sorghum. "We had it damn bad here until the last few weeks. We got some food here now, but wait till you see the way they work this. See that warehouse down there?" He pointed to a big building down the slope, by the river. "They get in a couple of tons of carrots, see? Then we eat carrot soup until they run out of carrots. Then they get in a load of turnips. We've been eating turnip soup for twenty-three days now."

"You've got nothing to complain about," Harry said, and leaned back against the mud wall of the hut. It was a bit chilly, but they had issued every two men a blanket, and he had around his shoulders the one that he and Tommy shared.

The unarmed Chinese political officer attached to their platoon of one hundred men walked past, talking with one of the GIs who was responsible for setting up work details. He looked in Harry's direction, and Harry looked away. Down by the river, under guard, some men were washing their clothes.

Harry sighed, and passed his hand across his face, feeling the nicks from where a fellow prisoner had shaved him yesterday with the one straight razor that had been issued to each hut of fifteen men.

You don't get it, Harry thought, looking past the Marine sergeant. This place is organized. Nobody's dying here. Not many, anyway. He gazed at the panorama of the big camp. On the far slope were scores of huts housing seven hundred privates and corporals from the different U.N. forces, most of them Americans. A road in the gentle valley between that slope and this ran down to the Yalu, and on this slope were the Chinese headquarters and the huts housing three hundred U.N. officers and sergeants. The Yalu flowed past, half a mile wide, and on both sides of the river were bare brown hills.

A column of men from the private-corporal side came walking through the camp, on their way to the lecture hall up by headquarters. Harry shook his head as he watched them pass. He had not yet been to a lecture, but he knew that, seven months after capture, he had arrived at one of the schools he first heard of the night he was taken by the Chinese. He closed his eyes. Again he saw the trim political officer on the snowbank across the stream, while he shivered without boots, sitting in the snow. Again he heard the political officer congratulating them on being captured, telling them they would soon be home, soon be released, just a little matter of a little march to a little school for a few lectures to straighten them out about who started the war. Now that they were here, the word among the prisoners was that the way to get along was to never let on that you owned so much as a car, back in the States. If they found out you had been to college you were suspect as a capitalist.

Harry rose and handed his blanket to Tommy Quinn. Moving over to the pail of water in which they rinsed their empty bowls, he stared across the river to Manchuria.

Well, he thought, we made it up to the Yalu. Just about a year after Charlie Company started marching for it in that big push.

"Purdick."

Harry turned, a bowl in each hand. The political officer who had been circling around the new arrivals for the past few days was pointing at him.

"Come with me."

Harry shrugged his shoulders, handed the two bowls to Tommy, and fell in beside the slender, erect Chinese. Walking along, he stole a look at the man's face. He had more of a hooked nose than the average Chinese, and a prominent jaw. His eyes were like sparkling black balls flashing under the heavy-hooded Chinese eyelids. He looked young, and nervous, and nasty.

"How is your health?" the man asked as they passed through the scattered huts, heading towards the headquarters building.

"All right," Harry said.

"Some of the men tell me you were able to walk long and hard."

"I had to walk long and hard."

"A strong spirit," the Chinese said. "You want to live, to return to your loved ones."

"That's right."

"My name is Chung."

Harry nodded.

The Chinese produced a cigarette and offered it to Harry as they walked past some men who were carrying pails of water.

"No thanks," Harry said, and then when the detail of prisoners were past, he thought of Tommy Quinn and said, "I'll take it." Chung handed him the cigarette, and watched as Harry put it away in his shirt pocket.

They crossed the porch of the ugly two-story wood and clay headquarters building, and entered directly into a room perhaps ten by twelve feet wide. A table sat on a straw mat on the wooden floor, with four chairs around it. Harry looked at the walls, expecting to see photographs or insignia or slogans or a bulletin board, but there was nothing.

"Please be seated," Chung said. He took off his khaki cap and sat across the table from Harry. There was a pile of papers on one corner of the table, and Chung picked them up and rifled through them until he came to one.

"This is the sheet of information about yourself which you were required to fill out upon arrival."

Harry nodded.

"You give your name as Sergeant First Class Harold Purdick, son of Mrs. Stephen Purdick, South Harbor, Maine."

"That's right."

"Your mother is a widow?"

"My father was killed by the Japanese in the Second World War."

The Chinese stopped and put down the piece of paper. For a moment there was a thoughtful expression on his face. "My elder brother, too. I'm sorry." He picked up the piece of paper again. "In your biography you say, and I quote, 'I was born of working class parents in a fishing village in Maine. My father was a lobster fisherman. I helped my father with his lobster traps. In 1945 I graduated from South Harbor High School. Then I enlisted in the United States Army, serving in Germany and various posts in the United States. At the outbreak of this war I was sent to Korea and am now a captive of the Chinese People's Volunteer Army at Camp Number Five, Pyoktong North Korea.' " Chung put the piece of paper down, smiled at it, and then at Harry. "I am a graduate in economics of Cornell University," he said. "I think I see in your speech, your gestures, your way of walking, what I often saw when I went past the fraternity houses I was not invited to enter at Cornell. I do not think I am in the presence of a little-educated fisherman."

Harry shrugged.

The political officer pushed the paper to one side. "You have a gift for leadership."

"No."

"Yes." Chung nodded. "You have in fact more of what I believe your Army calls 'command presence' than many of the officers here. Some of them are very poor specimens."

"It's very hard to have command presence," Harry blurted, "when you're sick and crawling on your hands and knees."

"You seem to make friends, even in these few days."

"I get along."

"Purdick," Chung said, "I need a new platoon leader. He will be responsible for one hundred officers and men. He can make the difference between their being ill or remaining in good health. I want you to try the job."

"No, thanks."

"Why not?"

"I'm not interested. I just want to mind my own business."

"Are you a graduate of the United States Military Academy at West Point?"

"Oh, for God's sake," Harry said. "No!"

"One of the men tells me you have a West Point ring in your possession."

Harry's eyes narrowed. Some stool pigeon in our hut.

Chung's fingers drummed on the table. "Do you have such a ring in your possession?" he asked, his voice rising.

"Yes." Harry's mouth was tight. He pulled the ring out of his breast pocket and put it on the table. "It belonged to a man who died on the way here." Harry's fists tightened in his lap. "If you'll look at the inscription in the inside, you'll see that this ring belonged to First Lieutenant Glenn W. Swann."

"How do I know that is not your name?"

Harry closed his eyes. "Well, for one thing, this biography you had us write is my first chance in seven months to get it on record that I'm still *alive*." Harry's jaw twitched. "This is the first time since I've been captured that anybody has asked for *my name*."

"We'll talk another time," Chung said, brushing the ring back across the table with the back of his hand. "We are not sending your names to the Red Cross yet, in any case. Because your capitalistic rulers continue to obstruct the truce talks at Panmunjom, we have lots of time."

II

The sailor got his small blue bag out of Bill's car and said, "Thanks for the ride."

"That's OK." Bill drove on from New York towards Cambridge, smiling. The sailor had been a pleasant fellow, home for leave after a cruise in the Mediterranean with the Sixth Fleet. The man's attitude was what Bill appreciated. He was in the service, but he did not feel that Bill should necessarily be in too.

It was the same way, Bill thought as he drove, around Cambridge. On week-ends some of his classmates from college would appear, some stationed at Fort Devens and some now ensigns in the Navy, but there was no ill feeling between those who were in the service, and those who were pursuing graduate work and had deferments to do it. Some guys were in, and some guys were not. It was a limited war.

III

This was the third of these lectures that Harry had been required to attend, but it was the first time he had heard Chung give one. Harry had a fever, and this morning everything came to him through a buzzing gray veil.

"How would you like it," Chung was saying, putting down

the prepared text and launching out on his own, "how would you like it if China was running its gunboats up your rivers as far as from New Orleans to Minneapolis? That's what you did to us." Then he went back to the prepared text.

Harry's mind wandered as Chung's voice became a monotone of "imperialists Wall Street aggression corruption true socialist development victory." There were two hundred men in the cold mud-walled hall, sitting on benches set on a dirt floor. At the front of the room there was a raised wooden platform, and on it, without lectern, holding the Peking-prepared lecture in his hands, was Chung. There was nothing on the wall behind him. He carried no weapon.

He'd do a hell of a lot better if he just gave these off the cuff, Harry thought woozily. When he puts in those little asides of his own, he sounds as if he really means it.

"The point," Chung said, putting the papers momentarily behind his back, "is that Communism is good *for China*." Then he began reading again about how South Korea had attacked North Korea, and about how the United States had been planning to invade China and that was the reason China had intervened in the war.

For heaven's sake, Harry thought, why try that on a bunch of us who know we were throwing our bayonets away and getting set to go home for Christmas?

There was a snore across the aisle from him, and Harry saw one of the Negro boys asleep, his head on a buddy's shoulder. The indifference to these lectures was like a cloudy cushion hanging from the thatched ceiling, but in that section across the aisle it ranged from a recognition and stirring when the American Negro's plight was mentioned, to a really icy resentment that any smooth-talking Chinese was going to tell them what the score was.

Chung folded the papers behind his back again. "Our problem," he said, "is that it is hard, living at one moment in history, as we all must, to see the large perspective of history.

But the truth is that all history has been one glorious revolution of the oppressed against the oppressors. At last we have the fully revealed doctrine of Communism, which explains what the past has been, and shows us how we can make the future be a time of splendid fulfillment of all the workers' revolutionary struggles of the past and present."

He really believes it, Harry thought. His fevered mind wandered again, back to his days in the freshman debating society at Harvard. He thought of that debate, "Resolved, that the Chinese Communists are Agrarian Reformers." He remembered it all, all that year, other debates, criticizing each other's techniques.

"Now," Chung said, "are there any comments?"

"Yes," Harry rose, still back in a pleasant dream of Harvard. "One of the problems with reading a lecture that you have not written is that you are likely to drone. That's very understandable, but you really have to guard against it."

Chung put the papers to his side. "You rude savage," he said in shaking tones.

Harry woke to where he was, and as he did he felt an electric surge of support hit him from behind, from the Negroes across the aisle. It almost propelled him down the center of the aisle. He rocked on his feet, and then said, "If there's any savagery being practiced around here, Chung, it's not by us."

Chung shouted, "The question was for comments on the *content!* On the subject matter!" The guards who had been outside came running in, unslinging the burp guns they carried across their backs. Everyone was awake by now, and Harry felt as if he were being lifted three feet from the floor.

"Well, as far as the subject matter goes, Chung, you can't make history jump through a hoop for you or anybody else. What you're giving us is just a theory of history, that's all."

"Purdick," Chung said as two guards took up places before the platform, "from this moment you are on no lists. Your name will not leave here. No one will know what has happened to you. Just as I thought, you are a capitalist agent. You are an enemy of the people, and a traitor to your fellow prisoners." He motioned, and two guards came down the aisle and pushed Harry outside.

On the hillside, one guard disappeared into a shack and brought out a shovel and a grub axe, while the other one kept Harry covered with his burp gun. The guard handed Harry the tools, and paced off a rectangle of the dun earth about four feet long and three feet wide.

I guess they're going to bury me in a sitting position, Harry thought, and started digging. From time to time he stopped, looking at the wide Yalu as it flowed across this dull brown prairie. The sky was a hazy gray-blue blanket, somehow horizonless, without a dome, more like a vapor than anything that could be called the heavens. The cold loam on his shovel smelled like buttermilk. Just down the slope a family of pigs grunted within a pen.

What a place to go out, Harry thought, and resumed digging.

When he had made the hole waist-high, the nearer guard indicated that he should sit in it. The other guard took the shovel and grub axe back and put them in the guard shack, and then wandered towards the inhabited side of the hill. The nearer guard squatted on his haunches, ten yards away, looking out over the river, and Harry shifted uncomfortably in the hole.

IV

The barn-like ballroom in the Hasty Pudding Club at Harvard was hot from the scores of flushed boys and girls who were dancing the 'Twenties-revived Charleston. Around the edges of the dance floor young men in sports coats and gray flannel slacks stood with drinks in their hands, chatting with each other and watching the gyrations of the couples in the middle.

The music came crashing to a halt, and after a moment the orchestra switched to the foxtrot strains of "You're Not Sick, You're Just in Love." The gray-flannel-suited young man with whom Anne had come to the dance disappeared as another Harvard senior tapped his shoulder, and she went dancing along, chattering about very little.

From time to time Anne glanced over her partner's shoulder, in the direction of the bar just off the dance floor. Bill was standing in there with his friends Peedy Adams and Ward Smith, and she was worried about him. She had not seen him more than two or three times this autumn, but each time she had, he had been high as a kite, at a cocktail party after a football game, or at one of these Saturday night dances. Tonight he was in really bad shape.

As she watched, Bill came veering out of the bar, went to the center of the dance floor, and cut in on a Radcliffe girl. Anne's face froze as she saw the girl take in the situation, try to dance around Bill's faltering legs, and finally suggest that they sit this one out. On their way off the dance floor, another man cut in on Bill. She saw Bill's lips moving, saw him arguing that they had stopped dancing, so the man should not try to cut in. Then the girl said something, and Bill drew himself up, bowed to both of them, and made his way back to the bar.

"Will you excuse me?" Anne said to the faceless creature who had her in his arms. "I have to disappear for a few minutes. No, no, don't bother to wait, that's all right." She walked into the bar. Bill was tearing drink chits out of a book, and motioning with them to the bartender.

"Hi," Anne said.

Bill turned from the bar. His defensive expression faded. "Hello, Anne."

"How're you doing, Bill?"

"All right, I suppose." The bartender came over, but Bill just shook his head at the man. "How are you doing?"

"All right, I suppose." A soft, sad smile touched Anne's face.

Bill looked around. "You OK, Anne? I mean, did somebody leave you on the dance floor, or something?"

"No, no. I just wanted to come and chat with you."

"Good." Bill looked at where his friends were standing, a few yards away. Peedy Adams nodded to her with his blond sheep-dog head of hair, and Ward Smith's heavy-blue cheeks broke in an encouraging smile. Bill pointed at them. "They're putting together the Pudding Show for Christmastime. Ward's Mister Words, and Peedy's Mister Music. Then Peedy takes the part of the leading lady."

"*Peedy* does?" Anne asked, looking at the slender, virile, blond-thatched young man.

Bill nodded. "Damn good, too." His eyes met Anne's, and saw the emptiness there. "Say — I don't know, but — "

"What?"

"I've got these tickets to the Yale game. If *you* were my date, maybe I wouldn't meet so many University Police that weekend."

Anne smiled at him again. He had straightened up as he talked to her, and the expression on his face was a combination of a protective feeling for her, and a need to be told that he was all right, that he was going to be all right.

"I'd be happy to," Anne said. Looking at him, she saw the catboat in Maine, saw the three of them out in it as children, as teen-agers. "Thank you for asking me."

Bill's face broke into a smile. "Thank *you*." He went over to Peedy Adams, handed him the book of drink chits, and started out of the clubhouse. A moment later he wheeled and strode back to Anne, quickly. "I won't forget," he said. "That's one thing I'll remember tomorrow morning."

"Good night, Bill."

V

The mists began to recede from the edge of the hole, and as the dawn broke he could see the cold river. It was the third morning since he had been placed in here. Harry turned his head as he sat in the hole, keeping an eye on the guard, who was pacing sleepily along the top of the hill.

Got to play him along again today, Harry thought. He did not know how long he was going to be in here, but he knew that nothing he could do would make the actual sentence any shorter. On the other hand, there were any number of ways of shortening the days. The guards had orders to let him get out of the hole for natural functions, but they watched him, and if he failed to produce, he was not allowed out of the pain-cramping postures of the hole the next time. So he had learned how to ration out even that. He was good for six trips away from the hole in day-time hours, and three or four long standing-up stretches at night. The Chinese saw like cats in the dark, but now he was a cat too, and the moment one of them disappeared into the shack for a smoke, he was up and on his feet and running in place in the waist-deep hole and waving his arms frantically over his head. At night he would do deep-knee bends, thirty, forty, fifty, keeping his head low. At first he had thought that calisthenics might only compound the terrible cramps around the spine and hips that came from sitting in cold earth for hours at a time, but the calisthenics relieved the pain. By comparison, whatever aches fifty deep-knee bends caused were not noticeable.

An American came over the top of the hill, carrying a wooden box in which was the one gourd of water and bowl of food he was allowed a day. Harry smiled as he saw the GI coming. He had no idea of what kind of a deal the American cooks had made with the guards to get him rice instead of sorghum and turnip soup, but every day it was a big wooden bowl of good rice, with sometimes chunks of cooked fish from the river hidden in it.

They packed the rice in so tight that sometimes it seemed the bowl weighed five pounds.

The guard closed in behind the GI who was bringing the food, making sure that there would be no word spoken between him and the man enduring this outdoor solitary confinement.

The GI bent down, gave Harry an encouraging wink, handed the bowl of rice to him, and made an obscene gesture in reference to the guard, keeping the upwards-pointing finger beside his chest as he bent over to leave the gourd of water on the edge of the hole. He gave Harry a final thumbs-up sign and walked off. Harry watched him every step of the way to the top of the hill, treasuring the American build, the American gait. When the man's shoulders and then head pulled down away over the top, he went to work on the rice. It amazed him that they could get it up here so hot, and he had an idea that the man who brought it ran until just the point where he came in view of this guard.

As he came to the last rice grains at the bottom of the bowl, Harry saw a piece of tightly folded paper there. Lowering the bowl into the tight angle formed by his trunk and his tucked-up knees, he slipped the piece of paper underneath him, and finished every grain of rice.

Late in the afternoon, when the light began to make it hard for the guard to see exactly what Harry was doing, he unfolded the piece of paper and spread it on his lap. Glancing every other moment in the direction of the preoccupied guard, who was doing something to the adjustable canvas sling of his burp gun, Harry read it. It was in pencil, with block letters that had been embellished with curlicues.

TO SERGEANT FIRST CLASS HARRY PURDICK, SECOND DIVISION, U.S. ARMY, TDY PYOKTONG, NORTH KOREA. HANG ON IN THERE. WE ARE WITH YOU ALL THE WAY. CHUNG IS STILL HERE BUT NOT ALLOWED TO GIVE ANY MORE TALKS. SINCERELY.

Then followed the signatures of twenty-four men, all of whom would be sitting in similar holes if this piece of paper were discovered. Harry tore it into pieces and began surreptitiously eating it. Looking at the sky, feeling the paper dissolving in his mouth, he felt no cramps at all for half an hour.

CHAPTER EIGHTEEN

"Simply delicious, Mrs. Purdick," Anne was saying. "And not just cranberry sauce, but cran*berries*."

Constance smiled as she watched Anne and Bill consuming the Thanksgiving turkey that she had cooked for them. When Bill had suggested that they have Anne for a midday dinner, before she had to join her family and some of their friends for an evening one, Constance had been a bit apprehensive.

I don't know, she thought, sitting back, her face smiling crookedly as she smelled the giblet gravy and dressing over which she had slaved. She brushed her white hair back from her forehead, and listened, not to what Anne and Bill were saying, but to the happy, bantering tone of their conversation.

I thought it would be awful. I thought we'd all sit here and it would make us think about Harry. Her blue eyes lit as she saw Bill's long, straight back lean forward as he said, "No, no, Anne, that's not the point," and Anne saying back, "Yes, it *is* the point." She had not seen Bill so animated for quite a while.

Constance rose to clear some space for dessert, and Anne was right beside her, helping. Bill was picking up the platter with the remnants of the turkey, and bringing it into the kitchen.

All three of them were always so nice with each other, Constance thought. Even when they were children. She felt tears in her eyes, and quickly bent to see how the mince pie was faring in the oven.

II

"Hey, Harry," Tommy Quinn said from the corner of the hut where he and another man were writing up the two hundred words of political discussion that were required each day there was not a lecture for their group, "we're gonna say it came as a big surprise to you to find out it was really the South Koreans attacked North Korea. O.K.?"

"Sure," Harry said, and went back to trying to mend a hole in his worn Russian brown shirt with a thorn and some thread he had pulled out of the inside seam of the gingham trousers. He shivered as he sat, bare to the waist, a blanket over his shoulders, working quickly on the shirt in his lap. It was becoming dreadfully cold here in December, and each blast from the frozen Yalu hunted down the smallest tear in their deteriorating summer prisoner uniforms.

"They've been making a hell of a big issue out of germ warfare," Tommy Quinn said. "I guess we better put down something on that." He turned to the man who was sitting in the corner with him. "O.K., Wuthers, what do you want us to say?"

Wuthers cleared his throat importantly, and Harry suppressed a smile. The little gnome was forty-two years old, and in twenty-five years in the Army he had risen to the lowest grade of sergeant. He had been a baker when the Chinese had overrun his Quartermaster unit.

"I'll tell you what to say," Wuthers proclaimed in his piping voice. "Just say what they told us the other day. Any country uses the atomic bomb, they can also be guilty of germ warfare."

Harry put down his thorn needle, and passed his hand across his face. Tommy Quinn had accepted the post of administrative squad leader because somebody had to see that men were detailed to go up to the kitchen to get the food, but the Chinese had made Wuthers the squad monitor. The monitor was supposed to be the political conscience of each fifteen-man squad of Americans, just as the Chinese had a political officer attached at every level in their own army. Wuthers had jumped at the chance. The only problem was that he could read very little and write almost not at all, so Tommy Quinn had to take over the task of writing the required reactions to the lectures.

"Why don't we say this about germ warfare?" Harry suggested. "Why don't we say that any country that can develop an atomic bomb must be able to breed a special kind of housefly that can stand the cold up here?"

Tommy Quinn grinned, and then he and Harry waited to see Wuthers get it. The past two weeks, the walls of the lecture hall had been covered with big blown-up photos of parachute-attached cannisters with bugs crawling out of them onto snowbanks in which they would have been dead in less than a minute. These were supposed to have been the secret disease-spreading weapons dropped by Americans. It had been so crude as to be pathetic, but Wuthers believed. The Chinese had raised him to the dizzying heights of squad monitor, and he believed.

"You goddamn guys," Wuthers said after a minute, his small eyes looking first at Tommy, then at Harry, then at the others huddled bored along the mud walls. "How about them confessions from the pilots? Huh? How about that? How about them signed confessions from the pilots who dropped them things?"

"Wuthers," Harry said, "when I was in that hole a few weeks ago, I would have signed *anything* to get out of it. I mean *anything*. The seventh day in there I didn't even know what I was doing. They never touched me; they just left me in the hole."

"You deserved it," Wuthers said. "You ruined a nice talk from Comrade Chung."

"Shove it up your ass," Harry said, and picked up the thorn needle again. The needle was shaking in his angry hand. He felt very much like walking across the hut and kicking Wuthers in his slack mouth, but he knew that Chung was backing his monitors all the way. It was Wuthers who had told Chung about Swann's West Point ring that he had in his breast pocket. Wuthers couldn't do much, but on the other hand, not much could be done to him, unless one were ready to go right back in that hole.

The hell with it, Harry thought. He finished mending the tear in his shirt, slipped it back over his head, and walked out the door.

"You can't go yet!" Wuthers cried out indignantly. "We haven't finished our discussion period yet!"

Harry stuck his head back in the door. "You tell 'em anything you want to, Wuthers." Harry's voice was choking. "Tell 'em we were all coming up to the Yalu with bayonets fixed and germ bullets in our weapons and lots of landing barges and we were going to cross the Yalu and march to Peking and rape their women and make their children do terrible things like vote in elections." Harry saw a pair of riding breeches moving up beside him, and then Chung was looking into his eyes. Chung's lips were quivering with rage at what he had just heard. His bright black eyes bored into Harry's suddenly frightened face.

"Go back in there, Purdick," Chung said in a steady voice. "Go back in there."

III

The Hasty Pudding Show, a spoof on the 'Twenties, opened its New York run in the Hunter College auditorium four days before Christmas, and was a howling success. As Bill and Anne stood talking with friends during the intermission, Bill overheard the bubbling voices of the New York homosexuals who always came to see these college shows in which the roles of both sexes were acted by young men. They were all a-twitter about Peedy Adams, who had shaved the hair from his chest, had been most effectively made up, and had put on some of the lithest, sauciest dances that anyone in the audience had ever seen.

* * *

When the final curtain came down, Bill and Anne were the first people backstage. Peedy had taken off his blonde wig, revealing his own waterfall of blond hair, and was standing there, his skirt still swaying as he pummeled the shoulders of his co-author Ward Smith.

"It was great!" Bill shouted.

"I know it!" Peedy roared in response, poking Bill's chest.

Anne kissed Peedy on his skillfully made-up cheeks. "You fooled *me*, Peedy," she said, and then shook Ward's hand in congratulations.

"But," Peedy said, lowering his voice, "the best is yet to come."

"What do you mean?" Bill looked at the pained expression on Ward's face.

"We're going on to the Stork Club."

"Well, what's such a big deal about that?" Bill inquired. "It isn't as if we hadn't all been in there three times this week."

"You don't get it," Ward said. "Peedy wants to go as my date."

The man at the inner entrance to the Stork Club held aside the velvet rope, and another dinner-jacketed headwaiter led them to a table for four beside the circular dance floor. As Bill pushed in Anne's chair, he was quaking with fear that Peedy might be unmasked. Peedy had switched to a brunette wig, but was wearing the dress from the show, minus the 'Twenties filmy frills. The hem of the flapper costume had been dropped in a fast piece of surgery with a razor backstage. A borrowed black-sequined cardigan sweater over the dress minimized the breadth of Peedy's shoulders.

"I wish I were dead," Bill whispered to Anne as he sat down.

The waiter was asking them what they wanted to drink. All around them were people they knew, many of whom had just seen the show. None of them recognized Peedy.

"I'll have a bourbon and water," Ward Smith said, and then he realized that he had not asked his date what he-she wanted. "What would you like, Petrina?"

"Oh, dear," Peedy said in feminine tones, batting his naturally long eyelashes at the waiter. "A little crème de menthe frappé, I suppose."

Fifteen minutes later, Bill was beginning to relax. Ward had taken Peedy out for one circuit of the jammed dance floor, and it seemed that Peedy's imitation was as good at close quarters as it was behind the footlights.

"I guess we can dance, too," Bill said. Anne rose and they moved off into the festive crowd, all young, all home from a score of prep schools and colleges. Her body came against him, warm and firm, and he reacted to it.

"Bill?"

"Yes?" He pulled his eyes back from watching Peedy as Ward led him through a samba.

"Tell me. Am I right in thinking that life looks better to you these days?"

Bill looked at the thoughtful, compassionate expression on her face. They passed the mirror nearest the bandstand, and for a moment, glancing at the two of them in it, at her neatly combed hair, the pretty deep-blue dress, he saw a montage of the other girls he had brought here on other, earlier vacations. Now they were gone.

"It looks a lot better. How does it look to you?"

"Better."

The orchestra was playing all the danceable old debutante-circuit favorites. They moved from "Love for Sale" to "You're the Top" without missing a beat.

"I read something the other day," Bill said as they spun relaxedly to the fast rhythm. "The idea is that the best is the enemy of the good."

Their eyes met.

"That," Anne said, "is a very interesting observation."

They returned to the table, where Ward had just seated Peedy after their second dance. The waiter brought another round of drinks.

"Excuse me," Peedy said, rising, and made his way through the dancing couples, in the direction of the rest rooms. Bill took a sip of his drink, watching Peedy go, and then he choked. Peedy had not turned right to go to the ladies' room, but was heading straight up by the bar, for the men's room.

"Get him!" Bill barked at Ward. Ward looked, his mouth opening, and then was off like a broken-field runner through the dancing couples. Watching, half out of their chairs, Bill and Anne saw Ward come skidding up to Peedy, grabbing his shaven and powdered arm just before he turned into the little hallway to the men's room door. He saw the two of them talking, and then Peedy was shaking his head, clearly saying that he was not going to use the ladies' room, and Ward suggesting that he come back to the table, and Peedy saying unmistakably, I've got to get to some bathroom somewhere. Ward nodded, waved a quick good-night to Bill and Anne, and propelled Peedy in the direction of the front door.

"How much mad money have you got with you, Anne?" Bill asked after a moment.

"Five dollars."

Bill sagged on the little chair. "I really wasn't counting on paying a bill for all four of us."

"Well, can't you borrow from one of these people you know in here tonight?"

Bill brightened. "Good girl," he said. "That's what I'll do."

IV

Harry sat against the wall of the hut, his face expressing a series of impatient smiles. It was Christmas Day, and the Chinese had allowed visiting back and forth between the officer-sergeant side of the camp and the corporal-pfc.-private side. Two men from Charlie Company had turned up. For an hour they and Harry and Tommy Quinn had compared notes on their experiences since capture, and whom they had seen die on the march north, and who might still be alive but not at Pyoktong. Then it had all dragged, and eventually the two boys had gotten up and shaken hands, and everyone had wished everyone else a Merry Christmas, and they had gone back over to their own hillside. As they left, Harry had found himself remembering that patrol with his raw squad on Christmas afternoon a year before, with Carmichael's ice skates sticking out of the boy's field-jacket pockets.

At the moment a great guy from Mississippi named Hump Jones was holding forth about his experiences as an MP desk sergeant in Japan before this war, doing imitations of the drunks and the junkies and the Japanese bar girl looking for the GI who told her all she had to do was drink one Coke a day and she would never get pregnant, that was why it was so popular in the States.

Harry rose. It had all started well enough, but it was two in the afternoon and all he could think of was Anne and his mother and Bill, wishing like a spike in his throat and heart that they were all sitting down to dinner, Christmas dinner in New York with Central Park soft and picturesque in optional snow into which they went only for a few minutes, and only for fun.

"Where you goin', Brother Purdick?" Hump Jones asked from where he squatted in the unmilitary posture that had caused his nickname. He winked at Harry, and the wink said, listen, son, I put out all this bullshit for the troops because it's going to get them through.

"Just get some air," Harry said, and he smiled back at Hump sadly, and Hump read it right: listen, brother, seeing Americans today just makes me think about the ones I really want to see.

Harry was three steps out the door when Tommy Quinn caught up to him.

"Thought I'd give you this when things started to go slow," Tommy said. "Merry Christmas." He held out a small package made of one of the sheets of lined paper on which the squad had to submit their discussions of the lectures.

Harry opened it. Inside there was a small metal chain, the type worn around the neck with dog tags.

"I thought you could use it for that West Point ring of Swann's," Tommy said. "The way you keep it in your pocket now, you feel for it every five minutes to make sure it's still there."

"This'll be a *lot* better." Harry looked down at the slim, worth-three-cents metal chain. "Where'd you get it?"

"I got it off a guy."

Harry looked alternately from Tommy to the ring as he slipped it onto the chain and then snapped the thin chain around his neck. He knew that the only way Tommy could have picked up something like this was by trading food or tobacco to get it. Harry turned away for a moment, blinking the sudden tears in his eyes as he stared at the frozen river and the smokeless huts on the snowy hillside.

Nobody ever made that much of a sacrifice to give me a present before. And I don't have anything for him.

"Tommy," he said, turning back, "damn it, I lost your present yesterday."

"Oh, that's OK," Tommy said. "You always let me have your tobacco ration."

V

Mabel Wiley came out of a falling dream, striking the bed with the flat of her hand, and then she was lying there, and Clarence was beside her, asleep.

She heard the laughter from the living room. It was New Year's Eve. She and Clarence had joined the half dozen friends of Anne's for a glass of champagne at midnight, and then gone to bed.

The luminous dial of the clock beside the bed said that it was quarter past one in the morning. Mabel stared up at the ceiling, welcoming the cold sheet of air that slipped into the overwarm room through the one raised window. The air sought her worried brow, and she leaned upward into it.

"Oh, *no!*" Bill's voice said from the living room, and there was more laughter.

Mabel sat up. She thought of slipping on her bed jacket, and then she remained upright in bed, letting the cool air brush her arms and the side of her nightgown. She was thinking of a year ago, with Anne poring over those pictures of the Marines retreating from the Changjin Reservoir. And now Harry was dead, and Bill's voice was saying something again in the living room.

Mabel put her hands to her face. There was something about this that her own deepest self had not yet told her, and now, starting this year of 1952, she wanted to know what it was. It was not that she minded Anne's going out with Bill. She and Clarence had always liked Bill, and when she saw Anne and Bill together, she understood why they were together. Because they had both loved Harry, together they could partly forget the sorrow. It was as if the sorrow had a fixed weight, and a ton of sorrow was easier for two to drag than for one.

Anyway, it's all almost childishly innocent between them, Mabel said to herself, so why should it worry you? You *wanted* her to start going out again. You didn't have Bill in mind, but the important thing is for Anne to get through her senior year in one piece, and if Bill helps her do that, fine. She has years after that to meet someone whom she'll marry. The important thing now is to keep her improving, and she is, she is.

Then why are you worried?

I don't know.

Mabel lay back again and slipped into a foggy dream, from which she suddenly awoke, sitting up and clapping both hands to her mouth. In her dream Harry had come up to her and begun talking quite matter-of-factly. He was wearing a helmet, and he was apologizing for being late for something.

That's it, Mabel thought, trembling. Everybody else knows he's dead, and underneath I think maybe he's alive. Oh God.

CHAPTER NINETEEN

Harry wandered about the bare snow-packed slope, not seeing the beaming GIs as they walked from hut to hut, reading each other the first letters they had received from home. To Harry it was all a wheel of cold oppressive gray sky above and frozen river below. This afternoon they had been called out before the headquarters building and told that, despite the objections of the American truce talks team at Panmunjom, the Chinese government had gotten some mail for them. Then letters from their families had been passed out to about one hundred of the three hundred men on this side of the camp. Harry had not been expecting any letters, since he knew all too well that Chung had not forwarded his name to the Red Cross along with the others. There was no way his family could know he was alive.

Harry saw a captain coming the other way, no letter in his hand; one of the two hundred men for whom there was nothing yet.

But for you there will be, Harry thought. There will be. What was flexing his face so hard that his teeth were bared was what had happened after that. Wuthers had come into the hut, with Chung behind him. To every other man in the hut, Wuthers had passed out one small air letter on which the men could write their first letter home. It was a single foldable piece of white paper, with a fat blue dove outlined on it, and the word "PEACE" in blue letters. Chung had looked on, nodding and smiling as the fourteen other men received their chance to write their families. Then Chung had nodded and Wuthers had turned away before he reached Harry. They had walked out, Wuthers with some extra forms still in his hand.

Harry looked up at the frozen sky. I swear I will get Chung. No matter how I have to do it, no matter how long it takes, I am going to get that man.

"Not even a letter to let them know I'm alive," Harry whispered. His face remained fixed, but his shoulders shook.

II

The taxi was stuck in crosstown traffic. Constance sat staring at the shiny cars, and the bundled-up midtown shoppers ducking in and out among them.

The taxi slipped forward a few yards, and Constance stared down at the package beside her. Today was her forty-seventh birthday. One or two old friends had remembered, in letters, but there were no presents. Bill had called from Cambridge last night, saying that his present was delayed.

Constance's blue eyes reflected a sad kindness. She knew what had happened; Bill had just remembered, yesterday, that today was her birthday. Her hand touched the package beside her. She had gone down to Bonwit's and bought herself a frilly bedjacket.

III

Harry was on his way back to the hut from the primitive latrine when he saw Chung standing just outside the hut in the dusk. The broken door was ajar, and as Harry came up quietly behind him, he saw what the Chinese was staring at. The other men were in exhausted sleep, two to a blanket, but Tommy

Quinn was kneeling on the dirt floor, as he did every night, saying his prayers.

Harry stopped, looking at the expression on Chung's face. Chung was trying to smile, but his lips were twitching in anger.

IV

Chung stood on the porch of the headquarters building, watching Wuthers bring Quinn up here in the cold noon light.

Wuthers came to a halt before the porch. "Reporting with Quinn as ordered."

"Thank you, Wuthers. You may go now." Chung smiled and motioned Quinn to follow him into the office. "Be seated," he said, and sat opposite Quinn. He stared at the honest-looking face under the flap-eared winter cap. Then he slid open the drawer of the table, and pulled out the pistol he was not allowed to carry in the camp.

"You received your first letter from home a few days ago," Chung said.

"Yes," Tommy Quinn confirmed.

"And you were given a letter form with which to answer it."

"Yes."

Chung nodded, and pulled a letter from the drawer. Handing it across the table, he asked, "Is this the letter you wished us to send your family?"

"Yes."

"It is my duty to read all letters from your platoon in order to correct any mistaken thoughts, or inaccurate information about conditions here." Chung gestured with one finger that he wanted it back. Tommy handed it over. "I will read you what I think is an interesting sentence in your letter, and I quote, 'Please tell Uncle Harold's family that I am sure he will be back from his trip up north as soon as the conference is over.'" Chung smiled. "Tell me about your Uncle Harold."

"Well," Tommy said quickly, "he works for a textile company in Worcester, and — "

"How would you know, on the border of China, anything about your uncle's movements in the United States?"

"In the letter I got from my mother," Tommy Quinn said, "they told me he disappeared when he was up in New Hampshire for a labor meeting."

"Do you still have that letter?"

"No. I threw it away."

Chung smiled. "Now let me tell you the truth. You and Harold Purdick were together in Company C, Ninth Infantry Regiment, Second Division. You were close friends then, as you are now. Undoubtedly you wrote your family about him. You have no Uncle Harold. If they had received this letter I have in my hand, they would have read through your past letters, and found his name. Then they would have located his family and given them the message, which is, tell them Harold Purdick will be back from the People's Republic of Korea when the Panmunjom truce talks provide a means for repatriation of prisoners."

Tommy said nothing.

"A costly gesture," Chung said. "*Your* mail privileges are also suspended."

V

The juke box in Cronin's was playing the music from *The King and I*; at the moment, "Getting to Know You" was drowning in the sound of hundreds of boys and girls chattering away their evening after-study hours in rhythm with the lifting of glasses of beer and the arrival of platters of hamburgers.

"I don't know," Anne said to Bill as she sat opposite him in one of the smaller booths in the great mustard interior of the barn-like beer hall. "I keep getting deeper into this thing. You know,

I started this one course in Far Eastern History because I wanted to understand what led up to this whole thing, but now — "

Bill nodded encouragingly. "Well, *do* you understand? I don't."

Anne shook her head. "No, but I mean, the whole thing is like a bottomless pit. Just the other day I was reading about the Second World War in the Pacific. The Japanese call it the Pacific War, and I was thinking, no you don't, it was the Second World War, in the Pacific." Anne reached for one of the French fries on the plate before her, and popped it in her mouth. "Then I thought, no, they're right to call it the Pacific War." She spread out her hands, palm upwards. "And they *are* right."

"I don't get it," Bill said.

"The point is, there were two separate wars. They just happened to be fought at the same time — one in the Pacific, and one in Europe."

"Now wait a minute," Bill said, holding up a hamburger. "There was a little something called the Axis, and Japan was part of it."

"No, but don't you *see?* I'm not saying that Japan didn't time some of its moves in relation to the European situation, but there was going to be a war out there anyway."

Bill suddenly straightened his long back, and an alert look crossed his face. "You know, that's damned interesting? My father was working on some idea like that when he was killed."

Anne stopped. "He *was?* I thought he was in American history."

"Yes, but when he was doing this history of naval operations out there, riding that carrier, he got thinking about the over-all thing. Some admiral had him conned into writing his biography, and then Dad foxed the admiral by taking it a step beyond that, and turning it into a book that would show how it was inevitable that a war had to happen out there."

"What happened to the book?"

"It went when the carrier was hit and Dad was killed."

Suddenly Anne began crying. Bill looked around, staring down a young man who was gawking from a table across the aisle.

"Anne," Bill said quietly, "would you like to go?"

"Yes," Anne said. "I'm sorry." She pulled out her handkerchief, and blew her nose. Bill rose and helped her on with her coat.

It was February slush underfoot on the Cambridge Common as he walked her through the dark, cold night. They had not said a word in the cold half mile from Cronin's. Crossing the wide street leading to the Common, Anne had grabbed at his arm as they skirted the icy side of a particularly big puddle, and he had kept her arm pressed between his elbow and his side.

In the mist, illumined by the dim cream light of a lamp near the statue of a Civil War soldier standing huddled in his greatcoat, Bill's steps faltered. He looked down at Anne's face.

"Anne."

Anne stopped, her arm still in his, and turned to look up into his face. Bill's mouth was slightly open, and his taut cheeks seemed to be quivering.

"Anne," Bill said, choking, "I hate to see you unhappy. You're the only person that makes sense to me any more."

Anne looked down at the shadowless electric light on the melting snow. Then she turned and kissed Bill's cheek. As she started to draw away she felt Bill's arms come around her. He held her, his face looking down at her.

He needs me, Anne thought. She closed her eyes and put her head against the chest of his coat.

VI

Harry walked slowly along the huts on the slope. It was the hour before this March dawn, and he was shivering. His body wanted to run back to his own hut and get back under the blanket he shared with Tommy, but his spirit kept him moving slowly through the irregularly placed huts that had once housed fishermen who worked the river below.

This was his hour. Everyone was asleep except the guards who walked the perimeter of the camp. No roll calls, no formations, no work details. No Chung peering around corners, no lectures, no farcical group discussions. Just silent huts, a graying night, and wind that bit like an animal.

Harry stopped, huddling in the lee of a hut. At night he dreamed grainy visions of pendulums, and great boulders pressing on his brain, and horses on tightropes, and of things happening that were breaking up his teeth. When he awoke, it was always with a lump in his throat. It was in these dawn prowls, his eyes darting like an animal's, ready to seize upon a piece of string, a square of cloth, a discarded pottery fragment, it was in these walks that his mind played him the rich colored film of home. As his straw-clad feet moved past mud-and-rush huts with thatched roofs, the inner screen of his mind took him into wood-paneled, mirrored elevators in apartment houses in New York, through bright wallpapered vestibules, into living rooms and dining rooms, into every bedroom he had ever seen. It all shone. It was all the Christmas vacations in New York rolled into one, all the gaiety and laughter and the girls in their long evening dresses and long white gloves, the boys in their dinner clothes, the cuff links and demi-tasse cups and silver forks.

But mostly it was rooms. In this hour before dawn, it was warm rooms. His mind would take him into a room he had been in only once before, a simple enough room in the house of a boarding-school friend whom he had visited only once, years before. He would see everything, to the last rug, to the curtain, to the books on the shelves. If he had not looked at the titles on the shelves when he visited there, then they were only books, standing exactly as they had been, but, if he had looked at the titles then, he could read the exact titles again now.

A prisoner came out of a hut down the way, heading for the latrine. Harry turned back. The spell was broken. With sunrise, fear and oppression spread like the light. The lectures were becoming more frequent, and Chung was once again giving his share. The interpreters spent more and more time listening to group discussions, during which everyone had to make an effort to say something. Men who seemed promising candidates for extra instruction were publicly told when to show up for it. Night after night, both collaborators and troublemakers would be summoned to headquarters. A man would come back and begin packing up his two food bowls and blanket.

"Where're you going?"

"I don't know where they're taking me."

And so they disappeared, men who had resisted the indoctrination, men who had lapped it up. And yet other reactionaries and progresssives remained.

Harry turned in the door of his hut. Tommy Quinn was just sitting up, a stunned thin statue in rags with one blanket about him on the cold dirt floor.

"You know," Tommy said, groaning to his feet like an old man, "some days I wonder why I bother."

Wuthers piped up, "I'll tell you why you bother, Quinn. You get up because you know them guards'd get your ass out of bed anyway."

Tommy looked over at the little gnome as if he had never seen him before. "You know, it's pretty damn sad when a man can't make the grade with his own people and has to go ass-kissing a bunch of people who captured him." He began folding the blanket. "What do you think they want you for, anyway, Wuthers? You think they really care about you?"

Wuthers came across the hut, furious, his finger wagging at Tommy Quinn. "Yes, they *do*. That's what's good about Communism — they care about *everybody*."

As Harry watched, Quinn's face broke into a surprised, bitter smile.

"Oh, they do?" Tommy said, looking around at the circle of ragged men who had stopped, some folding their blankets, some trying to comb their hair with old pieces of wood or pottery fragments, or the remnants of a belt buckle. "Look around, Wuthers."

CHAPTER TWENTY

ANNE WALKED down Massachusetts Avenue, on the other side of the slush-filled street from Harvard Yard. She had half an hour until her next class, in Emerson Hall, and she strolled along, her face pink in the wind, gazing at the offerings in bookshop windows.

How about some coffee? she asked herself.

Thanks. I will.

She started to turn into the Hayes-Bickford cafeteria when she saw Bill at the table in the back, chatting with a girl.

Anne stepped back, away from the door. Staring through the big plate-glass window, she saw him talking earnestly to the girl.

Well go on in, she said to herself. They don't own the place. Anne tried to make her feet move in some direction, but still she stood staring at the window.

Just some acquaintance of his, she thought. That's all.

Well then, go on in.

Anne swallowed, and then turned and walked down the street.

II

The seldom-seen camp commander was standing on the headquarters porch, serenely giving the assembled prisoners hell. His handsome, calm moon face reflected the expression of a man who might be reminiscing about something quite charming that had happened in his youth, and each sing-song stanza of Chinese carried a cheerful melody on the cold March air.

"The camp commander says knives are being made," Chung

translated. "This is of course forbidden and against camp regulations." The middle-aged tall commander resumed again, as if discussing a delicate philosophical point concerning which there might be many opinions.

"The camp commander says that these knives are being made from the metal shanks inside the combat boots of those who still possess the boots in which they were captured," Chung continued. "If any more knives are made, all remaining boots will be confiscated, and those men will be barefoot from now on."

Harry shivered in the cold, but a ghost of a smile was on his face. To one side of him was the tall, stooped MP sergeant, Hump Jones. On the other side was a paratrooper named Martinez who had volunteered for one-man reconnaissance patrols behind enemy lines until he had been captured. Beyond Martinez stood Tommy Quinn. All down the line, each thin face bore the same expression: screw you.

"All officers will be moved from this camp shortly," Chung said. He nodded to the interpreter next to him, a man known to the prisoners as Rat-Face.

Rat-Face took over the interpreting in his infinitely worse English.

"Camp commander says take note suggestion 'bout tooth b'ushes," Rat-Face said, gasping out the words. "Tells you no tooth b'ushes available. No toothpaste also. Also no soap still available." Rat-Face, having done his part, nodded to the last of the three interpreters who stood at attention on the frozen earth just in front of the headquarters building. Wu, whose English was much better when he read the Peking-prepared speeches than in more spontaneous situations, took over.

"Camp commander points out escape attempt three days before. Three men attempted escape. Three men captured after four hours. Three men now in hole. Very cold. Camp commander suggests you consider difficulties of escape. Korea not country where bananas grow on trees. Nothing easy to eat to pick up from land."

The camp commander said something with a smile. He seemed genuinely, pleasantly amused.

"Americans look very different from Koreans and Chinese. Easy to identify you if you try escape."

Harry smiled despite himself. Everybody hated the camp commander a good deal less than the three interpreters who did the lecturing and personal interviews. The camp commander had the air of an old soldier who knew the first rule of every army: go through the motions; don't fight the problem.

"Camp commander reminds you, Korea a —" Wu turned hastily to Chung, who whispered a reply. "Korea a peninsula. To north of you, China. East side, Pacific Ocean. West side, Yellow Sea. South side, maybe two hundred miles of Chinese People Volunteer Army before come to front line our army, then your army."

The camp commander spoke again, in his most reasonable, magnanimous tone.

"Camp commander hopes you appreciate fair trial system we now have. Because your suggestions, now automatic fair trial before all punishment. Before, only punishment. Now, fair trial and then punishment."

Hump Jones coughed away a laugh as he stood at limp attention beside Harry. "Real goddamn democratic," he whispered, and then it was Harry's turn to cough.

III

Anne and Bill sat in the Exeter Street Theatre, watching the Japanese movie *Rashomon*.

"That's a fantastic shot," Bill whispered in her ear as the screen showed a *samurai's* face through bamboo leaves.

"Mm," Anne murmured. She felt pricklingly conscious tonight. On the way into town, with Bill driving, she had mentioned casually that she had seen him having coffee with a girl at Hayes-Bickford.

"You should have come in," Bill said. "She's one of the few girls in the Law School. She was straightening me out on a pretty tricky thing in Constitutional Law."

That had taken care of that, and now there was this strange, beautiful movie. It portrayed the story of the wife of a *samurai*, ravished by the Oriental equivalent of a highwayman. The story showed it through the eyes of different people, and the blame and sympathy shifted with each character's version.

It's so kind of futureless, Anne thought, watching the slow movements, the misty backgrounds, the wet flagstones and ferns.

She felt Bill's hand seek hers, and gratefully she placed her hand in his.

IV

Clarence Wiley sat at home on a Saturday morning, his face furrowed as he gazed at the April rain breaking against the window. In the kitchen he could hear Mabel singing as she prepared the sandwich and salad that they would have for lunch, but, as he looked at the letters column in the *New York Times* once again, he did not feel like singing.

Here was a letter. A well-written, self-righteous letter, condemning Senator McCarthy.

Clarence rose and walked over to the window. The expression on his face was of a pain as real as if something were needling his flesh. He was a conservative, and yet he knew full well that this letter was right, that McCarthy was a menace to freedom of expression in the United States.

He put his head against the cold pane. What I don't understand, he said to himself, is why the liberals have abdicated any concern about Communism. They were hot against Fascism when Hitler was killing the Jews, but none of them seems to have given a damn that Stalin has put the padlock on Eastern Europe. You tell them that the Chinese Communists killed ten million people in China when they came to power, and they just aren't interested.

Clarence balled his big hands into fists. He glanced again at the open white wings of the newspaper flung on his armchair.

If the *liberals* would just get interested in the dangers of Communism, a man like McCarthy couldn't get so far. I know damn *well* the liberals have some of the best brains in this country.

"I wonder who the hell they think is minding the store," Clarence muttered.

"What?" Mabel came out of the kitchen, into the dining room, holding the dark wooden salad bowl.

"Nothing," Clarence said. "I was just feeling old and impotent, that's all."

V

The Fife and Drum Room in Boston was crowded on this Saturday night, and the dance floor was its densest part. In the dim light, couples moved slowly to the music from the three-piece orchestra whose wailing notes were lost against walls decorated in patriotic motif. Several imitation antique drums had been cut in half, and they hung against the dark walls, their rims painted red, and their blue sides carrying pictures of white eagles with their wings spread and heads turned to one side. A singer crooned, "It's the Loveliest Night of the Year."

Anne's face was warm against Bill's cheek. Once or twice he pulled his head back from hers, looked at her gravely as they

moved slowly about the floor, and then kissed her brown hair
where it swept down beside her temple.

*   *   *

Anne lay face down on her bed in Briggs Hall. She could hear
other girls coming in at the end of their evenings, some whispering in the corridor, giggles and "Oh, no, he didn't say anything
as corny as *that?*" Slippers slapped past to the bathroom.

She still had on the dress that had danced with Bill; her ears
held the slow, syrupy music, the sound of ice in glasses, young
voices. She saw Bill's face when he came over from Law School
to pick her up these evenings, the slow smile lighting his face as
she came down the stairs and his tall form rose from the couch
in the Briggs Hall living room.

Anne turned her troubled face towards the dim wall next to
her bed.

The best is the enemy of the good. The wise words came back
to her from that wild evening at Christmas when Peedy Adams
had gone to the Stork Club dressed as a girl. She remembered
Bill's face as he had said the words when she danced with him
that night. He was saying that he knew she could never love
anyone as she had loved Harry.

And still he comes over, Anne thought. And you go out with
him. And you do like kissing him. Harry's dead, and you have
to go on living, and you could make Bill happy.

VI

The log split. Harry put down the axe for a moment, and
passed the flowing sleeve of the tattered Russian brown shirt
across his sweating forehead. Chung and a guard had marched
a dozen of them down here to the area away from the camp
where the guard's quarters were, to chop some firewood for
them.

Wuthers and another progressive were sitting on rocks in the bright May morning, chatting with Chung, while Harry and Tommy Quinn and Hump Jones and Martinez did the work.

Harry picked up the axe again. Its blade was shaped like a wedge, and the rough round handle made it difficult to control the blow.

Under the pencil mustache he somehow managed to keep trim, Martinez smiled as he neatly cracked open a log with one stroke. "Jeez," he said, "and I used to gripe when my mom sent me down to the store on the corner for a loaf of bread." The olive-skinned paratrooper kicked the split wood to one side and set another log on the stump he was using for a block. " 'Gee, mom,' " he said in a falsetto, mimicking his younger self, " 'do I *have* to?' "

Harry chuckled, and Tommy Quinn and Hump Jones nodded appreciatively as they gathered up some of the already split pieces.

" — socialist principles," Chung was saying, and Wuthers and the young progressive were nodding. Harry's face clouded as he looked at the young soldier who was nodding eagerly. The boy was named Norden, and he was a good deal brighter than Wuthers. At the beginning, Norden had been like the great majority of the men, just going along with the lectures, just doing the minimum. But after a while he had begun nodding, and now there was a light in his eyes as he sat listening to Chung.

Harry wrestled another log into the proper angle against the heavy root, sticking out of a dirt bank, that he was using for a chopping block. He raised the axe and brought it down with everything he had, pretending that it was Chung's skull he was breaking open. The guard wandered past, the burp gun slung horizontally at his side.

A breeze sent a few pieces of bark skittering across the worn earth, and Harry raised his eyes and looked at the electric-blue flowers on the hillside. Just a year ago he had seen these spring flowers blooming, when Lee was bringing him the last miles to the Bean Camp.

Harry shook his head viciously. Those were the things he had trained himself not to think of; the passage of time, good things to eat, and Anne. That kind of daydreaming was like a fire. If you flirted past too near it you might end up like some of the boys in camp, who walked around all day saying nothing, or cried when spoken to, or opened their mouths and emitted sounds like dogs or cats, incapable of human speech.

Chung let out a gale of Chinese to the guard, who answered in a quick aria.

Damn, Harry thought, his face grave in the May sunshine, I wish I knew what they were saying to each other. It'd really be a lot more interesting. His axe bit into a log but did not split it, and he panted as he lifted the log into the air on the end of the axe, bringing it down again and again. He saw his earlier education, himself studying Latin as a little boy in a private school in New York, he and Bill both studying Latin and French, and then less Latin and more French in prep school. He saw all the pictures on the walls of those schools, Aristotle, Julius Caesar, Shakespeare, and all his books on European history, American history.

God, Harry thought, looking at Chung's tireless face as he continued preaching to his two nodding disciples, all that Latin and nothing about China. Not one word of Chinese. Not one thing except that they invented gunpowder.

He shook his head, thinking of all the plaques at Harvard, the Gutenberg Bible in Widener Library, the total European orientation of his education.

For a moment he saw his father again, in uniform in San Francisco before he disappeared into the Pacific Ocean for good.

We were all looking towards Europe, Harry thought. We were all looking in the wrong direction.

VII

Bill had brought over one of his books on Jurisprudence to study, but after half an hour of sitting with Anne in the same room downstairs at Briggs Hall, both of them pretending to study, they had risen and drifted into the May evening. They moved along the fragrant rain-fresh spring streets, holding hands, step matching slow step. Bill would stop and her lips would be there, her arms around his neck. Her body coming up close to him. Her eyes sad and thoughtful and hungry.

"When you graduate in June," Bill said softly, "why do you have to hunt for a job right away in New York? Why not come up to Maine? This summer'll be the last long vacation I probably ever have."

Anne looked at him as they wandered past a blooming lilac hedge, the flowers sweet in the velvet mist.

'If I come up — " she started, and then her mouth closed. If I come up, she thought, and we spend the summer right next to each other, we'll be so deeply involved with each other that we'll never get out.

"That's what I want," Bill said.

Anne's eyes widened. "What?"

"What you were thinking. That's what I want." His grip on her hand was firm, and then they both stood rigid, looking at each other in the light of a street lamp in mist. "Look, Anne. I want to marry you."

Anne swallowed. "Bill — not yet." She turned from him, trying to get her hand released from his, but the pressure held.

"But you will come up to Maine this summer?"

Anne said in a small voice, "All right."

CHAPTER TWENTY-ONE

Harry was on detail to carry buckets of water from the river back up to the hut. He had decided to get the water from slightly farther up the bank, since too many men were muddying the water with their buckets at the point to which they had been marched by Wuthers.

There were some bushes hanging low over the water just around the bend, and Harry parted two of them and started to dip his first bucket into the river. Then he saw it. It was partly hidden even from here, a big log ten or twelve feet long and about ten inches in diameter. Harry moved towards it on his hands and knees under the bushes. It had drifted ashore here, washed down by the spring-flooded river. It was huge, compared to the little logs he had been splitting for Chung. Most of it was still afloat, but its front was wedged firmly into the river bank.

Harry waded in, still carrying one bucket with him. Looping the bucket's handle over his arm, and keeping low in the cold May stream, he pushed the floating part of the log even further ashore. A wild strength came over him, and in one minute of pushing and tearing at it with his hands, lifting and sliding, he had it up on the bank. Then he squatted by the edge of the sandy little strip between water and bushes, filling the pail, but staring wild-eyed at the log. If a Chinese guard saw it, it would be a log, but to him it was a boat. Swimming beside it, he could get out into this river, and the river flowed down to the sea. If he clung to this log, and steered it, it would take him there. At the mouth of a river, by the ocean, there would be fishing boats.

Harry beamed as the vision rose pure in his mind. Little fishing boats, pulled ashore at night. Little fishing boats had sails. He and Tommy could steal a fishing boat at night, and sail out to sea. Yellow Sea or Penobscot Bay, there was one thing he could do: sail a boat. This river belonged to North Korea on one side and China on the other, but the ocean belonged to the United States. If they could get out there where the patrol boats were, the airplanes and the helicopters and the destroyers —

Harry filled both buckets and headed back towards the rest of the working party.

*   *   *

Tommy Quinn's face was that of a gambler calculating the odds. "You know those crackers they're giving us for lunch now?"

"Right," Harry said softly as they waited outside the kitchen to carry the evening pails of millet and carrot soup back to the squad.

"Well, if we worked up a stock of about fifty apiece, maybe two weeks' worth — "

"Right."

"I can quit smoking and trade off your tobacco ration and mine for that poncho Martinez has."

"Good."

"Then we could put the crackers in the poncho." Tommy's face fell. "There's one thing. I can't swim."

"Listen," Harry said. "You're going to learn."

II

Mabel sat up quietly in bed, listening to Anne and Bill laughing in the living room. They had come down to New York for one cheerful week-end before going back to take their respective final examinations.

Clarence rolled over in the other bed pulled close beside her own, and Mabel looked down fondly upon his half-open mouth as he began to snore in a new key. Then there was laughter again from the living room, and she sat up even straighter, a chill along her spine. Below, on the avenue, a bus moved off in a heavy metallic whuush-um; the street lights threw a white rectangle upon the dim ceiling of the bedroom.

Clarence opened his eyes.

"What's the matter, Mabel?" he asked, totally and suddenly alert.

Mabel put her hand on his shoulder as if she were listening to something from a great distance.

"Would you think I was crazy — " her voice faltered " — if I told you I sometimes think Harry Purdick is still alive?"

Clarence rose on one elbow; with the other hand he took her arm above the elbow, and squeezed it

"Mabel," he said, "we *buried* Harry."

"I know," Mabel said. "I know."

III

Harry sat on the bench along the wall of the room at headquarters that housed the tiny prison camp library, reading a copy of the New York *Daily Worker*. This was the safest place to come if you wanted to be sure that they would not grab you for some work detail, and today of all days he did not want to be tired when darkness came. Tommy was spending the afternoon recopying the squad's reactions to recent lectures, another occupation that the Chinese encouraged, so they should both be fresh as daisies when it came time to leave.

The interpreter named Wu came into the room, and the American sergeant who was librarian rose to his feet.

"What you read?" Wu asked the sergeant in a friendly voice.

"Upton Sinclair."

"You like?"

"Very much."

Wu nodded and came towards Harry. Harry rose. He was thinking about how Wu had an ass just like a woman's. He knew, because he and Tommy had been down by the river every day, pretending to bathe but actually teaching Tommy how to swim, and Wu was also a daily bather.

"How you like *Daily Worker?*"

"Fine," Harry said.

"Too bad about Monte Irvin."

Harry smiled despite himself. There was a sports column in the *Daily Worker* written by a man who signed himself lester rodney in small letters, and in this latest, two-month-old issue, there was the news that the Giants' Monte Irvin had broken his ankle and was out for the season.

Wu motioned for him to sit down. "You think Willie Mays be drafted?"

"I don't know." Harry still could not stop smiling at the absurdity of it. The Chinese had found out in a hurry that lester rodney's sports column was the thing everybody turned to first, so now they were trying to display an interest.

The best part of it, Harry thought, is that I'm the one guy in camp who couldn't care less about baseball.

"You think Willie Mays should go in Army?"

Screw it, Harry thought. I'm leaving tonight, let's tell him what he wants to hear. "Nobody should go in the Army. Everybody should have peace."

"You good boy, Pu'dick. Some day truce talks finish, you go home your loved ones."

I'm not waiting for any truce talks to finish, Harry thought, still smiling at Wu. He knew Wu had extremely limited English, even though he had to stagger through giving the prepared talks. Everyone tried to use their most complicated words on the interpreters who had bad English, and then to define the words improperly when the interpreters asked their meaning.

Wu said, "What you think about steel strike?"

"I think our steelworkers are very uncooperative about prosecuting the war effort, considering the expressed wish of the elected federal officials."

"I suppose so," Wu mumbled, and left.

The sergeant who was librarian shifted on his chair. "I don't see why you had to do that," he said, still looking at his book.

Harry stared at him. "What do you think — is Willie Mays going to be drafted?"

*   *   *

They had blackened their faces with mud to help them remain invisible as they passed the guard shack, and now that they were at the log they moved fast. They took off everything but some makeshift breechcloths they had made from the ragged tails of their Russian brown shirts, and slipped their clothes into the poncho, along with their hoard of crackers. They tied the folded-over poncho onto the log with some straw twine taken from a bag of rice.

Tommy looked over at Harry in the night, and Harry nodded. They lifted the log, set it in the water, and slowly sank in on either side of it like two seals. Harry nodded again, and they began moving it out slowly into the stream.

Harry felt the bottom fall away, and looked over at Tommy, who was out above his head for the first time. Tommy's arm was tight around the underside of the log, and Harry could feel his body rigid beside him in the water, but the current was taking them now. The camp slid past slowly, almost majestically, with the lanterns in the guard shacks and the lights up at headquarters, and then they were alone in darkness, floating in dark water between Korea and China.

IV

Bill sat at the wheel of his car, whipping along the Wilbur Cross Parkway on his way down from Boston to New York. In the back seat were all his clothes, the ties flapping wildly in the June air that poured through the windows, and in the trunk were his cartons of law books and notes. This morning he had finished the last exam of his second year. By late afternoon he would be at his mother's in New York. This evening he would have dinner with Anne, who had finished her exams and come down to New York for a few days before going back up for her graduation.

He whistled through half-open lips, sometimes exultantly inhaling as he hummed along in the light mid-afternoon traffic. The clear road matched his mood. The darkness of the past sixteen months was lifting; he saw sunlight ahead.

V

"Time to head in?" Harry whispered to the drenched head on the other side of the log, and Tommy Quinn nodded agreement. There was a touch of gray in the night sky; Harry estimated that it was about half past four in the morning. This had been their fifth night out, and they had it pretty well organized now. They would head in to shore and leave the log almost anywhere on the bank. The log was not a suspicious object, and they devoted their efforts to finding a thicket in which they could sleep during the day.

Harry swung around behind the log to its other side, and he and Tommy both began kicking it towards the northern shore. For the first four nights they had stuck fairly close to the southern shore, about two hundred yards out, but tonight the river had narrowed, and they happened to be near the opposite side. A few hours before, a boat had come downstream and they had thought they might be discovered, but it had gone on, its single lantern swaying and a man with a sweep-oar standing in its stern.

Harry's stomach writhed in hunger. OK, OK, Harry said

to it, you'll get a couple of crackers soon. His face was intent in the darkness. The crackers were going a lot faster than he wanted to see them go, but they were agreed that they had to keep up their strength or it was no go anyway.

The deserted shore pulled over to them, ghostly bare hills and always the blessed few thickets along the shore.

Tommy pointed towards a dark area, and they slid up towards the bank. Harry's hunger vanished, and his stomach became a knot of fear. This was the bad part, stepping off into the new unknown each night, hoping that the bank would not erupt in shouts and lanterns, or even pinpoints of rifle fire from nervous sentries.

The soft clayish mud slipped into place beneath their feet; they were sliding the log ashore. Tommy untied the poncho, and then like Indians they passed over rough grass and into the bushes.

Harry sat deep in a thicket, wolfed down the crackers that Tommy handed him, and then pulled on his gingham trousers and collarless Russian shirt. He felt the skin of his arms, his stomach, his neck. It was wrinkled like an old man's from the hours of water. The fatigue hammering him was like the terrible impulse to stop moving that had come upon him on his march north in the snow.

Harry curled up on the dry inside of the poncho that Tommy had spread out for both of them.

"Hey," Tommy whispered, "you know what? We're in China."

"Huh," Harry said, and was asleep.

VI

Constance sat in her apartment in New York, a drink in her hand and a bottle not far away. Bill had come in an hour before, looking flushed and happy after another evening of seeing Anne.

In three days they would all, Purdicks and Wileys, go up to Radcliffe to see Anne graduate, and then go on to their neighboring cottages in Maine.

I cannot get in the mood of this Anne and Bill thing, she thought. I cannot get in the mood. I wonder what the Greeks thought of this, or the Romans, or all those people. Suppose she had married Harry instead of just being engaged to him? How would those old Greeks feel about her going out with her dead husband's brother?

She looked at the picture of her own dead husband in his naval uniform. You would have known that one, Steve, you would have known. She stared at the gold stripes on Stephen Purdick's sleeve in the photograph. I don't know.

"My men have all been the wrong age at the wrong time," Constance said to the empty room, and poured herself another drink.

VII

The storm came up at two in the morning. It had been dead quiet above the river for a few minutes, no wind and the water warm. The log had even been leaving a tiny rippling wake on the surface. Then it came, wind pouring out of Manchuria, lightning blasting the sky a fog-deep red, rain pelting the river so that it was like swimming in a sea of firecrackers. The waves began rolling the log, and Harry moved along its side, to check the straw twine holding the food-carrying poncho to its top. The log spun in his hands, and a wave slapped the poncho partly out from underneath the twine. Harry grabbed at the wet twine and tried to hold it tighter. He cursed himself for keeping his clothes on tonight in this water, in an effort to stop this painful wrinkling of his skin. Every move now was desperately impeded. The log was pitching; its back end disappeared in a trough in the waves. In flashes, he could see the top of Tommy's water-darkened head in the lightning barrage, and see one of Tommy's arms gripping the log and the other flailing to keep balance in the lurching water.

A wave rose under the log, tearing it one way and tossing Harry the other. Frantically he kicked back to it. He saw the poncho slipping out from under the twine, and then the poncho was gone and he was hand-over-handing it back along the log and Tommy was gone.

"Tommy!" he shouted into the thunder. The log whirled away from him.

Harry trod water for a moment, looking towards the nearer northern shore. He looked back once in the lightning. There was nothing, only rain-needled waves. Harry swam for shore, gasping as the waves clubbed his face.

VIII

The warm evening stopped at the doors of Christ Episcopal Church in Cambridge. Anne knelt in a pew near the rear, a gauzy blue-and-white scarf on her head. Tomorrow everyone would arrive for two days of ceremonies and festivities connected with her graduation; tonight was her chance to be alone.

Anne slid back into a sitting position in the pew, and looked at the church's shadowy white-and gray interior.

I wish I was better at praying, she thought, and then a smile crossed her face. She was remembering an evening a few months before, when she had been discussing her lack of a strong faith with a girl in the dormitory who seemed always serene. The friend had asked her if she went to church often, and Anne had said, "No." The friend had asked her if she often prayed when she was by herself, and Anne had said, "No."

"Well," the friend had observed, "it's like anything else. It takes practice."

The smile left her face, and she began thinking of her years here, and the kind of education she had received. If there was one thing, she said to herself, if there's one thing they never do at Harvard or Radcliffe, it's to teach you what to think. They give you tons of information, and leave the conclusions up to you. It sounds great. Perfect objectivity.

Anne shook her head. She was smiling no longer.

There are moments, she thought. Sometimes when you're reading, or listening to a lecture, or just thinking about something, and then you see, you *see*, and it's great. But all you see is just one little monument of thought. You never see a whole big sky with stars twinkling and everything balanced and in order and moving.

The smile returned to her face, but this time it was rueful. Well, she thought, tomorrow morning you graduate *cum laude* in history and you don't know a thing. You've skated through an elective education. Elective courses. Elective thoughts. Elective beliefs. Pure intellectual freedom, and it leaves you sitting in a church on the eve of your graduation, wondering who's here and what He wants.

She stood, and walked to the door of the church. Standing with her back to the dim white pews of the interior, the cool green Cambridge elms freshening the air above her, she wished for a sign, for some conviction to seize her heart.

All she heard was the sound of birds chirping in the trees.

CHAPTER TWENTY-TWO

HARRY SAT against a brick wall in this Chinese village to which he had been brought by the farmers who had found him lying on the shore. When he had arrived three hours before, two or three hundred of these young Chinese soldiers bivouacked here had crowded about him, fascinated to see the enemy they were en route to fight. Now they were leaving him alone as he dozed in the sunshine with a finished bowl of rice beside him, but still they stared at him as they went about their work details.

Harry blinked, and slowly rose and stretched. The tattered clothes had dried. The snapshot of Swann's wife, the one that looked like Anne, was lost in the river. Swann's West Point ring still hung from the little chain Tommy had given him for Christmas. He did not seem to be under guard, and they were right in thinking it was not necessary. He did not have the strength to get a quarter of a mile from here without collapsing.

A young soldier passed, and gave him a friendly smile. I'm sure they're Infantry, Harry thought. No weapons. They'll get those at the front, picked up from the guys who are dead. They don't want to harass me; they know they might be prisoners themselves in a few weeks.

He made his way shakily across the hard-packed earth of this brick-walled compound. For the past few minutes he had thought he heard planes, and he wanted to find out what they were.

There was an elaborate wood-carved gate to the village, with its doors open. He stood in it, ignoring a farmer coming past with three pigs and some soldiers carrying mortar shells that would cross the Yalu into North Korea and go down those trails up which he had been brought. From this vantage point he could look south across the Yalu. As he watched, a silver plane skimmed above the glittering surface of the morning-after-storm river, and dropped a bomb on something on the opposite side. He jumped behind the heavy wooden gatepost, crouching against it, and then he realized that pigs, farmer, soldiers, were all going about their business. Timidly he rose, still keeping his body behind the heavy carved post, and watched another plane with Air Force markings zoom in at whatever it was across the broad river.

What the hell's the matter with you? he said to the Air Force pilot. Can't you see three hundred men over here, walking around in broad daylight? Come on over here and get them before they ever get to the front.

Three young Chinese soldiers came up to him. One took a deep breath, stepped forward, and said, pointing at the planes, "No come China."

Harry looked at him, and at the Infantry replacements passing through this village in a steady stream.

"That's swell," he said, and walked back across the courtyard.

II

The first evening that he arrived in Maine, Bill drove the old Ford convertible to a place near the Bay. Getting out of the car, he walked uphill through the pink sunset light falling upon the blueberry bushes. It was all granite and ragged carpet of twig-studded moss.

He came to the big rock where he and Harry had played when they were children. Climbing atop the granite boulder, he stood in the sunset, his hands on his hips, his head turning slowly as he saw again his most beloved place. Behind him the lake was tucked firmly into green-farmed hills and stands of birch at its edge. Before him lay the spruce-covered granite islands dotting Penobscot Bay. They were slowly blackening as the light pulled west across the water.

Harry, Bill said, I hope you don't mind me loving Anne. At the beginning I didn't think about it, I just saw her, and when I saw her I didn't drink so much. I don't know, I just didn't feel so bad when she was around. At the beginning I didn't think about it, and now I don't think about anything else. She hasn't said yes yet, but I'm going to keep trying. I can't help it, Harry. He climbed down from the rock where they had played as boys.

III

Harry's face fell as he saw in the distance the hut-dotted slopes of the Pyoktong camp. This morning he had crossed the Yalu in a sampan with these infantrymen who had been assigned to return him on their way south to fight. Except when he thought of Tommy being whirled away into the storm, something which he could not yet grasp, the five days' march back to here had been the best time he had had since he was captured. Each night they had stayed in a village on the Chinese side, eating lots of millet flavored with salt and dried peppers. This party of infantrymen were a cheerful lot, sharing everything with him equally and delighted with the few words of Chinese he had picked up from Lee after his first escape attempt fourteen months before. As they marched, the Chinese peasant boys would point to their eyes or noses or ears, and Harry would tell them the name for that in English, and they would teach him the word for it in Chinese. Their memories were remarkable. He had no idea what dialect they spoke, but he now knew, in that dialect, the names for most of the parts of the body, for trees, roads, houses, sorghum, turnips, and millet. He was in the best health since his capture, and for the first time in seventeen months he felt the sex urge returning to his wasted body.

The Chinese stopped well outside the village beyond which the camp lay. They said, "tsai cheeyen, good-bye," and held their thumbs up and smiled at him with encouraging nods. One of them, the one who had impressed Harry as being the most educated, shook his hand and said, "Ho Hwei Yu Chi." He said the syllables deliberately, and repeated them as if he wanted Harry to remember. Then they assembled about him in a formation of heavy guard, as if he were a dangerous animal to be guarded on all sides, and marched him down the road to the village, where the guards from Pyoktong were quartered.

Two guards were waiting for him in the village. The infantrymen vanished, and Chung came storming out of a hut, in a frenzy. Harry stared at him. Chung was literally frothing at the mouth with rage: spittle, foam, bubbles.

"Pig! Inconsiderate and ungrateful!" Chung was gesturing, walking around Harry in circles, his face working. "We treat you well, we gave you benefits, we gave you chance learn true direction of world development, now do this!"

My God, Harry thought, he's so angry he's losing his English.

"Worry about you!" Chung shouted. "Worry about your safety! Why no Quinn!"

"Quinn is dead," Harry said quietly. "In the river."

Chung screamed. "Fool! We so good to you, now do this!" Chung gestured to one of the guards. The guard tied a straw rope around Harry's wrists, behind his back, and off they went up the road to the camp, the guard holding the end of the rope so that Harry was like a dog on a leash, then Chung in single file, then the second armed guard.

The men began coming out of their huts as the word spread. Chung had the lead guard parade Harry through the entire camp, first the private-corporal side, then the sergeant side, so that everyone could see they had him back. To each American platoon leader that he saw, Chung said loudly, "The other one is dead in the river." Harry tried to walk erect, but the guard yanked at his wrists when he did, so most of the time he kept his head slumped forward.

The faces of the men standing outside each hut were masks of sorrow. Everyone had hoped that someone might make it out and tell the world what was happening here.

"Tough luck," a voice said in the silence, and, rounding the corner of another mud hut, Harry heard another voice, "Sorry you didn't make it." Chung marched on, oblivious, and they were going up the steps of the headquarters building, into the room that Harry had been in before.

The camp commandant was sitting behind the table, and the interpreter Wu was sitting beside him. Wu had many sentences written in English on the paper before him. Harry was barely through the door and standing, tied, before the table, when Wu began.

"You were brought here before — because we are going have fair trial. You have broken a very important rule of camp commander leaving camp without permission. If we find you guilty doing this, you will be punished, but if you are not guilty, we will not punish you." He glanced at the camp commander, and the moon-faced man, who knew no English, gestured impatiently for Wu to get on with it. "Did you leave this camp without permission?"

"Well, I left the camp."

"Who gave you permission leave the camp?"

"Well, nobody gave me permission."

Wu translated for the camp commander. Harry could hear Chung, just behind him, scraping his feet tensely on the floor. The guard behind him tugged at the straw rope on his wrists, to show he was in the spirit of the thing.

The camp commander said a word, and Wu asked, "Why did you leave the camp?"

"I wanted to go home to my family."

"Why do you lie?"

"I'm not lying."

Wu blew up. "You lie! You lie! We treat you good, we take care of you, we feed you well, we protect you from warmongers, we liberated you from fighting, we give you our side of story — you leave camp no permission, cost us much money, we worry about you, then you here now we give you fair trial, and fair trial you tell lies!" About twenty seconds passed. "Why you no answer?"

"I didn't think you were asking me any questions."

"You must answer!"

"What do you want me to answer to? What do you want me to say?" Harry's face was red, and he felt like crying. He was disgusted, frightened, ill from it.

Chung interjected something, and the camp commander said two words. Wu nodded eagerly. "You see Quinn die in water?"

Harry's eyes closed. In terrible clarity he saw that somebody higher up was chewing their asses about this escape. The last thing they wanted was to think Tommy Quinn could still be loose.

"Don't worry," Harry said, his eyes still closed. He started to add that he knew that Tommy could never have gotten out of that maelstrom with his few swimming lessons, but he realized that even that was not good enough. "I saw him die."

This was translated to the camp commander, who went into a measured few sentences, his voice emotionless, his handsome middle-aged face lecturing Harry.

"Camp commander say you responsible for death of Quinn."

"I think you're right." Harry closed his eyes again, and the guard tugged the rope for effect.

"You very dishonest man," Wu said. "I see you in water many days practice with Quinn, but not understand. Day you go, I see you in library reading *Daily Worker*. Very dishonest."

Harry remained silent. He could not imagine that this was going to end in any way but his death. He felt it like a huge bird beating its silent wings about the building.

The camp commander said something more.

Wu translated, "You must tell truth why you escape. You must tell camp commander you going back your Army fight Chinese People's Volunteers again."

"Look," Harry said, "all I want to do is to go home to my family." He suddenly felt it was all over, that nothing he said would make any difference. Turning his head, he felt Swann's West Point ring move on the chain that held it against his chest. The picture of Swann's wife, the one that looked like Anne, had been lost in the river, but the ring was still here. "If I had gotten back to my lines," he said slowly, "I am sure they would have sent me home. But if they had sent me back into combat, I would have done it."

"Your government is no good." There was another long pause. "Why you no answer?"

"What do you want me to say?"

There was more discussion in Chinese, with the camp commander turning to Chung again.

Then Wu looked at Harry. "Camp commander says you are guilty."

Harry nodded.

"Camp commander says you will be punished."

Harry nodded. There was more palaver in Chinese.

"Your punishment will be one week in the hole and one month hard labor. Do you understand?"

Harry opened his mouth and looked at a point well above their sitting heads. The bird had gone away.

"You must write confession."

Harry swayed on his feet. Suddenly he could not keep his eyes open. "OK. I'll write confession tomorrow."

Wu screamed, "You write confession when I tell you write confession! You write confession now!"

"Look, I'll write a confession at any time that is most convenient for you."

Wu stopped. "What 'conven'ent' mean?"

"I will write the confession whenever you say."

Wu shifted on his seat, satisfied. "You write confession to-day. You confess you left camp to fight against Chinese People's Volunteers and not to go home to family."

"OK."

*   *   *

The guard handed Harry the shovel and the grub axe, and stepped off the dimensions of the hole he was to dig.

"I know," Harry said. "I know."

CHAPTER TWENTY-THREE

Constance waited inside the door of the house in Maine until the taillights of the car disappeared down the driveway in the night, and then she stepped back out onto the dark porch. Bill was not yet home from taking Anne to the movies. Constance had been at a dinner party at the cottage of friends in South Harbor; this pleasant widower had come for her and driven her back here.

She saw the lights of his car appear again, moving along the road at the near end of the lake, heading back towards South Harbor. Then the headlights were tilted towards the foggy sky as he went over the hill, and his tail lights were gone into the same glow.

A sad smile clung to her lips. She knew that he had wanted to come in for a drink. He had been a pleasant man, about fifty, widowed three years before. He was lonely, but he had taste, and she could sense about him that easy women were little comfort to him. He would marry soon again.

A loon cried above the pond, the haunting call across still, muffled water. She put her hands on the wooden railing of the porch, smelling the damp spruce trees, feeling the dark fog on her face. The man's voice stayed in her ears; she saw again the friendly, cooperative expressions of her friends who had given the dinner party.

That is one thing, she thought, that comes with age. People get less coy about things. They think I should marry, they serve up a single man; if it takes, fine; if it doesn't, fine.

She passed a hand across her mist-softened cheek. Her friends were quite right, she thought, and yet they were wrong because they had access only to the less important facts. They saw a woman forty-seven, widowed for seven years almost to the month. They knew she had one son dead, and the other going into his last year at Law School and seeing Anne Wiley every evening. On that data they could reach only one conclusion: let's get Connie Purdick married to somebody nice, soon.

The sound of her high heels echoed on the wooden boards as she went back to the door and entered the cottage. One friend had said to her on a picnic in July, when they had sailed out to Ram Island, "Connie, you've lived so long for other people, it's time you lived for yourself."

Constance went out to the icebox and pured herself a glass of milk. She saw herself as she did it, saw all the contradictions; the schoolgirl grown old, drinking milk at the end of the evening when others were having a nightcap, just as she had started drinking wine in Paris as part of the meals during her year at school there, while her friends here had been still drinking vanilla jerks.

Leaving a light in the kitchen for Bill when he came in, she climbed the broad brown wooden steps to her bedroom. How can you explain it, she thought, without being what the kids used to call corny and then they called it icky and now God knows what they call it?

In her room was a picture of Stephen, not the one in his naval uniform, but one she had taken up here in the 'Thirties, Stephen with his shirt open and white flannel slacks, and a book he had been reading, put aside as he smiled at her. Looking at his thoughtful face, she was back in that moment, fumbling with that camera with the front that slapped down and the lens that came sliding forward on a little black bellows. She felt the sunshine on her back, the shouts of Harry and Bill, little boys then, playing on the lawn. After she snapped the picture, she advanced towards him, looking down into the lens finder, seeing him come closer and closer in the ground glass. Then she was standing above him, still smiling, and Stephen swept her into his lap and kissed her.

I don't see anything so mysterious about it, Constance thought as she took off her shoes. That's my husband. He happens to be dead.

II

They had done very well to come in second in the race, considering that they had no third person for a crew, and that Anne had handled the Seventeen's spinnaker by herself, while Bill stayed at the helm. Now the small fleet was sailing relaxedly back into South Harbor, with cheerful, tired shouts of congratulation or condolence passing across the dark salt water.

"Here," Bill said, motioning to Anne. "You sail her in and I'll straighten things up."

Anne gave a grateful, tired sigh, and slumped down beside the tiller, letting the main sheet run out a bit. Bill disappeared into the small cabin and tossed a sailbag out to the cockpit floor.

The wooden tiller vibrated slightly, and Anne changed course until the tremor left the rudder. With her left hand she pushed her hair back on both sides of her salt-burned face.

"Here's the boom crotch," Bill said, handing the long piece of varnished wood up from the cabin.

"OK." Anne smiled at him and put it at her feet. She gazed at his tall form as he worked inside the cabin, his tanned arms reaching for things, his torso in the white T-shirt moving back and forth in the little companionway. Then he was out and moving barefoot along the deck, up to the foredeck, taking the jib down and stowing it in a sailbag. He came aft and took the tiller from her.

"Anne," he said, "I have to tell you something, and this is as good a time as any." His voice was tight.

Anne's eyes widened, and she looked away for a moment, at the other boats across the water. Then her eyes were riveted on Bill's long, handsome face.

"Unless you agree to marry me," Bill said quietly, "I am going down to Cambridge tomorrow morning and get a room there and get a job for the summer. Then I'll stay in Cambridge next year and finish Law School, and you'll be in New York or wherever, and when I graduate I'll get a job in a law firm that's in some city where you're not, and we won't see each other any more." He shook his head. "I can't take any more."

Anne put out a hand towards him. Her mouth was open. "Do I have to say yes right now?"

Bill looked away from her, across the water. "I'm getting in that car tomorrow morning. If you have something to say, say it by then."

*　　*　　*

Anne lay in her bed, staring at the moonlight on the screen over her window. The lake made the gentlest of slapping sounds on the narrow strip of beach.

She slipped out of bed and stepped to the window. On the moonlit water the little catboat rode at her mooring. Through the mist-lightened birch trees she saw the Purdick's cottage. A million disjointed memories swept her. Anne swayed on her feet. She remembered one morning long ago, when she had measles. The boys had come over, carrying a box of blueberries for her. She had come to this screened window, and they had looked up at her, awed by illness, shifting nervously from foot to foot.

We picked some berries for you, Anne, Bill's voice said in the moonlit, misty night.

I'll bet you bought them at the store, she had said with a weak smile.

Like heck we did, they answered in chorus.

Anne felt her heart beating fast. I can't let it go, she thought. I can't let it all go. It's me as much as it is them. If Bill goes, it's all gone.

She crossed the room, turned on the light, and began to get dressed. She picked her favorite cotton print, the one she had worn to the Yacht Club dance with Bill last Saturday night. She put on high heels, and a white cardigan sweater, and combed and brushed her hair, and put on lipstick. Then she turned off the light, went downstairs, and out of the house.

Her feet knew the path even in this luminous night, even in high heels. She walked swiftly, confidently.

The brown-shingled side of the Purdick's house looked silver. She picked up a handful of pebbles and threw them up at Bill's second-floor window.

There was no answer.

He's gone, she thought, her heart beating wildly. He's gone. It's too late. She reached down among wet ferns and moss, scooped up another handful, and flung them up at the screen.

Bill's face came to the window as Anne was starting to bend for a third handful of pebbles.

"Were you *sleeping?*" Anne asked in an indignant whisper.

"Sure," Bill said.

"Bill," Anne said, "the answer is yes. I mean, I'd like to very much."

"You just stay right there," Bill said. From within there was a rumble of his feet coming down the steps, and he was running across the porch. He vaulted over the porch railing in his pajamas, and she was in his arms.

After a few seconds the screen door opened, and Constance came padding across the porch in her nightgown, a wool wrapper, and floppy slippers, a flashlight in her hand.

"What on earth — " she said as the cone of light fixed Bill and Anne in an embrace, Anne fully dressed and Bill in pajamas.

"Mother," Bill said, looking from the flashlight to Anne's relieved, excited face, her eyes sparkling in the moonlight, "we're engaged."

III

Harry stood beside a hut, watching four of the Turk prisoners teasing one of the Chinese guards. The guard's orders were to pace up and down before the warehouse that held the food, and not to leave that area in front of the warehouse doors. The swarthy, mustachioed Turks would sneak up to the opposite side of the corrugated-iron roof of the warehouse, and toss stones over it in a quick volley before retreating behind the nearest hut. The guard would come tearing around the edge of the warehouse, brandishing his burp gun, but by that time the Turks would be out of sight, and the guard's orders allowed him to go no further in search of his tormentors.

Harry stood in the lavender sunset, watched the Turks throw two or three more volleys of stones, and then headed uphill towards his own hut. He had eaten the sorghum-paste supper an hour before, and already he felt pangs of hunger. Ahead lay another long evening with nothing to do, not even a candle for light in the hut. Another night to lie sleepless, seeing Tommy drowning in the rain-lashed river, to remember Interlicchio dying in the snow trying to hold off the Chinese Army with his light machine gun, to remember Anne standing there at the Port Authority Terminal in New York as his bus pulled out for the last time.

As he came nearer the hut, he saw Norden coming through the gathering evening, down from his daily extra instruction session at headquarters. Looking at this boy who had nodded more and more convincedly as the lectures progressed and Chung and Wuthers worked on him, Harry sensed that something was up. Each day they had nothing to do but look at each other, and even the slightest change in mood was easy to feel.

"Hi," the kid said.

Harry stared at him. Even in these rags, Norden looked like the All-American Boy. "Hi."

"I'm going," Norden said.

"Where?"

"I don't know."

Harry nodded, and they walked along together. So now they're shipping Norden out to someplace where they can really work on him, without any of us political deadbeats poisoning the atmosphere. A look of sorrow crossed Harry's face, and he found himself blushing.

You should have tried to say something to him. You should have tried to straighten him out before Wuthers and Chung finished him off.

The hell with it. He might have told Wuthers, and Wuthers would sure as hell tell Chung, and Chung's riding me hard enough as it is.

"Well," Norden said in an uncertain voice, "good luck."

Harry just kept walking beside him.

"Purdick, won't you even wish me good luck?"

Harry kept looking straight ahead.

IV

The bouquets were trembling in the hands of the maid of honor and the one bridesmaid.

"Now," the woman at the back of the church said, and the bridesmaid stepped off down the aisle. The strains of "Here Comes the Bride" rose higher as the bald-headed man at the small organ pressed and pedaled it so that the entire little wooden church in South Harbor rang to the chords.

"Now you," the woman at the back said, and the maid of honor stepped off. At the front of the aisle stood Bill, erect and solemn in a white linen jacket and gray trousers. Peedy Adams stood beside him as best man, identically dressed, smiling and pushing his waterfall of blond hair from his eyes. In the front pews, across the aisle from each other, Mabel Wiley and Constance Purdick, in silk print dresses, kept their eyes fixed on the back of the church.

Anne came down the aisle on the arm of her father. Clarence was wearing a white linen jacket, the same as Bill and Peedy, and Anne was in an ivory wedding dress that just touched the floor. Her face was serene; a sudden trusting smile lit her face as she approached Bill and the altar.

V

Harry sat as far back as he could get in the hot stuffy lecture hall, his mind tuning in and out on today's attacks on Wall Street and imperialism and corruption in Washington, interspersed with expressions of sympathy for the oppressed working class in the United States. Ever since Chung had been reinstated as a lecturer, he never departed from the text until it came to a few planted questions at the end.

Everyone was getting his hair cut regularly now, and Harry stared at the rough-shaven backs of the Negro and Caucasian heads sitting row upon row ahead of him. It was strange that the backs of heads could be so expressive. These were slumped in boredom, or cocked to one side in skepticism. A tiny minority leaned forward eagerly.

"Only the imperialist capitalist rulers want nuclear war," Chung's voice was saying. "The people's republics have a consistent record of attempting to have complete nuclear disarmament. The only reason any people's republic remains armed is because of the constant aggressive actions of capitalist rulers." Harry sighed. "If these capitalist rulers would stop being aggressive and attempting to maintain their colonial empire in

Asia, all the world would have peace. That is all you want; that is all we want."

Harry looked down at his wrists. He had picked up a kind of poison ivy gathering bundles of brush on a detail that went out to a nearby hillside. He smiled as he looked at his wrists, and the itching bubbles on the back of his hands. After what he had lived through, it seemed so amazing to come down with something slight like poison ivy.

VI

"You do *not* have to do the dishes." Anne pushed Bill gently out of the kitchen of the apartment they had rented in Cambridge. The Law School would not be in session for another month, and they were having a marvelous time. It was the continuation of their honeymoon, but with the added feeling that everything around them was theirs.

Anne sang as she washed the china that had been Constance's wedding present to them. She knew that many young brides used their best china only when they had guests, but she felt differently. She wanted the candlelight and the crystal and china now, the linen napkins now, every night, now. She was enrolled in a cooking school on Brattle Street, and she could do things like pancakes for breakfast and even a rather tentative soufflé.

Bill sat in the living room, staring out at the bright summer evening on the lawn and the tree-lined street. He had never had so much fun in his life. The days were a strange new adventure of painting over the dull green bathroom walls, and trying that chest in a new spot, of shopping for things for the apartment, of Anne watching him try on a new suit down at Brooks Brothers in Boston. There was nobody you had to check in with; if they suddenly wanted to drive the thirty miles to Singing Beach with some cheese and a bottle of wine, they did.

His eyes turned from contemplation of the grass and trees, and he watched Anne as she stood at the sink, humming as she did the dishes. There were moments when he looked at her and could not believe that she was his. Gazing at her now, he shivered as he thought of their nights. It came to him in shadows and whispers and the sound of warm limbs traversing crisp linen. Oh, Bill, her soft voice, oh, Bill. That feels so beautiful. That feels so wonderful.

VII

There was an ungodly squeal in the distance. Harry sat bolt upright on the dirt floor, his blanket falling from his shoulders. The other men turned in their sleep, shivering in the foggy September night that thrust itself in the hut's open doorway. Two figures bounded through the door and dove into their blankets. Three minutes later, as everyone lay silent, a lantern pushed through the doorway, a flat suspicious Chinese face looked from under a short khaki visor, and the lantern withdrew.

After two more minutes Harry sat up and addressed the mud-walled room at large. "What the hell was that all about?"

"I got me a pig's tail," said the Southern accent of Hump Jones, the tall, stooped *raconteur* who had been an MP sergeant in Japan.

"What do you mean?"

"Me 'n Martinez, we got it, boy." In the dimness Hump held up a slender tapering object that looked as if that was just what it was. "Son, we *will* have flavorin' for ouah greens."

Harry grinned. He remembered the three or four pigs in a pen on the slope where he had been twice in the hole. Hump sometimes dug up greens near there, and boiled them in water. Once or twice he had spoken of cutting off a pig's tail and using it to dip in the boiling water to add flavoring, but everyone had thought, well, that's just Hump talking.

"How'd you do it?" Harry asked admiringly. Men were clustering around to feel the tail, and there was excited whispering and giggling.

"Found me a piece of glass," Hump said. "Then me an' ole Airborne Ranger Martinez here, we jus' executed us a commando raid on the pig pen."

Harry reclined on his blanket and looked up at the dark shadows of the ceiling. He could hear Hump telling it again for the men at the far end of the hut, whispering, with more exultation and men punching each other's shoulders in delight at how pissed off the Chinks would be about this one. A strange protective feeling swept over him, hearing the men chuckle, as if they were children and he was some kind of uncle. He found himself thinking of Hump's oft-told tale of how he had been captured. The Chinese had smashed his division's front, and Hump's MP captain had told him to keep traffic moving down the road, and then to hitch a ride out on the last vehicle. Hump had kept waving them past, jeeps and trucks and tanks and artillery, and suddenly the road was empty and there was no more last vehicle.

Harry grinned as he thought of how Hump had told it, but still the protective feeling remained. A light appeared beyond the next hut; everyone skidded back into their blankets on the dirt floor. The guard came back in, this time with Wuthers, who had been promoted to platoon commander and now lived in a hut filled with progressives.

The Chinese guard held the lantern high as he and Wuthers peered around the hut. Wuthers shrugged his shoulders, and they started out. Just as Wuthers stepped through the door, one of the men let out a tiny, rat-like squeak. Everyone in the hut choked with laughter; it was a perfect one-sound summation of Wuthers.

I don't know, Harry thought as the whispering about him resumed. I sure as hell would like the United States to know where the last vehicle is. Sleep was coming on him now, but so were the memories; Carmichael with his Christmas-present ice skates sticking out of his field-jacket pockets; the big Negro Pete Murphy half-carrying him through a snowy night on the march north, a night when he had fallen and cut his head on a rock and would have been dead if Pete had not practically carried him under his arm. And always, always, Tommy Quinn and Interlicchio in that hole in the snow, dug in, the two of them waiting for the Chinese Army.

Take the pictures away, Harry asked. I don't want to see them any more. Please. I don't want them to be my special responsibility. This isn't some religious vision, it's just guys getting killed, that's all. Don't make me think about it. He turned restlessly on the dirt floor, wishing he could be as interested in the pig's tail as the others. The men around him were giggling in the darkness again, like kids in a cabin at night at summer camp when the counselor has told them for the last time to shut up.

What do you want me to do about it? Harry said in angry silent words to the dark thatched roof above him. I can't watch out over all these guys. I couldn't even get myself to talk that kid Norden out of this stuff they keep putting on us.

Socialist principles future development working classes justice golden future justice equality end to oppression solution of all problems.

Harry turned over and lay face down, his forehead feeling the cold earth through the one frayed blanket about him. He flew away, his mind taking great powerful bounding strides, and he was back in that spruce-scented night in Maine, walking the darkened road with Anne, both of them eating ice cream, each taking a bite from the other's different flavored cone, and then stopping, kissing in the night.

I'll get out of this, he swore in silent iron. I'll get out of this. Harry's fist struck the cold earth beside his head.

We'll all be together. Anne and I, we'll go sailing, and we'll be married and we'll have all our lives ahead of us. He saw the kitchen in Maine, his mother cooking, and then he was tossing a football around on the lawn with Bill, and they were all together again, and he was back and they were glad to see him and it was his wedding at last, my wedding, Harry thought.

My wedding. His lips moved the soundless words as he turned over, staring at the dark ragged rush ceiling pyramiding into blackness. He felt the cold, wet night air on his face. Anne. Oh, Anne. How beautiful. His eyes closed. He saw Bill coming up here to Pyoktong to get him, Bill and his college friends and all the guys he had known along the way, all in green fatigues marching into this camp to get him and take him away from the Chinese.

Please, his lips said. Please.

VIII

Bill took from his green bookbag the ledger-like notebook he had bought for this course in Estate Planning, and opened it as the first lecture began. He jotted down the date, September 21, 1952, and waited, his new ball-point pen poised, for the professor to get through the usual saber-rattling about the importance and difficulties of the area of the law on which they were about to embark.

" — turning to more substantive matters," the lecturer was saying, and Bill fidgeted, his pen still poised above the page. These opening classes were in such contrast to the good hours at home. Last night Anne had kidded him about the way he kept their silver carving set in the gray cloth bags in which it had come, retrieving the silver knife and fork from her after she had washed and dried them, putting them back into the gray bags, and then putting the bags back into the box in which the set had come as a wedding present. He had flared up and told her that he supposed the people who made the carving set knew how it should be kept. She had shot back that it was an awful lot of trouble, the bags in and out of the box and then the knife and fork in and out of the bags, and he had said, all right, all right, we won't use the set any more.

But I *want* to use them, Anne had said, and then somehow they were laughing and then they were kissing and for half an hour the knife and fork were left quite unattended in the kitchen.

" — in the disposition of *any* estate," the lecturer was saying.

I have to try to take this more seriously now that I've got Anne to take care of, Bill thought, but still his face turned sour as the lecturer's words bored in. Once he had heard a record, "Seven Beers with the Wrong Woman." These were the first hours of his third year of studying to become a professional partisan, a pin-stripe pug, the guy you hire to fight for you in a ring where the referee wears black robes.

If two years of it didn't drive me crazy, Bill thought, automatically jotting down the meaty tenth of what the professor was saying, I don't suppose a third year will.

CHAPTER TWENTY-FOUR

Harry's face wore a frightened look as Wuthers escorted him up to headquarters. He looked back over his shoulder. Some barge-like boats were lying in a cove on the river bank, and all the sergeants in the camp were standing down there in line, with their blankets and food bowls, waiting to be herded on board for a trip to somewhere. He had been standing down there shivering with the rest of them, discussing how they had found two guys in an empty hut yesterday, having homosexual relations. Then Wuthers had come up to him and told him that the camp commander wanted to see him. Not Chung, not Wu, but the camp commander.

Wuthers swung the door open, and Harry made his petrified legs carry him into the room. The camp commander was behind the table, looking extremely harassed in the midst of this move of a large part of the population of his camp. Sitting beside him was Rat-Face, the interpreter Harry knew least. There were all sorts of lists scattered about the table, with one column written in Chinese and the other column written in English. There were also some totally typewritten lists, bearing an embossed red cross at their top.

"Please be seated," Rat-Face said, and the camp commander composed himself and made a graceful gesture towards the chair.

I don't want to be seated, I don't want to stand, I just want to get the hell out of here and go wherever the guys are going. Harry obediently settled into the hard chair.

"The camp commander has discovered your name has never been given to Red Cross," Rat-Face said. He appeared embarrassed and worried. "Because of this, there is no record on American side you are here. Do you know anything about this?"

"You're goddamn right I do," Harry said. "Chung kept me off the lists."

The camp commander seemed to need no translation on that one. He said something in a low voice to a guard, who left the room so quickly that for a moment Harry thought that the man was going to go through the wall instead of the door.

"As a result," Rat-face said, "I suppose you have received no mail from your family. Since they do not know you are here?"

"That is right," Harry said. "Chung did not let me send any letters home."

The camp commander tugged at Rat-Face's sleeve, and a fast explanation took place.

There was the sound of running feet, and the door opened behind Harry. The camp commander went out through it almost as fast as the guard had, but before he snapped the door closed, Harry saw Chung at attention on the porch, looking in at him in surprised hatred. He could not hear a word that was said, but the camp commander reappeared thirty seconds later. He said half a dozen quick things to Rat-Face as he resumed his seat.

"Your name is now going to Red Cross. Your side's representatives at Panmunjom will add your name to lists. Your army will be informed. Your loved ones will be informed. Is this satisfactory to you?"

"Yes."

"You have no complaint?"

"No."

The camp commander nodded, pulled open a drawer, and handed across the table one of the white air letter forms with the fat blue peace dove and the word "PEACE" on it. He said something to the interpreter.

"Your government will inform your family soon, probably by some electric way. So you may write this letter now, and it will come after official notice to your loved ones. Please write it now before you leave this camp to go to new camp." He produced the bottle of ink and two straight broad-nib pens which Harry had last seen when he had to write his confession after his escape attempt.

The camp commander rose, and said something more to the interpreter. His tone was a strange one, and Harry rose in some kind of deference to the situation.

Rat-Face nodded. "Camp commander wishes me to tell you his usual job is commander of large tank group. Not using so many tanks in Korea either side now. His usual job not policeman. Also wishes me to tell you he once escaped from Japanese prison camp."

"I see," Harry said, nodding at all of them as if they were drunks who had to be humored, his eyes fixed on that single white sheet of paper. When the camp commander had gone and Rat-Face was waiting for him to write the letter, Harry sat down in front of that single small white rectangle. He looked at it carefully, trying to calculate how many words it would hold, and then took up the pen. He dipped the pen in the inkwell and began, "Anne Darling." Then he stopped and stared at his handwriting. It was like that of a nine-year-old child.

I didn't know you could get out of practice like that, he thought. He stared at the words, thinking that his handwriting must have been like this when they had made him write that confession, but that he must have been too rattled to notice. "I am alive and all right and I love you," he penned quickly. "Please wait for me." He looked at it, and as he did he realized all the fears about her that had beset him in the year and eight months since his capture. He had never admitted that she might not wait, he had never allowed himself to think that. "We will be married as soon as I return from here." Harry looked at his big, crazy childish handwriting. He was already halfway down the small page. "Please give my love to Mother and Bill. Of course to your parents, too. Please tell Harvard to hold a place for one more senior whenever I get back. Please have everybody write right away. I think I can receive mail now. With all my love, through everything, Harry."

II

Constance regained consciousness. She was lying on the floor in her apartment in New York, just where she had been standing when she casually opened the telegram. It had fluttered a few feet away, and now she crawled to it, snatched it up, and pulled it close to her face. The words kept moving before her eyes.

HAPPY TO INFORM YOU YOUR SON
PREVIOUSLY REPORTED KILLED IN ACTION
NAME APPEARS ON LATEST LIST
PRISONER OF WAR STATUS

She rose, her eyes closed, and stretched her arms above her, a beautiful smile on her face. She spun as if in a waltz and paced exultantly back and forth across the room, her eyes wild with the triumph of life, panting, her fingers grasping at her skirt, her blouse, her hair.

My baby is alive. My boy is alive.

She fell into a chair, laughing. Harry. You're alive. We've done it. You are here and I'm here and you're alive and there you are the nurse bringing you to me, little closed-eyes face.

She sat up. As if the books on the shelves were falling in upon her, she saw set among them the wedding picture of Bill and Anne.

Constance rose, straightening her back, and went to the telephone. When she got the person she wanted, she wasted no words.

"Clarence? Constance Purdick. I'm sorry to call you at the office, but there is something extremely urgent. I have to talk to you. Do you want me to come down there?"

"Just stay right there," Clarence's calm voice said, "and I'll be there inside of thirty minutes."

*   *   *

"You're not too cold out here?" Clarence asked her as the special Army ferry boat to Governor's Island slapped through the gray October waves.

"I need the fresh air." Constance stared across the water at the skyline of lower Manhattan, the Statue of Liberty pale green under a dark sky, the neat low buildings of First Army Headquarters on Governor's Island sliding towards them.

Thank God for Clarence, she thought, looking at his big hands as they rested quietly on the railing near her. I never would have thought of this.

*   *   *

The Army psychiatrist listened with eyes wide, smoking one cigarette after another as the three of them sat around his desk in the hospital.

"It's very hard to know what a man in captivity over there could stand hearing about," he said when they had told him. "We haven't had even one man escape from any of those camps and make it back here, so we don't know what the conditions are in there. The International Red Cross has only been in to one camp so far, and I'm sure they took them to some kind of showplace. Even that wasn't too good." He offered his pack of cigarettes again, and lit one more for himself. "The way the war is going in those hills, and the way those truce talks are deadlocked, it might be quite a while before he gets back, so he might have to live for quite a while with whatever you tell him. Now. The girl — " he jabbed his cigarette in Clarence's direction, "your daughter — she and her husband haven't been told yet?"

"Neither one of them knows yet," Clarence said. "My own wife doesn't know yet."

The doctor coughed. "Well, let's go through the possibilities.

Would your daughter want to get a divorce or a separation or an annulment or something, and go back to waiting for this man?"

Constance drew in her breath.

Clarence looked at Constance, and then shook his head. "They seem quite happy to me."

The doctor nodded, and looked at Constance. "And we can assume that her husband feels the same way?"

Constance cleared her throat. "I'm sure Bill wants to stay married to Anne."

"Well, in that case, your son — the one who's a prisoner — is obviously going to have to face this situation sooner or later." The psychiatrist thought for a minute. "I'd say later. If you leave it until he gets back, at least he'll be in a more congenial environment when he gets the news. If it's a shock to him — even if he goes into shock — you'll be there. There'll be facilities — medical facilities — my kind of facilities, for that matter — for taking care of him."

Constance shuddered.

Clarence drummed his fingers on the arm of the tubular steel and imitation leather chair in which he sat. "It makes sense, but what is he supposed to hear in the meantime? Harry thinks she's still his fiancée. She can't *not* write him."

The doctor stubbed out his cigarette. "You'll have to make the final decisions on this, but my advice is that he should be allowed to believe that things are the way they were. He's in a very tough spot. I don't think you should take away anything that might help him get through."

"I buy that," Clarence said. He looked over at Constance. She nodded, and they rose to leave.

* * *

Well, Constance thought numbly, now I know what a family council looks like. A white-faced Anne was sitting rigid on the hassock in her parents' apartment. Bill had forgotten to bring a necktie with him when they had started driving down from Cambridge. He sat on the couch in his open white shirt and tweed jacket, nervously crossing and recrossing his long, gray-flannel-clad legs. His face was a mixture of excitement that Harry was alive, and worried confusion about what was to come next. Clarence sat like a rock, and Mabel had brought in some tea. No one was touching the tea.

"All right," Clarence said when they were all seated. "You know what that doctor at Governor's Island thinks. Anne — " his voice softened — "how does it strike you?"

"I don't know." Anne's voice seemed to come from a cave. "I just think — " she stopped, her lip trembling, looking over at Constance. "I just think Harry could *tell*. I don't know if you could pretend a thing like that, even in a letter."

Bill thrust his hands into the pockets of his tweed jacket. "It's all right with me for you to try, Anne."

Mabel spoke up. "After all, Anne dear, couldn't you write him in vague terms? You can tell him you miss him. You can tell him you look forward to his getting out. You can tell him — oh, lots of things. Tell him you hope he's all right."

Anne stared at her mother. "That won't be hard."

"All right," Clarence said, an invisible agenda before him. "So Anne will use our address, return address Miss Anne Wiley, and we'll forward his letters to you, Anne. In fact, you'd better send yours to him, to us here, first, in an outer envelope. Then we can mail them here and have a New York postmark on them. All right? Now, how about Bill? Are you going to write him?"

"I don't know," Bill said. "It seems to me one of us lying to him is enough."

"Well, that's *just great!*" Anne cried, leaping to her feet. "Why should I be the only one — "

Constance looked at her. "You're the one who was going to marry him."

"That's right." Anne's eyes were blazing. "Bill is only his brother."

"Come on," Clarence said. "What's your reasoning on this, Bill?"

"Look." Bill stood and walked over to the window. He leaned half-sitting against the covered radiator, his arms folded. "When Harry gets back, it's going to be bad enough as it is. At least I think he'll be able to understand why Anne has written him this way. But he'll *never* be able to understand it if I write him as if everything was fine. It'll just make him bitter. It's just gratuitous. Anne is the one he needs to hear from, Anne is the one he wants to hear from, Anne is the one who can help him live through this. I'm willing to let her do it. Anne, and Mother. That's enough."

Constance muttered, "I think he might like to hear from you, too."

"Mother," Bill said, exasperatedly letting his folded arms come apart, "I'd love to write him if things were *different*. But there's no use telling two lies when one is going to do it."

Mabel chimed in, "It doesn't have to be lies. She can write him in vague terms."

"Sins of omission," Bill said, and walked over to the couch and sat down on it heavily.

Clarence rubbed his hands on the fronts of his trouser legs. "Bill, he's going to think it's funny if he doesn't hear from you."

"I've gone to the Antarctic," Bill said. "Mother can write him I'm in the Navy, on an Antarctic expedition. That'll take care of me."

"All right." Clarence looked at all of them in turn. "I guess we have our signals straight. Now the only remaining problem — "

"There's only *one?*" Anne shot in.

"The only remaining problem *at this moment*," Clarence continued, "is to try to make sure that none of Harry's friends mention anything about Anne and Bill if they write him."

Constance raised her hand. "I'll try to take care of that. I'll drop a note to all the boys who might write him." Bill looked at her gratefully.

CHAPTER TWENTY-FIVE

Harry lay twisted on the wooden floor of the schoolhouse that was his home in this new camp by the Yalu, his face pale and his hands clamped to the lower right side of his stomach. It had hit him on the barge coming up here, and grown steadily worse this past day. He could feel the hot swelling in there, feel his own tight nausea, and this time he did not need to have the disease first and learn its name later. He knew it was appendicitis. If that swelling hot thing in his right side broke, poison would run through all his veins. In his present hungry, weak condition, suffering from exposure after the open barge traveling the October Yalu, a ruptured appendix would kill him.

He stared around the forty-by-forty bare classroom with the sad mistrusting eyes of an animal in captivity. Hump Jones and Martinez had gone to see if they could get help for him. The others were outside somewhere, building a dirt wall in this cold despite the shredded condition of their fourteen-month-old gingham summer uniforms.

Harry stared up at the ceiling, gazing right through holes in the wooden slabs to the leaden winter sky above. Wind whistled around the edge of the schoolhouse.

Feet came across the wooden floor, and Hump Jones was bending down, with slender dark Martinez beside him.

"Buddy," Hump said, "they got some kind of doctor in the town down by the river. Chung n' Wuthers said they're not goin' to detail any extra men to carry you, but if we kin get you there, OK."

"Let's go," Harry said, feeling the hot heavy pus burning at the bottom of his stomach. They pulled him to his feet and set off, the tall stooped MP on one side of Harry, and the slight olive paratrooper on the other, Harry's arms outstretched across their shoulders, a walking crucifix.

The Chinese guards quartered in the town by the Yalu stared impassively, but they pointed to the hut for which they were looking.

Hump knocked. There was a word in Chinese from within, and Hump knocked again. The door opened, and a dark, shaven-headed Chinese officer six feet tall looked out. The instant he saw Harry's face as he hung between the two men, he swung the door open. He motioned them to bring him across the room to a wooden stool beside a table covered with anatomical charts.

"What seems to be the problem?" he asked in a soft British accent as he seated Harry on the stool.

"My appendix," Harry said in tight tones.

"Ah." The doctor had Harry take his shirt off and slide his pants down, and since he had no underpants, Harry was naked except for the West Point ring hanging from his neck. The doctor had his wrist and was feeling his pulse. "We will be at least half an hour," the doctor said to Hump and Martinez. "Can you wait?"

"All the time in the world," Hump said. Martinez walked with his panther gait over to a small brick stove that was radiating heat in the mud-walled room. The doctor picked up a leather case the size of a pack of cigarettes, and opened it. Harry saw a row of what appeared to be gold hatpins inside. The shaven-headed man selected a needle, and then squatted beside Harry's right knee. His strong hands examined the area just below the outside of the knee, and he nodded.

"Doctor," Harry said, "it's my *appendix*." He pointed to his stomach. "Up here."

"I know where the appendix is located, young man," the doctor replied. Hump and Martinez were looking at the gold needle in the Chinese doctor's right hand.

"What's that?" Martinez asked in his husky breathing voice, "anesthetic, doc?"

"No." The doctor placed the needle firmly against the skin of Harry's leg, three inches below the knee. "Cough."

Harry coughed and the doctor painlessly screwed the needle about half an inch into Harry's leg. He removed his hand from it, leaving what appeared to be a slightly thicker handle on the base of the needle sticking out into the air. Then his hand took Harry's wrist again.

Well, Harry thought, this is it. He felt like laughing. I got through combat and then twenty months of this, and finally get to a doctor and he's polite and wants to be helpful, and what does he do for appendicitis? He sticks a needle in my leg.

The doctor remained squatting, studying the needle and continuing to hold Harry's wrist in a firm, gentle grip. Hump and Martinez alternated between warming their hands over the brick stove and coming back to peer at Harry, naked on the chair, with the needle sticking out of his leg and the doctor squatting beside him.

"How is the nausea?" the doctor asked after five minutes.

Harry blinked, and said in a small, surprised voice, "Better."

The doctor nodded. The brick stove kept up a pleasant hissing sound. After fifteen minutes the doctor moved his hand to Harry's stomach, the first time he had touched the area affected. "Does it feel cooler?"

"Yes."

Another fifteen minutes, and the doctor said, "Cough." Harry did, and the doctor began withdrawing the needle with his steady hands. After a minute the needle was out. The doctor rose, gesturing to Harry that he should put his clothes back on. He wrote something on a piece of paper, using a thin long-handled writing brush and a small metal can of ink to do it.

"You'll be a bit weak for one or two days more," the doctor said. "This chit tells the authorities up there to let you remain absolutely still for at least two days. Keep this chit. If there should be any further trouble, come back and see me. I don't think there should be."

Harry rose, light-headed. He felt his stomach. It was no warmer on the right side than on the left, and the swelling was gone.

"One more thing. Eat very lightly for the next three days."

"That's easy," Harry said. "Thank you, doctor."

"Not at all."

The three of them walked up the road, Harry going slowly, but under his own power.

"Just coincidence," Martinez was saying doggedly, his fierce face with its pencil mustache turned towards them. "You didn't have appendicitis after all. Just a bad stomach ache is all it was. It just went away while you were down there."

Harry walked along, silent and wondering and serene. "You know," he said to Hump just before they reached the compound, "these really are the damnedest people."

II

Anne sat at the kitchen table of their apartment in Cambridge. In the evenings Bill used this table for studying, but it was afternoon, and in front of her was the letter from Harry, the one he had sent just before leaving Pyoktong on the barge. Her eyes were red as she looked at it for the hundredth time, the cheap paper, the dirty smudges of his hands, the handwriting that proclaimed that they had made him almost an illiterate. The cold of North Korea seemed somehow to sweep across the autumn leaves on the sunny lawn outside, howling up off this sheet of dirty white paper, this fat silly blue peace dove. His handwriting looked as if it was not simply unpracticed, but as if his hands had been cramped and twisted with cold. She would never have thought that any fifty words written on soiled paper could have moved her so much.

Before her was some of her old monogrammed paper, bearing her maiden initials. She stared down at it and at her pen, still not knowing what she was going to say. She felt hungry, yet she had eaten only an hour before.

"Harry darling," she wrote, "It was the most wonderful moment of my life when I found that you were alive after all." Her pen flew. "I love you, I always will, and I will marry you if you want me."

Her pen stopped an inch above the paper, and she looked at what she had written, slain by the truth it spoke.

Anne pushed back the chair as if a snake were wriggling across the table. She fled into the bedroom and threw herself down on the big comfortable double bed.

Only last night, she thought, sobbing, only last night Bill and I lay right here and we made love so that my toes fluttered. Marriage. I'm married to Bill. I promised, on that altar. That's why we have promises, because people don't always feel like doing what they said they would.

"Harry," she whispered, "one of us should be dead. Either you or me."

Twenty minutes later she sat again at the kitchen table. She left what she had written, and continued.

"I do not know if you realize that you were not reported just missing in action, but reported killed in action. The Army sent back a coffin they said had your body in it, and there was a funeral attended by almost everyone you ever knew. Naturally, quite a few people went on about their lives after that on the assumption that you were dead. You will have to bear this in mind if you find some of your friends a little confused when you get back."

She paused, wiped tears from her eyes, and wrote more. "Even after the telegram saying you were alive, we didn't know where to write you until your letter came. I am afraid this may not reach you before Thanksgiving, but I hope you have the best possible one under the circumstances. I miss you, we all miss you and love you. This will all come to an end, and you will be back here and then we can discuss just what you want to do about the future. The important thing is to know that you are all right."

Anne left the letter again, and wandered around the living room she had been trying so hard to make nice. She went into the bedroom, dizzy, and stopped before a picture of Bill. He had not wanted a picture of himself on the bureau, but she had insisted. Now she picked it up, and studied the long, kindly face.

I don't want to hurt you, Bill. That's the last thing I want to do. I want it to work. How could I know Harry was *alive?*

Anne stared at her reddened face in the mirror. How do I know what it'll be like when Harry gets back? He may not want me when he finds out what's happened. He may be so changed from this thing, he may not want me, we may have nothing to say.

He may not get back.

Don't even think that.

Anne moved back to the table slowly, and stood, one hand on the chair, staring at Harry's smudged letter and her own monogrammed stiff sheets in reply. After a long time she sat down slowly and picked up the pen as if it was of great weight.

"Harry, I never understood religion emotionally, but I am doing more thinking about it now. I pray for you, and for all of us, and I hope that you will do the same. It seems to me that at the very top of the spiritual ladder the distinctions between individual human beings become meaningless, and our prayers should go to that end, so that we do not worry about the smaller things that can cause human beings to argue or to have grief. When I say 'smaller things' I realize that some of them seem big to us, inevitably, but they *would be* small if we could just see them right."

She rested her forehead on her hand as she wrote. "Harry, the important thing for me and for all of us is that you take care of yourself and get out of there all right. I will be waiting for you."

Anne scribbled a few lines about friends of his that she had seen, and what they were doing, told him his mother was looking well, and signed it "Love, Anne."

CHAPTER TWENTY-SIX

W UTHERS WAS TRYING to get them to march in step as the column from this compound moved down to the soccer field. They had been issued new padded blue cotton uniforms with short-visored blue caps that reminded Harry of the one he had worn as a little boy at school.

"Hut two, hut four!" Wuthers was shouting, and the Turks in line just ahead of Harry were mimicking him and making obscene gestures behind his back. As they marched onto the field for the first orientation talk since they had arrived here, Harry saw two other long columns snaking onto the hard-packed earth where the Chinese were waiting for them. One column was composed of Negro sergeants and the younger white sergeants, whom the Chinese had segregated into a compound down the road. The other column was composed of two hundred older white sergeants, who had the compound next to Harry's. In Harry's column were the men of Compound A: one hundred and twenty American sergeants, thirty-five British Commonwealth sergeants, the twenty-five Turk wild men, and two Frenchmen. At the tail end of Harry's column were twelve American sergeants of Japanese, Chinese, and Philippine descent, whom the Chinese had put in a one-room shack at the corner of his compound.

The other two columns, each of two hundred men apiece, were standing in place when Wuthers brought Compound A to a halt in front of the raised wooden platform in the middle of the field.

"The camp commander will now address you," Wuthers said solemnly, trying to confer dignity upon his piping tones.

A stocky Chinese they had never seen climbed the steps onto the platform. In a row before the wooden platform were six Chinese interpreters, including the old favorites from Pyoktong — Chung, Rat-Face, and Wu.

Here we go again, Harry thought. New camp, same old political lecture, I suppose. He glanced over at the Negroes standing in the cold, the blue-cotton pants legs flapping in the November wind. A lot of them had come from Pyoktong.

"You are now at Camp Number Four at Wiwan in the People's Republic of North Korea," the camp commander said in correct but halting English. Harry moved his feet inside the black basketball sneakers that had been issued, feeling the cold coming up through the ground and wishing that they had been given some socks, too. "You will be obedient to the camp regulations. You have already built a wall to form the boundary between Compound A and Compound B. You have also built brick stoves in your barracks. The wood you are using to heat them was cut by other prisoners who arrived before you. Therefore tomorrow you will begin to carry wood from the countryside to here. Also some knives were made from inside part of U.S. Army boots before you received new uniforms. These knives are illegal." Harry smiled. The camp commander was not going to lose face by asking for them to be turned in, because he knew they would not be.

The camp commander looked at them for a few moments before he said the next thing. "There will be no lectures in this camp. We have told you our side of the story, and intelligent men understand our side of the story now. Therefore it is unnecessary to continue your political education."

A rustle of whispers came down the ranks.

"They've kissed us off, son," Hump Jones whispered from behind Harry. Martinez, next to Harry, was grinning like a wolf.

The camp commander went on with his do's and don't's, but Harry felt his breath going out in a great sigh. They had held out. Hour after hour in that year at Pyoktong, cold in that damned lecture hall in the winter, stifling in summer, and now the Chinese had had it. They had plucked out the fifteen per cent who responded, they had picked up a Wuthers here and there, shipped out a Norden who started nodding and couldn't stop, but here stood six hundred sergeants labeled "no sale."

Harry looked over at the Negroes, who as a group had resisted next best to the Turks. There were some pretty broad grins under the little blue cotton caps.

The camp commandant was droning on about regulations.

Well, Harry thought, here it is. When the big moment comes, no trumpets, just a lot of cheap blue cotton pants flapping in the wind. He looked around at the men in the ranks about him, delighted.

I wonder if you guys really understand, he thought, but there was a glow on them. They understood. Hungry thin faces from Gulfport and Abilene and Holbrook, Arizona, and they understood.

Harry looked to the front again, studying the faces of Chung and Rat-Face and Wu as they stood unarmed in front of the platform on which the camp commander was giving his harangue. He wondered if they were getting it. They had held all the cards, they had shipped out of Pyoktong the men who resisted hardest and the men who seemed most promising, but most of the student body was standing right in front of them, silently telling them to drop dead.

"Despite the objections of your government," the camp commander said, "we have managed to bring you mail from your loved ones." He motioned, and two guards came forward with sacks of mail. The camp commander went down the steps of the wooden platform, and walked off the soccer field. Rat-Face began calling out the names of men who had letters. Harry stood tight as man after man went forward.

They promised I could have mail like everybody else, he thought, watching Chung. Chung was standing to one side, nodding pleasantly when a man from his platoon would trot forward to pick up a letter that Rat-Face held extended towards him.

Harry teetered on his feet, and then began trembling in rage. *I should have known. A new camp, a new commandant, Chung can do any goddamn thing he wants to. He can tear up anything coming in or out of here.*

The old wound in Harry's shoulder twitched, and then the face of the shaven-headed needle doctor down by the river rose in his mind. He heard the man's British accent, his kind voice, felt his strong, soothing hands.

That man, Harry thought, *that man*. Harry's eyes narrowed. *That man could get another letter out for me.*

II

Constance could not understand what this officer from First Army was getting at. He had called and asked to come up and see her, and here he sat in her apartment, drinking a cup of coffee that she had made for him. His face was red from the December cold, but Constance thought he was somehow blushing as well.

"About the body," he said finally.

"*What* body?" Constance asked wildly.

He held up his hand, the palm towards her. "The one that was mistakenly returned to you. The one we thought was your son."

"Oh."

He took another quick swallow of his coffee. "It's still there, isn't it? Where you buried it?"

"Of course."

The officer looked relieved. "We thought we could disinter it and bury it at Arlington. We don't know who it is either, but I assume you don't want it there, since it's not your son."

"I see." Constance gave him a reassuring smile. He looked so uncomfortable about the whole thing. "Why don't we just leave the poor boy where he is?"

III

Harry came walking down the road to the Yalu, away from the compound and towards the knot of little houses where the Chinese guards were quartered. Chung had been furious when Harry showed him the slip that the needle doctor had given him, with the Chinese characters on it saying that Harry could come back for further treatment if necessary. Finally Chung had let him go, and he was walking down the road, thinking how strange it was to be unguarded.

I suppose they know damn well none of us have any heart left for trying to escape, Harry said to himself, his breath smoking the freezing air. They didn't make too many converts at Pyoktong, but they sure as hell converted us to the no-escape idea.

He came to the little mud house, and knocked on the door. As before, the door opened, and the tall, dark-faced, shaven-headed man looked out.

"Doctor," Harry said, holding out the chit the man had given him, "you said I could come back if I needed any treatment."

"Certainly. Won't you come in?" The doctor motioned him to the same stool in the corner by the stove. Harry took off his little-boy cap and sat on the wooden stool, feeling the wonderful heat from the stove sink him into sudden stupor. He shook it from his brain.

"Doctor, the appendix is fine, but I have an old wound in my shoulder. It's been kicking up."

"Take off your shirt."

"Yes, sir."

The big Chinese bent over behind Harry, and the reassuring hands began feeling the point where his neck joined his spine.

"It's to the left of there, doctor."

"I can see the scar very plainly, young man." The doctor continued feeling the base of Harry's neck. Then he straightened and went over to where his little pack-of-cigarette-sized leather box of gold needles sat atop the anatomical charts spread on the table. He selected a needle that had a tiny metal arrowhead on its tip.

"I'm surprised it's giving you pain," the doctor said. "It appears to be very satisfactorily healed. When did you get it?"

"Just about two years ago, doctor. In the first big attack when your Army came in."

"Oh, yes." The doctor smiled as he came around behind Harry again. "I was in Hong Kong then."

That explains the British accent, Harry thought. He felt the doctor's thumb resting itself just to the left of the base of his neck, and then he was aware that somehow the needle was in him.

"Does that cause you any pain?"

"No, sir."

"Fine." The doctor left him sitting there with the needle sticking out of the point where his shoulder joined his neck, and came back a moment later, carrying another stool. He placed it a yard from Harry, and sat down on it. "It will take perhaps half an hour. How is your health otherwise?"

"Well, I have another wound in my buttock, but that only gives me a twinge every now and then." Don't play it down too much, Harry thought. You may need a half dozen excuses to come back here before you think the time is right to hit him to get a letter out for you. Harry looked longingly at the sheets of paper stacked at one corner of the table on which the anatomical charts were spread. If the doctor would let him, he could write a letter on any one of those sheets, explaining to Anne about how Chung was stopping her answer to the one letter he knew had gotten out from Pyoktong.

Just take it easy, Harry said to himself. Don't rush this. You're ahead of the game right now. You're sitting here in a warm room instead of being out on a work detail. Just take it easy.

"Have you ever been to Hong Kong?" the doctor asked.

Harry stared at him for a moment. It was the first personal question that the man had asked him. Staring at the kindly face, Harry thought, my God, he really wants to talk. I've found the one educated man along the Yalu River who doesn't have a political officer's axe to grind, and he wants to talk.

"No, doctor," Harry replied, "I haven't. What's it like?"

IV

It was Christmastime in New York. The darkness of the winter's early afternoon was kept at bay by thousands of brightly lighted store windows heaped with silks and leather goods and toys. Package-laden men and women strode past bell-ringing Santa Clauses. There were wreaths in windows, and pink cheeks in the street.

Anne stepped out of the building just around the corner from her parents' apartment. By its door were the dulled brass plaques of the doctors whose offices were on the ground floor. She walked down the street, as if she were holding herself together, her face blank.

Anne turned in the door of her parents' apartment house, and rode up in the elevator. She let herself into the apartment. As the door opened, her mother came quickly into the hall.

"What did the doctor say?" Mabel's face was glowing in anticipation.

Anne nodded. "Yes. I'm pregnant."

"Oh, *darling!*" Mabel threw her arms about her daughter. "How absolutely wonderful!"

Anne took off her coat and walked into the living room, her mother moving excitedly beside her.

"I'll telephone your father right away," Mabel said happily.

"And when Bill comes in, he'll be so *thrilled!* And you'll have to call Constance Purdick right away."

"Yes." Anne sat down on the hassock, her arms folded over her knees. She smiled weakly at her mother. Everything was changed. It was plunging through her mind, the child within her, a child, and Harry out there at the end of the world and the guns still pounding in the hills out there and the rest of the world going on. The child. Harry was the child's Uncle Harry.

"Maybe we can call it Harry," she said in a voice so low that Mabel bent to hear her. "If it's a boy." Then she began laughing hysterically.

"You're just upset by this, dear," Mabel said.

"Yes." Anne choked, and began laughing again. "Yes, I am." She started to slide off the hassock, and Mabel was holding her up, looking at her daughter's turned-aside suffering face, holding her up as if she were a rag doll.

V

It was seven o'clock in the morning of New Year's Day, 1953. Harry stood shifting his cold sneakered feet on the snowy ground in front of the schoolhouse where he was quartered. A big Turk named Ali was barking unfamiliar commands at the twenty-five Turks as he marched them over from their separate small building to join this formation that had suddenly been ordered by Chung. From the corner of the compound, the twelve Nisei and Hawaiian and Philippine sergeants, nicknamed "the U.N. Squad," were bringing their light frames across the shadowy area on the double.

When everyone was mutteringly in place, a small column of Chinese officers and guards entered the compound. Something clicked in Harry's mind; it brought back the picture of the day the American doctor captain had been forced to make his public confession at the schoolhouse, with the formation of guards escorting him up the long stone steps.

Harry peered at the column as they came closer. Chung was at the head of it. Behind him were two of the Chinese guards who had been sentries in this compound. They were without their omnipresent burp guns, and their caps were missing from their heads. Behind them came a phalanx of the camp commandant, the interpreters Rat-Face and Wu, and another dozen guards, all carrying their burp guns. The column came to a crunching halt in the snow, and Chung pushed the two hatless guards forward before the ranks of blue-clad prisoners. Harry could see now that they had their hands tied behind them.

"These men have been guilty of corruption!" Chung shouted. "They cannot speak English, but their presence here this morning is their apology for giving such a poor example of proper socialist dedication!"

Corruption? Harry thought, looking at the two guards. They were just kids, and in fact these two were the nicest of the bunch, sometimes smiling, and usually staying out of the way, burp guns and all. Corruption? There's nothing left to corrupt.

"These men have been guilty of giving certain prisoners extra leaves of tobacco in return for the stamps on your letters from the United States," Chung said sternly. "A man who can be bribed for an airmail stamp can be bribed for other things! You are guilty of offering the bribe, but they are doubly guilty, because they have had the privilege of being exposed to true fraternal socialist principles!" Harry stared at Chung. The beak-nosed interpreter was working himself into a rage. The two young guards stood in their sand-colored quilted jackets, their heads bowed, their hands tied behind them.

Beside Harry, Martinez murmured, "A couple of stamps, for chrissake."

"These men will be transferred and sent immediately to the front," Chung said.

Hump Jones cleared his throat behind Harry. "Sonofa-bitch Chung's never been *theyah*," he drawled.

Chung shouted a command, and the two guards did an awkward about-face in the snow. Harry looked at the face of the camp commander, and Wu, and Rat-Face, in the gathering gray dawn. They looked uncomfortable. The column marched off.

"Happy New Year," Hump said, and the formation turned into little knots of individuals, heading back into the barracks or getting set for work details. Harry shrugged his shoulders and started across the compound, the needle doctor's slip in his hand. The guard at the gate passed him through, and he headed down the road for his daily drawn-out morning session with the doctor.

* * *

"No," the doctor said, "you're not making that one quite right." He took the writing brush from Harry and drew the Chinese character once more. It stood out amidst the big, sloppy approximations of it with which Harry had filled the sheet of paper. "Once you start the character," the doctor said, "be decisive. It's like drawing any letter of your alphabet. The important thing about a 'W,' for example, is that it should *look* like a 'W.' It doesn't have to be geometrically perfect, but it shouldn't waver about."

"I get you," Harry said. He pressed his lips together and drew the character swiftly.

"Much better." The doctor stopped looking over Harry's shoulder, and checked the needle in Harry's back.

Harry drew the character once more, enjoying the reckless sensation of drawing it fast. He was not quite sure just how these Chinese lessons had begun, but now the daily ritual was for him to take off his shirt, have the pin put in, and then bring his stool over to the table on which the anatomical charts were spread. He would spend the half hour that the pin must stay in, drawing.

First came a review of the five he had learned, and then each day came a new one.

"Here." The doctor placed a cup of tea beside Harry's elbow.

"Thank you." Harry put down the writing brush and sipped at the tea. Looking at the doctor's pleasant, slightly amused face as the big man studied his latest efforts with the character for "I," Harry felt ashamed. The man was being so pleasant, and he was not going to like it when he realized that all this had been for the purpose of softening him up to get a letter out.

I can't help it, Harry thought, taking another sip of the tea. I really do like the guy, and I really like learning what all these squiggles mean, but he's my only hope to let them know at home why I can't write.

"Middle," the doctor said, suddenly. It was his way of testing.

" 'Chung,' " Harry intoned, and then he stopped. "Doctor, that's not the same 'Chung' as the interpreter here?"

"No, no. The 'chung' that means middle is pronounced as the straight tone, just as you did it. His 'chung' is pronounced differently, and written differently. His 'chung' means nothing, just as 'Jones' means nothing. Now draw 'middle.' "

Harry quickly drew the square with the line bisecting it vertically.

"Very well. Now back to 'I.' "

Harry drew the complicated character for "I" once more. He smiled as he looked down at his jet-black marks all over the page, in various stages of drying. He felt as if there were a whole world under these characters, as if he could walk through them and enter another dimension.

Ho Hwei Yu Chi. The words came back to him, the young Chinese infantryman shaking hands with him just out of sight of Pyoktong when they dropped him off there after his escape attempt in the river with Tommy Quinn. Ho Hwei Yu Chi, that one had said, and then they had been gone, on down towards the front.

"Doctor," Harry said, "what does 'Ho Hwei Yu Chi' mean?"

The doctor started, and then he grinned. "I can't believe you heard that from one of these interpreters."

"No. It was just some regular troops. We were saying good-bye. They taught me those few words I told you about — you know, like for hand, and head."

"Yes, but you have to practice those words to get the tone right," the doctor said. "The tone has to be right, or it means something else." He took the little gold-tinted metal teapot and poured more in Harry's cup. "That phrase with which they said good-bye to you," he said musingly. "I suppose the nearest thing in your culture would be tales of Sherwood Forest. Robin Hood. That sort of thing. It was said by adventurers, soldiers, when they met in the hills, each hiding from different authorities. It means, 'a time will come when we shall meet again.'" The doctor smiled. "It's a rather admiring phrase, really. It also carries the implication that when that time comes, it may be that you shall have to fight each other."

"All that in just four syllables?" Harry asked.

There was a rap on the window, and they both turned. Chung was standing there. Then he moved from the window, and knocked at the door. The doctor's face became blank. He moved to the door. Harry took the page of scrawled characters, balled it up, and threw it into the stove just as Chung strode in.

Chung began talking in Chinese, his voice steady. He pointed to the cup of tea near Harry, he pointed to the writing brush and then pointed to the window. Harry needed no words of Chinese, none at all, to understand that Chung was telling the doctor that he had been watching at the window for some time.

The doctor turned to Harry. His face was a mask, and his voice seemed to come from a deep, metallic tunnel. "I was just telling Comrade Chung," he said, "that with this session our series of treatments is concluded." He stepped behind Harry and began slowly unscrewing the needle from the back of his neck.

Harry stared at the wall. Chung was standing by the door, his arms folded, waiting.

"Put on your shirt," the doctor said in brusque tones.

Harry rose. The room was echoing with emotions. The doctor, frightened, humiliated, being distant and impersonal to save himself; Chung, vindictive, self-righteous, triumphant at having caught Purdick, seething with hatred for him.

As Harry dressed, his eyes looked away from Chung, because he was afraid that Chung might read what could be seen there. With the visits to the doctor gone, there was only one way to stop Chung from tearing up the letters for him.

*   *   *

The wind whined about the dark little wooden latrine building in the corner of the compound. It was midnight. Harry slipped through its door. There was Martinez, sitting on one of the holes, his trousers down so that it looked legitimate if a guard poked his nose in here.

Harry slid down his trousers and sat on the next hole over. The wind came screaming up through the hole. Harry's eyes closed, and he began shaking, big, body-shaking shivers. Slowly, through chattering teeth, he began to explain what he wanted to see Martinez about.

"That's no good," Martinez whispered when he had heard the problem. "I'd lend you my knife, but that's not the way." He thought for long moments as the snow hissed against the thin wooden boards of the building. Harry stared over at the straight back of Matinez' head, the pencil mustache.

I was right to come to him, Harry thought. Ex-member of the Comanches in East Harlem, Airborne Ranger, one-man patrols behind Chinese lines. Got a problem? See your friendly neighborhood killer.

"Purdick," Martinez said after a minute, "what we got to fix up for Chung is an accident. That way we all come out smelling like a rose."

CHAPTER TWENTY-SEVEN

In the light from the streetlamp, big snowflakes whirled against the window of their bedroom in Cambridge.

Bill lay in bed, looking up at the ceiling, feeling Anne's soft breathing beside him as she slept.

Women, he thought. What you don't know about women could fill a book. Since they had come back here after his Christmas vacation from Law School, it had been a new Anne with whom he was living. In some ways she was even nicer than she had been before, quiet and efficient and affectionate, but at times he saw a sorrow on her face, deeper than her expressions after they all thought Harry had died. It was as if a permanence had descended on their marriage, a permanence which had nothing to do with him. She cooked; they chatted; they went to parties. But she was living for the child.

Bill turned on his side, staring at her sleeping face on the pillow. Strangely enough, it had been in class, and sitting over books in the library, that he had come to realize that to live with a woman was not the monopoly of her that he had always assumed. You could sleep with her, be received in her arms, be father to the child within her, and still another man could control her soul.

When you get back, Harry, he said silently, you're going to think you're the big loser. You're wrong. Anne's the big loser, and you and I are tied for second. But the thing is, Anne and I have never talked about it, but she and I don't want the baby to lose on this, too.

II

Harry staggered down the road in the dark February afternoon, carrying over his shoulder a tree trunk nearly the size of the log he and Tommy had used to escape from Pyoktong. He had been carrying it for five miles, back to camp, where it would be chopped up for firewood. Every hundred yards he stopped to rest. Chung seemed to be everywhere, watching the prisoners as they struggled with their loads. The area where the trees had been felled and trimmed was ten miles from Wiwan. Everyone in the compound would march up there in the morning in a group, but on the return trip men were strung out for five miles, depending on their strength, and the size of the load assigned to each man by the interpreters. Chung saw to it that every day Harry ended up under something the size of a small telephone pole.

Harry stopped for the eightieth time, letting the tail end of the small tree trunk rest on the ground behind him. He shifted the rags that each day he stuffed under the right shoulder of his padded blue jacket. The rags were the remains of the Russian shirt he had worn for fourteen months, before they issued the blue cotton.

"Purdick," Chung barked, "you will be the last one again!"

Harry nodded, balanced the eight-inch-thick pole on his shoulder again, and resumed his slow walk in the snow. You're right about that, Chung. I'll be the last one in every day, believe me. A sad, choking expression came upon Harry's face. That was the plot. Every evening he was getting back to camp in darkness. Chung seemed content to walk beside him, and let the armed guards go on ahead. What Chung did not know was that Martinez was getting back in with a lighter load as fast as he could every day, having a drink of water, and then coming back out on the road. The guards let men come back out, once they had brought in one log, if they wanted to help their friends who had drawn heavier loads. Few men did this, but it gave Martinez the chance to walk back up the road past the strung-out guards and struggling prisoners, until he had a chance to slip off the side of the narrow road. Each afternoon now Martinez had been hiding up in thickets on hillsides, shadowing Harry and Chung as they came in behind the others.

I wish I didn't have so much time to think about this, Harry thought as he moved along under the two-hundred-pound timber. He could remember Clarence Wiley talking about the law, saying that two things were needed to prove first-degree murder; premeditation and deliberation.

I wonder where justifiable homicide figures in, Harry thought, wincing as a foot slipped to one side and the twisting log tore open a blister on his frozen raw red palm. Chung is giving me the biggest log out there every day. He knows damn well I *have* to be the last one in.

*　　*　　*

"Didn't you notice?" Martinez whispered excitedly as they sat in their nightly conference in the latrine. "He was carrying his pistol under his jacket today!"

"Do you think he knows something?"

"I don't care if he does or not," Martinez said. "If he's got a gun, then he can commit suicide! We don't need any rockslide or hipping him into that ice pond or anything!"

"What do you mean?"

"The Chinese commit suicide, don't they?"

"Sure. Sometimes, I guess."

Martinez gripped Harry's arm. "Sure they do. He's an unhappy sonofabitch anyway. Even the other Chinks don't like him. Listen, tomorrow you've got to be the *latest*, man. When I sneak up and mug him, drop that log and help me hold him down. I'm gonna shoot him with his own pistol, leave it in his hand, and then you and I are gonna come shagging back to camp under your log. O.K.?"

Harry took a deep breath and nodded. "O.K."

"Just make sure he doesn't get you back here before dark."

"Don't worry," Harry said. "He yells at me, but he really doesn't push me after he's got me loaded."

*   *   *

It was dark on the road, and the snowflakes were falling. There was a moon somewhere, but all it did was leave a gray glow behind the windless falling flakes.

Chung was about five yards behind him as Harry carried the biggest timber thus far. Harry's face was expressionless; everything was on automatic pilot. The other wood-carriers and guards were easily half a mile ahead of them in the cushioning snow, and Martinez was out here somewhere, ready to move in.

"Purdick."

Harry stopped under his load, let the rear end of the log down, and turned under it so that he was facing Chung.

Chung came two yards closer to him in the snow. "Purdick, do you believe in what I think is called the law of the jungle?"

"I didn't use to," Harry answered, leaning forward slightly as he supported the log.

Chung took his pistol from under his jacket. "I used to see cowboy movies when I was at Cornell. Sometimes the sentiment was, this town isn't big enough for both of us."

Harry almost fainted as he saw the dull blue gun pointing at him through the falling white flakes. Let's be friends, he thought frantically. Let's forget the mail, let's forget you put me in the hole, let's stop here.

"Why don't you say something, Purdick?"

"How are you going to explain it when I'm missing?"

Chung cocked the weapon. "It was expected that some men would fall by the roadside in a project such as this." There was a quick whistle from right behind Chung, and as Harry threw aside his log he saw Chung spin around, right into a ferocious tackle by Martinez. Harry dove at Chung's pistol as it flew off to the right, and then he had the pistol and was crouching over where Martinez had Chung pinned from behind.

"Hurry up," Martinez panted. "Anywhere, just so it doesn't go through him and get me!"

Chung stopped struggling, and held open his mouth. His eyes indicated that Harry should put the pistol there. Harry nodded, slipped the muzzle deep into Chung's mouth, and as Chung began to gag, he fired. Blood and tissue spurted from Chung's mouth, and he fell away from the gun.

"O.K.," Martinez said. He took the pistol from Harry, and began smoothing down the signs of struggle in the snow. Chung lay twitching, one knee convulsively rising in short jerks and then slipping down again. Harry bent over, rubbing his blood-splashed hand in snow, and packing fresh snow over the stains. Martinez fixed the pistol firmly in Chung's hand. Harry picked up the log while Martinez smoothed down the signs of the end of the log having rested here. Then they were both under the log and walking back to camp in the falling snow.

III

Anne sat looking at this second letter from Harry.

Anne Darling,

I am afraid you will have to start all over again if you have written me any letters. I am pretty sure you must have had one from me just before I left the last camp, but there has been a hold up on my mail which seems to be over now.

I love you and want to marry you as soon as I get back. I am all right and I think of you all the time. Please write immediately. I can only write one letter each time, so please give my love to Mother and Bill. Also please tell Harvard to save a place for me when I get out. Best regards to your parents.

With all my love,
Harry

She put her hand to a button of her blouse, jerkily yanking at it. Her nails closed on a fold of material, starting to tear it, and then she put her trembling hands in her lap. She stared at the oppressive March morning at the window.

I can't give you what you want. It's no longer *possible* to give you what you want. I'd like to give you what you want, but I can't.

"It's going to be harder to write this one than the last one," she whispered, and picked up her pen and told him that she loved him and was waiting for him. I hope you can live on this much, she thought, because I'm living on even less. I'm living on duty and mutual good will, and it tastes like ashes.

IV

Bill sat at the back of this small classroom, only half listening to what this man from the Department of Justice was saying. He had come to this meeting only because of a guilty conscience. The other day, chatting with half a dozen of his friends as they ate lunch at Lincoln's Inn, he had realized that they all already *had* jobs, even though it was three months until they received their law degrees. Clarence Wiley had been asking him to come into his law firm upon graduation, and all at once, at that lunch, he had realized that he very specifically did not want to work for his father-in-law. So, when it had been announced that the Justice Department would see people, he decided to come on over. At least he could say he had looked into it.

"In another division of ours," the little man was saying, "the Office of Legal Counsel handles a broad range of problems involving such things as civil rights, housing, and aid to education. This protects the average citizen, in ways that he could not possibly protect himself."

The man went on, and Bill found himself listening carefully.

It's funny, Bill thought, but the man from the Justice Department is really talking about justice.

"Even when a given matter is not a federal case," the man said, "we can open our files to help those who are working against discrimination in housing, against local racketeers who are demanding protection money from merchants and small businessmen, against the denial of the right to vote."

I wish he wouldn't sound so smug, Bill thought. Why do liberals always have to sound as if Moses has just handed them the tablets?

Still he listened, and as he did, his eyes brightened. There were no two ways about it; the man was talking about justice.

I'll be damned, Bill said to himself. For three years I've been working with this stuff, thinking all it was good for was to make a living as one guy's gladiator when he wants to sue the other guy.

Mentally he reviewed his equipment. He knew how to write wills for old ladies, but he also knew how to spot an unconstitutional statute, a dummy corporation, an agreement in restraint of trade.

"In the Solicitor General's office the job is to spend one's full time representing the United States in the Supreme Court, a practice which no other legal office can hope to match. This means that you are working for what is believed to be the best interests of the nation as a whole, on every case." The man smiled. "Of course, this is not the more profitable side of the law. That should be understood. You just get a salary. No fees. No partnerships."

I think it's pretty well understood, Bill thought, looking at the tiny turnout. Of his class of three hundred, only twelve men had come to hear this pitch.

"On the other hand," the little man continued, "for just this reason, in our Tax Division, for example, after a short training period, you will regularly be appearing on behalf of the government against corporation lawyers who are considerably older and more experienced than yourselves. You don't get much money for doing it, but you get experience you would otherwise have to wait many years to acquire."

I'm not greedy, Bill thought. The only thing I'm greedy for is something I can believe in.

"And now, if the rest of you will wait around, I'll talk to you one at a time up here at the desk. I've got application forms, and so on." The little man's face had a pleading expression.

The meeting broke up. Of the twelve who had come, five put on their overcoats and walked out. Bill looked around at the remaining handful. They were not the men who were going on to the big firms and the glamor jobs. They were not the hotshots who were on Law Review.

Seven of us, Bill thought. Seven from the whole class, even interested in the Justice Department. He walked up and got in the line waiting to talk to the man.

CHAPTER TWENTY-EIGHT

Harry's face was taut as he stood in this formation on the soccer field. It was the first time that they had all been called out here since the time, just after they arrived, when it had been announced there would be no more lectures. Now all three compounds stood here, six hundred blue-bag scarecrows under a fair April sky.

I hope it's nothing about Chung, Harry thought, feeling Martinez standing rigid beside him. In the six weeks since Chung's death, not a word had been said, not a question had been asked. Another interpreter had replaced Chung, and that had been that.

The stocky camp commander mounted the little platform. "Because of the efforts of the representatives of the Chinese People's Volunteer Army, we have arranged for some sick and wounded men to return to their loved ones. Hostilities are continuing, but these men will be returned through truce talks area at Panmunjom. This is called Little Switch. In return we are getting back wounded heroes of the Chinese People's Volunteer Army who have been mistreated by your side at Koje Island."

I don't know what that's all about, Harry thought, but I hope we mistreated the hell out of them.

"Following men will be here at four o'clock this afternoon with all possessions for truck ride south to repatriation area."

The ranks buzzed. It sounded real. The commandant began reading names from a list in his hand. Some of the names were of men who were indeed sick, or had been wounded, but interspersed were the names of some collaborators and stool pigeons, most of whom had had their chance to shine at Pyoktong.

"Lettin' the fair-haired boys go first," Hump Jones muttered.

" — Wuthers." The camp commander droned as he came to the bottom of the list.

Martinez snorted. "He's about as sick as I am."

"Sonofabitch has got a disease called gullibility," Hump threw in.

The commandant let the list fall to his side. "Despite the objections of your representatives at Panmunjom, we have been able to procure some more mail for you." He left the platform, and the guards came forward with the bags.

This is it, Harry thought as they began calling names for letters. His heart was beating from half a dozen causes at once. The meeting had not been about Chung; some men really were going home; he was about to find out if the death of the man who had blocked his communication with his family was going to pay off. He looked down at the hand that had jabbed a pistol into Chung's mouth.

All the perfumes of Araby cannot sweeten this little hand, he thought, and grinned.

" — Purdick —" Harry sprinted forward through the ranks for his letters.

*　　*　　*

Harry wandered around the back of the schoolhouse as evening fell, staring but not seeing the American cooks cleaning up pots outside the cookhouse. In his hands were the two letters he had spent the afternoon reading — one from Anne, one from his mother.

He looked down at the one from his mother. "The day that you come back will be the happiest in my life," she said. "Harvard will have a place for you, Anne is waiting for you, and you know what it will mean for Bill and me to see you again." Then followed little things, about Maine and New York, each of which he had read a hundred times.

Harry looked from the letter to the pale-blue flowers blooming on a distant hill. The evening was just closing them out now.

That's the third time I've seen those flowers bloom, Harry thought. He winced. The first time, walking north with Lee after his first escape attempt, on the way to the Bean Camp. The second time, at Pyoktong. The third time, here at Wiwan.

An ox cart moved past on the road outside the compound. Harry looked at it, and then at the letters from another world, a world where they had more than ox carts. The last truck he had seen had been when they burned the schoolhouse where he had walked with Swann, and the three trucks had taken them north to Pyoktong. Harry's hand came to his chest. The West Point ring still hung there, on the dog tag chain that Tommy Quinn had given him two Christmases before.

Desperately he turned to the letter from Anne. "I love you and am waiting for you."

Harry's head hung to one side. These letters drained him and filled him and drained him again.

He saw a figure drifting alone by the barbed-wire fence. It came closer, and he saw that it was a Turk. The stocky man had a letter in his hand, and tears were running down his brown cheeks. Harry turned in the twilight and walked back to the schoolhouse building.

II

The smell of roast lamb was exquisite, and Bill sniffed appreciatively as he came through the door. It was a crisp May afternoon outside, his studies were under control, and he had received an encouraging letter from the Justice Department.

"Anne!" he called. "Where are you?"

Anne emerged from the bedroom, wearing one of her new maternity dresses, and gave him a mischievous smile. "I have something that I think will interest you," she said. Her voice had a strange, excited edge.

"Well, what?" Bill said. He put down his green cloth book bag and reached towards her, his hands gently taking her arms above the elbow.

Anne took his right hand and placed it firmly against her protruding stomach. He felt an animal-like punch against his palm. Bill grabbed back his hand and stared at Anne in awe. She was smiling delightedly.

"The baby just started doing that this afternoon."

Bill put his hand back again, gently, and again Anne's hand closed on his wrist and brought him firmly against her tight stomach. It felt like a fish in there, slapping its tail and squirming.

"He's doing the Charleston in there," Bill said, leaning down as if he could somehow see through the dress and her skin.

III

Harry lay in the sunshine in front of the schoolhouse, sunbathing in the June afternoon. These days they were finishing their work details in the morning, and in the afternoon they were free to lie around or play soccer or toss the softballs the Chinese had recently supplied. The problem was that they were still not getting enough to eat, and twenty minutes of soccer exhausted most of them.

"Check."

Harry looked up. An American named Jack and a Frenchman named Jacques were playing one of their endless chess games, using hand-carved wooden chessmen on a flat piece of driftwood they had found down by the river.

Harry stared at the chessmen, made from two different kinds of wood, and then looked at his own stupid hands. That was the thing, he thought. He had been educated to be fluent in speech; these men had been raised to be fluent with their hands. It was a different world, and a rich one, quite uncomprehended in any-thing he had ever read.

"How ya goin', mate?" An Australian acquaintance of his sat down beside him, tugging at the weird shorts they had been issued, long blue things without a fly, held up by a drawstring.

"How was the soccer, Bob?"

"Fair enough. One of those bloody pommies is a beaut."

Harry smiled. He knew from this Aussie that all Australians called the British "pommies" because they thought their com-plexions were like pomegranates.

The black-haired Australian stretched out in the sunshine. "Don't forget to wake me if anything interesting happens," he said sarcastically, and went to sleep.

Harry nodded. Sitting in the sunshine, he felt a mortal sadness. It was as if they were all cavemen, or children, back at the begin-ning of the world, doing little tasks and playing little games. Men who could repair airplane engines, reduced to whittling wood. Men who had children growing up without them, spending their time repairing a high dirt wall they had been ordered to build to keep themselves inside. He looked listlessly at the men com-ing up from the soccer field, tired and doubly hungry after run-ning the frustrations out of themselves. They were trying to keep smiling as they tossed the ball back and forth on their way back to the schoolhouse and a meal of turnips and the long hol-low night ahead.

*   *   *

He was not able to sleep, and he paced around the back end of the schoolhouse. The night was cool. Turning the corner, he stared in the direction of the Turks' little building. There were big orange cones of light over there in the darkness. The Turks had been the first to catch on to the fact that a form of marijuana grew wild along the banks of the Yalu, and each time they were allowed to bathe down there they brought it back in armfuls and dried it here. To get the full buzz on you needed to pack it lightly in a big open cone of leaf tobacco, and then puff on it energetically.

I'd rather have them puffing than staging one of those fights, Harry thought, watching the orange narcotic light. About once a week all hell would break loose over something in that little house, and then there would be mustachioed Turks being thrown through the windows and leaping to their feet and rushing back in and being thrown out again. No one ever seemed to break any bones, but with the dawn there would be some awfully cut-up swarthy faces.

The orange light held him, and the murmur of Turkish within. He grinned as he thought of the arrangement that they had reached with the Turks about the use of the latrine. After the Americans had built the twelve-holer outhouse, they had found that the Turks were using it by squatting on the top of the holes, and using water from cans that they held in their hands, rather than the toilet paper which was available for the first time since they had all been captured. Harry had been one of the sub-terranean spokesmen for the GIs who had met with the Turks about this, and he had made friends with them as a result of the negotiations. The agreement reached was that the Turks used only the two holes at the far end, on the right, and each nation went on feeling that it was the only one that knew how to do these things properly.

Harry turned and moved off in yet another direction through the darkness. As it did every night now, the face of Interlicchio rose before him, the thin, hook-nosed Florentine coin of a face, the boy from the Bronx under his helmet, getting his light machine gun set in place in that hole in the snow. He was looking straight ahead, waiting for the Chinese Army, but he seemed to be waiting for Harry to say something, to do something.

"I can't help you, buddy," Harry said. He looked up at the stars, feeling hunger bite his stomach. Then he saw Tommy Quinn in the cookhouse at the Bean Camp, the flash of his gold tooth in the dimness.

Fellas, this is Purdick. He's a friend of mine. He's a cook, got it?

· And then he was back with Anne, a hundred times with Anne, sailing in Maine, just fooling around, Anne in a long dress at a dance in New York, white gloves, a string of pearls around her neck, her clean skin flushed from dancing, Anne beside him at the movies, Anne beside him in a car, the old convertible, the top down and a night like this in Maine, a summer cool night like this, driving somewhere, laughing, chatting, the rustle of her skirt on the seat.

Don't think about it, Harry said. Don't think about it or you'll be like the guy who started rolling around on the ground the other day.

He stopped short of the barbed wire, looking towards the road that led down to the village by the river. The needle doctor's face came before him.

That guy is OK.

Harry stood thoughtful in the dark. He had stayed away from the needle doctor, stayed away from everything that would bring him to the attention of the Chinese, since Chung's death. The boys in the schoolhouse had put him on the committee to talk among themselves about problems, but he stayed away from any dealings with the Chinese.

In the night a breeze touched him, and he saw Chung pulling out his pistol and talking about the law of the jungle. It frightened him, and he walked swiftly into the schoolhouse and lay down among the other prisoners.

IV

Constance Purdick came fighting her way out of an afternoon nap in the cottage in Maine. She had just dreamed that she was at a funeral for Bill and Anne's baby, that it had just lived a few hours and died.

She sat up in bed, her heart beating and her face cold. Outside the June late afternoon was gray, and the cry of some seagulls who had flown too far inland came snipping through the mist and low clouds.

The baby isn't due until September sometime, she said to herself, breathing deeply. It'll be fine. You're just upset about Harry and everything. It'll be fine.

She got up, slipped her feet into a pair of mules, and moved quickly down the stairway to the old wall telephone in the kitchen. Constance gave the operator their new number in Washington, where Bill was starting with the Justice Department, and then went into the living room and sat down, waiting for the call.

It came in five minutes. Constance ran into the kitchen.

"Hello? Anne dear, how are you? Oh, *good*. No, I suppose Bill *isn't* home yet. Well, that's all right. What?" Constance held on to the wooden box, one hand holding the earphone and her mouth practically inside the fixed black speaker in the middle of the box. Her free hand was playing distractedly with her white hair where it fell across her forehead. "No, I just wanted to call and see how you all were. That's all. You've moved in all right? Bill liking his work? Oh, good. And you're — fine? Good. Yes, I'll *bet* it's hot down there. Give Bill my love. And you too, dear. Good-bye."

V

Harry slipped into the latrine. The other members of the Policy Committee were already there. The Turks were represented by Big Ali and his interpreter, a British-educated Turk named John, who was the only Turk without a mustache. Hump and Harry represented the Americans, and an old Scot named Rutherford was the Commonwealth. The chess player named Jacques had insisted that France should have a vote, although there were only two French prisoners. A Nisei from Hawaii, Kato, came slipping in from the direction of the little segregated outfit that had come to be known as the U.N. Squad.

"What's up?" Harry whispered.

"We're bringing the prisoner in as soon as Martinez can slip him over heyah," Hump answered.

"What's the charge?"

"Stealing food. This guy took some of that puffed-up bread they gave us the other day. Harrington was saving it up, and this guy stole it."

Harry's face was a study. "What the hell was he saving it for?"

Hump shrugged his big, stooped shoulders. "How do I know? Maybe an escape. That's his affayuh."

Harry nodded. "Well, why didn't they just beat him up when they caught him?"

The little Scot leaned forward. "We seem to be developing a bit of discipline or some'at. They wanted us to take the case."

There was a light breeze as the door swung open, and Martinez propelled a lanky figure in ahead of him.

"Sit him on the floah," Hump whispered. The prisoner sat down cross-legged. Harry looked at him. He was a boy from Maine. Once or twice Harry had chatted with him about Maine, but the boy came from inland, from the potato-farming country.

"Very well," Rutherford said. "Who's in charge of this court?"

"Purdeek," the Frenchman said, and Big Ali and John the Turk nodded approval.

Harry looked at them. "O.K." He bent forward in the darkness at the thin silver face of the boy sitting on the floor, looking up at them as they sat along the row of holes on the raised wooden part of the latrine. "Did you take it?"

"Yes." The answer was a scared hiss.

"I don't have to ask you why you took it, you were hungry. We're all hungry." Harry stared at him. "What do you think we ought to do to you?"

The boy was trembling. "Maybe take my food away from me for a couple 'a days. Give it to Harrington. Then we're even."

"*Pas mal*," the Frenchman murmured.

Harry looked to the other faces in the darkness. John the Turk was whispering a translation to Big Ali. Both Turks nodded.

"Heyull," Hump whispered to the Turks, "if *you* fellas think that's enough, it's all right with me."

The Nisei spoke up. "Would you rather have a beating?"

The boy thought for ten seconds. "How bad of a beating?"

"That's enough," Harry said. "We have a majority right now. Two days without food. Martinez, get him out of here."

VI

A gin-and-tonic party, laughter and ice cubes on a cool evening lawn in Georgetown. Bill stood just behind a madras-jacketed man who worked for a senator from Virginia, waiting for the chance to refill his and Anne's glasses. A few yards away, Anne was talking with a couple they had known from undergraduate days at Harvard and Radcliffe.

Bill smiled as he plunged his hand into a tall paperboard drum containing cubes of ice. It was a good party, pleasant people and good canapés and plenty to drink. The work in the office was interesting to him, and he liked the kind of people who seemed to be everywhere in Washington; bright, interested, involved in things that affected lots of people.

He splashed in some gin, and then poured the tonic in the glasses. Turning, he looked at Anne and saw that she had been watching him out of the corner of her eye, a fond expression on her face. He winked at her, and, without stopping what she was saying to the young woman beside her, she smiled.

Bill grinned and moved towards her across the lawn, keeping the glasses steady in his hands.

VII

One of the British prisoners was Knocker Edwards, who had been a cartoonist on a London daily paper before being conscripted. The interpreters had given him permission to give a show in the compound this late June afternoon.

Harry looked around as the Turks came over in a group and sat down on the hard ground before the steps of the schoolhouse.

" 'Lao, Harry," Big Ali said as he sat down.

"How you doing?" Harry asked.

"OK." That finished Ali's English, but he grinned lovingly about him. To the Turks, a friend was a brother. They would share anything they had with a friend.

John the Turk sat down beside him. "Bit of entertainment, eh?"

Harry smiled. Looking around at the crowd, all stripped to the waist in the sun and wearing their long drawstring shorts, he felt as if they had all known each other forever. Earlier today he and Hump had figured out that it was June 25. It was exactly three years since the North Koreans had attacked South Korea.

And here I am, Harry thought, sitting with a bunch of Turks who shave off their pubic hair and grow big mustaches.

"Ladeez and gentlemen!" It was Hump Jones, who could have run for Congress from Wiwan any day. "Although I know you are all sick of having so many special USO shows arrivin' here, including of course those stars Esther Williams — " cheers, "Jane Russell — " cheers, "Betty Grable for the retreads — " laughter and cheers, "we have today something really special for

you, from the teddibwy distinguished Bwitish contingent —"
There was more laughter at Hump's Mississippi approximation
of a British accent. "I give you — you kin have him — Mister
Knocker Edwards from London England!"

The little Englishman with a mustache strode out the front
door of the schoolhouse as if coming on stage, and walked to the
crude easel that had been set up on the steps. Taking a piece of
charcoal, he began rapidly sketching something on one of the
big pieces of yellow paper that the Chinese, who were watching
from the back, had given him for his show. He stepped back,
and there was a caricature of the upper half of Hump Jones,
huge and stooped, with an MP armband.

"He seems to be looking at something," Knocker said in mock
confusion. "What could it be?" Then he quickly drew in little
legs under Hump, running frantically when he realized that he
was supposed to catch the last vehicle in the retreat, and had
missed it. Everyone had heard the story of Hump's capture;
everyone roared.

Next was a caricature of Martinez, showing his prominent
teeth and olive skin and the pencil mustache that made him look
like a killer wolf. There was a round of applause, and not just
for the artist, but the subject. Martinez was a tough man even by
the standards of this camp, but they liked him.

"Monsieur Jacques," Knocker said, waving to the little
Frenchman to come up and stand on the steps. "*S'il vous plait.*"
There was more applause. Jacques stood up there, cocking his
head and grimacing, and Knocker portrayed him as a chessman,
a knight with a little *tricouleur* at the end of his lance. Jacques
went back down the steps, flushed and pleased, holding the big
yellow sheet with the picture on it.

"Gentleman Harry Purdick! If you please." Harry's eyes
widened, and then he was on his feet, making his way forward
through the seated sun-tanned skinny backs. They were applauding, and they kept talking approvingly as he stood there

on the steps. Harry looked out at them once or twice, with a mistrusting glance.

"C'mon Purdick!" a GI shouted. "Hold still for your picture!" Harry grinned and held still, but still his eyes looked out at the two hundred faces. It had never occurred to him that he was popular.

He turned his head and looked at what Knocker had drawn. It showed Harry's face under a silk hat, wearing a turtleneck sweater with an "H" on it. In one hand he held the scales of justice, and in the other was a dripping writing brush which had just drawn a Chinese character on a piece of paper. Sticking out of his neck was a huge version of one of the needle doctor's pins. Beside him was a Rube Goldberg-looking machine, with wavering lines about it to show it was vibrating.

"And that, Mister Purdick," Knocker whispered, pointing with his charcoal to the weird machine, "is counter-mortar radar, in case you've forgotten what it looks like."

My God, Harry thought as Knocker handed him the picture, these guys knew every damn thing. He went back into the audience as Knocker had one of the Turks come up.

"Draw anything you like. Anything at all."

The man drew a single oval shape, like an egg, and handed the charcoal back to Knocker. Half a dozen quick strokes, and Knocker had transformed it into a naked woman. Everyone went wild.

"How about one of the Chinese?" Knocker asked politely. "Comrade Wu?" He waved invitingly. Wu and the other interpreters stared at him and then huddled among themselves. As Knocker continued to beckon him, Wu came stepping through the crowd seated on the hard dirt, and mounted the steps.

"Draw anything you like," Knocker said, handing over the charcoal.

Wu thought for a moment, and drew a big square.

"Thanks very much," Knocker said, and filled in the Union

Jack. Everyone came to his feet, applauding. Wu stood looking at it for a moment and then, erect, walked back down the steps and straight through the laughing crowd.

* * *

At one in the morning there was a meeting of the Policy Committee in the latrine.

"All right," Rutherford said. The little Scot's face was tense. "They've got Knocker up at headquarters. Suggestions?"

"I've got me an idea," Hump said. "They've been mighty strong on this athletic meet they're goin' to let us have. They want to take photos and everything, show everybody how good they been treatin' us. Suppose we tell Wu everybody's goin' to be sick those days? Just won't have the strength to make it out to the soccer field?"

John the Turk said without hesitation, "We will all be sick at your convenience."

"Charming," Jacques commented. "Perhaps we could say we 'ave V.D. The Chinese would be in a confusion about the source."

The little Nisei put in, "They could force us onto the athletic field, even if we said we were sick."

Harry shook his head. "I don't think the camp commander'd take a chance on that. Once they get the soccer teams and the softball teams out there, they don't want anything to go wrong."

Rutherford nodded. "I think Hump has it. Offer them a trade. Knocker for soccer."

* * *

Harry came trotting to the sidelines as another man went into the game. He sat down on the sparse burnt grass in his long blue shorts and black basketball sneakers, panting from the exertion. A Chinese photographer moved along the sidelines, taking pictures of prisoners of war enjoying themselves in benevolent captivity.

"You don't have to smile that much!" Hump was yelling to the American team from the sidelines. "Just kick the ball, as long as youah in theyah!"

CHAPTER TWENTY-NINE

THEY STOOD in ranks on the soccer field, wondering what it was now. Harry's throat was dry. Any time they departed from the regular routine, he was afraid that they were going to pull him and Martinez out and execute them publicly for the death of Chung.

The camp commander mounted the little wooden platform. Today he was dispensing with the row of interpreters. It was only him and six hundred prisoners, with the burp-gun-carrying guards fanned out behind the formation.

"Despite the objections of your side, and through the efforts of the Korean People's Army and the Chinese People's Volunteers, an armistice has been signed. The armies have stopped fighting and each side is now backing up two thousand meters."

The ranks were motionless. They heard him, but they could not take it in.

"I am very happy for you because now you can return to your loved ones. Please be patient. You will be returned as soon as possible. Remember that all camp rules and regulations remain in effect. Remember that all offenders will be punished." The camp commander stepped down from the platform.

"Damn," Hump Jones murmured, "I hope we get across down theyah befoah some asshole pulls a trigger by mistake."

II

Constance sat looking at a copy of *Life*. The pictures showed the death of a soldier who had been wounded just a few minutes before the cease fire. It showed him expiring on an operating table, a bottle of blood plasma being held beside him, and a clock on the wall showing how very nearly this boy had made it through.

I'm going to church right now, she said to herself, and stay on my knees until I am awfully sure that God wants me to get up.

III

The needle doctor's dark-complexioned face gave a slow, delighted smile of recognition when he saw Harry standing at the door.

"I thought I'd come and say good-bye," Harry said.

"Good for you," the doctor answered, waving him in. For a moment he appeared embarrassed. "How is your shoulder?"

"Fine. I had to tell the guard it was hurting, to get down here."

"Mm. Perhaps I'd better just put a needle in you somewhere, in case anybody should appear."

"Fine," Harry said. "Anywhere you like, doctor. It doesn't hurt anyway."

The needle was in Harry's right leg, just above the black baseball sneakers. He had rolled up the blue cotton trouser, and, as usual, the needle could not be felt. They were both drinking their second cup of tea.

"What will you do," the doctor asked, "now that you're able to return?"

"Well, I want to finish school."

The doctor looked surprised. "Aren't you a bit old to be going back to school?"

"I'm twenty-six," Harry said. "And this time, by God, I'm going to make it through." He paused. "And I've got a girl.

She's waiting for me. We'll get married as soon as I get back."
The doctor beamed. "I wish you many sons."
"Thank you."
"And what will you study?"
"Well, I was studying American History before. Now — "
Harry finished the cup, and the doctor bent forward and poured
him more. "Thank you. Well — my father was writing some-
thing about how Japan and the United States sort of collided in
history — " Harry sipped the tea. God, he thought, that doctor's looking just about as pleased as I am that this war is over.
"Anyway, I want to study a little bit about this part of the
world, and how this whole thing happened." Harry gulped at
the tea. It was so much better than anything he had tasted in
months.
The doctor sat back on his stool. "That seems a wise idea."
He looked down at his tea cup. "I understand there were books
at some of the camps. Books in English. Did you read them?"
Harry put down his cup. "You know, that's something I
really don't get." He knew he was speaking in a rush, but he
couldn't stop. "Here's China, right? Five thousand years of
civilization, right? And what do you give us? Marx, Engels,
Lenin. *Upton Sinclair*, for chrissake. The social protest novels
of Upton Sinclair."
The doctor flushed. "In any event," he said slowly, "I think
it would be a good thing if you took a course in our history.
Perhaps you've had enough Marxism. If you want to understand the Chinese people, I think perhaps you can go directly to
a study of Chinese history."
Harry finished yet another cup and the doctor bent forward
and refilled it. Harry looked at the anatomical charts spread on
the table, but his mind was far from them. I'll be damned, he was
thinking, I started saying some of that stuff to him just to say
something, but I really believe it. I really *am* going to study
how this thing happened.

"China must take its place," the doctor said, suddenly. "It is absolutely essential that we be allowed to take our place."

"But not over my friends' dead bodies."

"Then remove your friends from Asia. We must be allowed to take our place." The doctor leaned forward on his stool, his mask-like face tight. "Please do not assume that we share the same values. You value the individual, and freedom. That is your concern. We value the family, and order. That is our concern."

Not even him, Harry thought. I can't even be friends with him. I just wanted to come and play, and now he says things I can't understand.

Harry rose. "Thank you very much for the tea."

"It was a pleasure. I wish you a safe journey home, and a good life in the future."

Harry paused at the doorstep. How did that go — a time will come when we shall meet again. "Ho Hwei Yu Chi," he said, and started up the road to the compound. He was twenty yards away when he heard the doctor running after him.

"The needle!" the doctor said, out of breath. Harry looked down and saw that his trouser leg was still rolled up, and the gold needle sticking out above the black sneaker. The doctor bent down and began slowly pulling it out, and then they both began laughing.

"Good-bye, doctor," Harry said, in much better humor. "Thanks for everything."

"All the best. Really." The doctor looked around to see if anyone was watching, and then shook hands.

IV

There was a tremendous thunderstorm slapping rain onto the square canvas tent outside of Kaesong. Harry looked over at

Martinez, the one other man who was still here of the ten who had originally shared it. Every other evening the Chinese held a roll call, and men would pour out from all over Tent City. The Chinese would call off one hundred and twenty names, and march them off fifteen minutes later to a building a mile away. From that building, within a day or two, they were taken by trucks to Panmunjom and then released. Night after night Harry had fallen out with the others. He had seen Hump go out, and the Turks go out in a group, and the Commonwealth boys go out, and now there were only about a hundred men left in this camp through which twenty-five hundred had passed.

Harry stretched out on his bunk, looking at the wind rippling the pyramidal dark-brown canvas above him. It was an incredible luxury to lie on a cot for the first time since he had been wounded southeast of Seoul in October of 1950. Now it was August 30, 1953.

He looked over at where Martinez was boredly rearranging the packs of cigarettes that had arrived, a carton of them, in the Red Cross package for each man.

They're going to catch up to us, Harry thought. They're playing with us right up to the end. They're going to call the last roll call and then take me and Martinez into some room and tell us they know about Chung and we'll be the two guys that don't make it out.

And even if they don't know. Harry listened to the thunder rumbling down the valley and the crack of nearer lightning. What about that thing Hump said? What if some trigger-happy jerk shoots somebody in the No-Man's Land and starts the whole thing up again? I can just see them putting us in the trucks again right now. Heading back north. This time they'll probably take us all the way to Peking.

A head was stuck in the tent flap. It was a Negro boy who had been at Pyoktong, and his eyes were rolling. "Hey, Leatherbee jus' got killed by lightnin'!"

"Cut it out," Harry said, sitting up. Martinez moved to the tent flap in his fast, light gait.

"Not kiddin', man," the Negro boy said, coming in. "Leatherbee, man, he was runnin' from the mess tent to his own tent jus' *five* minutes ago, man. Lightnin' come down and hit the spoon in his breas' pocket. Chinese are havin' a *fit*, how they goin' to explain this when he don't come out."

Martinez nodded and went to the Red Cross kit. "You better have a drink." He pulled out a small earthenware crock and offered it to the drenched boy.

"Where'd you get that?" Harry asked.

Martinez smiled. "Not from the Red Cross."

Harry moved to the door and stared up at the torrential sky, and the water gushing down the muddy trails among the hillside tents. Then he looked up at the sky again. "What are you doing up there?" he shouted, his head thrust back in the wind and rain. "What are you doing up there, anyway?"

CHAPTER THIRTY

I'LL BELIEVE IT when I see it, Harry thought. I'll believe it when I see it. They were aboard the last of a three-truck convoy heading down the road from the building where they had been taken from Tent City, two nights before. It was ten thirty in the hazy morning, and they were heading south.

"Smoke?" Another prisoner was proffering one of the clean white cigarettes from the Red Cross packages.

"No, thanks." Harry looked at the set-up in the canvased-over back of this Chinese truck. As in the two trucks ahead of him, there were eight men down the benches on either side, and then eight straddling the middle bench. They had been seated in accordance with some list. There was a Chinese driver in front, and Rat-Face, unarmed, was sitting at the tail end of the bench on the right.

"Look at that." A freckle-faced boy had lifted the canvas behind him. Along the side of the road were endless American combat boots and fatigue jackets and trousers, thrown away by the truckloads of Chinese who were being sent north up this road, back to their own forces.

"Damn fools," Harry said. He had heard that they were doing this, along with shouting anti-American slogans every mile of the way. "It'll be years before they see another pair of shoes as good as those."

"Maybe they ain't so dumb," the kid said thoughtfully, letting the canvas flap drop. "Maybe they got to impress their bosses how much they hate us."

Harry nodded and looked at the man directly across the way from him. The man had fallen and scraped some skin off his wrist this morning, and within five minutes the Chinese had rushed a doctor to the spot. They had bandaged him from his wrist to his elbow, and lifted him aboard the truck as if he were a crate of eggs. Looking at that white bandage now, Harry found himself thinking of that first march north to the Bean Camp, and the first schoolhouse, and being in the hole at Pyoktong. Then the men were pointing at something, and he looked out the rear. A Chinese equivalent of a jeep had turned into the road behind them, and was keeping its interval about forty yards back. There were two Chinese in it, and an older American wearing a dark suit, white shirt, dark tie, and a short-visored blue prisoner's cap like the one Harry was wearing.

"Prob'ly some old master sergeant been hiding up in the hills," the freckle-faced boy said. "Most likely didn't know the war was over."

You think the war is over? Harry thought, and then asked himself, why the hell did you say that?

The truck slowed and turned a corner. An American MP stood there, tall, white-gloved, sparkling brass whistle and enameled helmet liner, waving them on. Everyone's jaw dropped. They were in.

"You know, Rat-Face," Martinez said quietly from where he sat opposite the interpreter in the back, "you really are an ugly bastard."

"You really are," another man said. "I been too scared to tell you till now. If I ever catch you on even terms I'll kill you."

"Talk nice," Rat-Face said, backing out practically over the tail gate. "You going home to your loved ones, now. I am going home to my loved ones." He looked towards the Chinese jeep behind him.

"I hope you and your loved ones die of cancer," Martinez said. "Rat-Face, you people treated us worse'n animals."

A big Negro chimed in. "You'n all your bullshit 'bout your

revolution. Easy to make people tear things down, but what you got at the end?" He shook his head. "What you got at the end is a *drag*, man."

Rat-Face said soothingly to the truck in general, "Be good boys, be good boys."

Martinez leaned towards him. "Rat-Face, I am *so glad* we held you bastards here and not on the West Coast somewhere."

"We don't want West Coast," Rat-Face said with deep conviction. "We come here stop you attack China."

Martinez looked back at the jeep still following, and stamped the floorboards in frustration. "Rat-Face, you people want the whole world, and you can't have it." He jabbed one forefinger towards Rat-Face, and the other hand towards his chest. "I'm gonna re-enlist and every time you boys come poppin' out of your rat-hole you're gonna see *me*."

The trucks were stopping, and then they were backing up, side by side, into a semicircle. Harry looked out the back, and rose at what he saw. In the foreground stood a Marine major in fatigues, holding a sheet of paper in his hand. Behind him at a respectful distance were hundreds of GIs in clean starched green fatigues, all watching, all waiting.

The Marine major came to the tailgate of the truck. "This is the last shipment of prisoners in your hands," he said to Rat-Face. "Is that correct?"

Rat-Face rose with dignity, between the major's official coldness and the pure hatred in the truck. "That is correct."

"Very well." The major backed off and began calling names. The men from the other trucks jumped out, and then he was calling the names from this truck.

Harry was the last man off. Rat-Face looked at him as Harry swung over the tailboard and landed on the ground.

"You be good boy, Pu'dick."

Harry turned. The men in front of him were milling around, and there was a moment more to speak.

"Did you really mean that," he asked, looking up from under his blue schoolboy cap to where Rat-Face was standing in the back of the truck, "did you really mean that you people came into the war because you thought we were going to attack China?"

"Yes."

"But we *weren't* going to attack China," Harry said, his face working. "You mean the whole thing was a misunderstanding?"

"Yes."

"Good God," Harry said. The truck pulled away in one direction and Harry turned in the other. There was a corridor of enlisted men with armbands, pointing the direction in which he should follow the other men. Beyond the lines of guides were the crowd of GIs, hands shading their eyes in the hazy sun, looking for missing friends, missing cousins, missing brothers.

Two enlisted men with Red Cross armbands were holding open the door of an ambulance, and Harry climbed in to join five others from his shipment. They took off down the road. Harry's mind was blank. It seemed to him that he was collapsing, sinking, that it required an attentive effort to breathe. In. Out. In. Out. His eyes closed. Then the ambulance stopped and the doors were opening. Harry was right at the back, and in the sudden light he saw starched fatigues with white cloth stars all over stiff field caps and collars.

"I'm General Mark Clark, Commander, Far East," said one of the two generals who had opened the ambulance doors. He shook Harry's hand. "We're very proud of you men. You've done a wonderful job." Harry saluted.

The other general stuck out his hand. "I'm General Maxwell Taylor, Commander, Eighth Army. You men have been on our minds constantly." They shook hands, and Harry saluted.

An enlisted man motioned him to start walking towards something that looked like an airplane hangar. As he moved along behind the guide, Harry saw an American jeep pull up beside the two generals. The older American in the blue Chinese suit and prisoner's cap who had been behind them on the road got out, and then the two generals were embracing him and slapping him on the back.

I wonder who the hell that old sergeant *is*, Harry thought, and went through the door of the big arch-roofed structure.

"Name?" said a sergeant sitting behind a table.

"Harold Purdick," Harry said. "I mean, Purdick, Harold. Sergeant First Class, Ninth Infantry, Second Division."

The man looked down the list. "You are now a master sergeant. The promotion is backdated to the day after your capture. What day were you — "

The American in the Chinese suit came through the door, accompanied by General Mark Clark and General Maxwell Taylor. Harry started to move aside.

"That's all right, son," the tall man said from under his Chinese cap.

"What date were you captured?" the sergeant behind the desk asked Harry.

"I don't know. Around February fifteenth. 1951."

"February fifteenth, 1951. Right."

Harry moved away from the desk, waiting behind the blue-clad backs in front of him.

"Name?" the sergeant asked the tall man.

"Major General William F. Dean. Former commanding officer, Twenty-Fourth Infantry Division."

The sergeant behind the desk leapt to his feet, and Harry's head spun on his shoulders. The line was moving along, and Harry moved past a plyboard partition. There were chaplains standing there. He saw Martinez kneeling beside a bench where a Catholic chaplain was sitting. Martinez' lips were moving. The chaplain nodded, and his lips began moving in turn. He made the sign of the cross slowly, and Martinez rose. The priest took him to a small altar in the corner, and Martinez knelt in his Chinese blue garb, his cap in his hand, and then the priest was holding a chalice and bending forward.

After Martinez moved on, Harry went up to the Catholic priest.

"Excuse me," Harry said. "I want to tell you about a couple of friends of mine named Interlicchio and Quinn. Maybe you could pray for them or something."

II

Harry looked at the clock on the wall opposite a shower in the hospital in Tokyo. Dimly he realized that he had been under the water for forty-five minutes, alternately soaping himself and soaking and never getting out from under the hot steady flow. They had flown them here yesterday from a hospital at Inchon, and life consisted of milk and more milk and scrambled eggs yes I would like some more and steak I don't care if it's medium or rare or what and beautiful mashed potatoes, the first potatoes he had had in two and a half years, he had had no idea he missed potatoes so much, and orange juice, and coffee, real American coffee.

Harry turned off the shower and took the thick white beautiful towel from its rack outside the open shower stall. He dried himself, polishing each limb, smiling. He dried off Swann's West Point ring, still hanging from the chain that Tommy Quinn had given him. He felt relieved, tremendously relieved. Everything was fine. He was in a hospital, not because they had found anything wrong with him, but because he had never been to a hospital after his second wound, the one in his shoulder when the Chinese first came in. There was a regulation that one had to be checked up if one had not been in a hospital for the last wound before capture. It was fine with him. This way he would get a ride home in a plane, instead of by boat. He had asked a Red Cross lady to place a call to Anne and when he got Anne he would tell her to let Harvard know he would be there in time to start his senior year. Today was September sixth. He had one or two things to do, like getting married and finding an apartment for Anne and himself in Cambridge, but he was sure that school would not start before about the twentieth. Everyone here was taking care of him, was pulling for him.

Harry put on his pajamas and the maroon bathrobe. He walked down the corridor and past the MP guarding the ward in which the last group of returned prisoners was lounging about.

Harry smiled at the MP. The man was there because the POWs were objects of curiosity, and his job was to keep out curious people. Harry smiled at a couple of guys who were leaving the ward, heading for the Ginza on pass.

It's great to have a guard that keeps people out instead of in, Harry thought, and stretched out on the beautiful white linen of the beautiful soft bed.

*   *   *

The Red Cross lady came into the ward just as Harry was laying out his new uniform on the bed. He already had on the shiny sand-colored trousers, and now he was pinning the badges and ribbons onto the shirt. The tailor had sewed on the master sergeant's stripes, three chevrons up and three rockers across on each sleeve. The big Indian head patch of the Second Division was on his right shoulder, to show that was the outfit with which he had been in combat.

"About that overseas call to your fiancée," the Red Cross lady said. She looked at him strangely. "She — she's not in New York right now, but they said your mother is. We've fixed it up so that your mother should be calling you in about ten minutes."

"Great!" Harry looked at the new wrist watch he had bought in the hospital PX.

"The booth is right down the hall," the lady said. "It's reserved for you. She paused. "You know, you'll be flying back to the States on the first flight after your last de-briefing session. That's probably within a couple of days, and you may not have any time to get down to the Ginza. I wonder if you'd like me to buy you any presents for home."

"That's a great idea," Harry said. "Thank you." He pulled out his new wallet and took out a hundred dollars of the partial pay he had received. "I'd like something for my fiancée, and for my mother, and for my brother. What's a good thing to get them?"

"Well, pearls are an excellent buy."

Harry looked at his new wrist watch and nodded. He wanted to be at that booth before ten minutes were up. "O.K. Why don't you get two presents of pearls, and — "

"Well, what?" the lady smiled. "I mean, necklaces, or bracelets, or pins?"

Harry stared at her. God, he thought, I haven't seen a necktie for two and a half years, and she's asking me about necklaces and bracelets. "Whatever you say. How about a samurai sword for my brother?"

"They've all been confiscated by the Occupation."

"Oh. Well, just get him something exotic. Thanks a lot." Harry put the hundred dollars into her hand and strode to the telephone booth.

"We have New York now," the operator said, and Harry clamped the receiver close to his head.

There was a hissing on the wire, and then he heard his mother's voice say, "Harry?" It was flat and metallic, but it was she. It was.

"Mother," Harry said. "How are you?"

"Fine, darling. It's so *wonderful* to hear your voice! Are you all right?"

"Fine. Everything's fine. Treating us very well here. Where's Anne?"

"She's out of town. Darling, when are you getting here?"

"Within a few days. First Hawaii, then San Francisco. Then home."

"Darling, can you meet me in San Francisco? I mean, could you?"

"Sure! I can get *discharged* in San Francisco."

"When shall I come?"

"Better give me a day to get processed out. Why don't you make it four days from now?"

"All right. Four days from now. I'll check in at the St. Francis Hotel. When you get through with whatever it is, just come to the St. Francis."

"Great," Harry said. "Bring Anne with you!"

*   *   *

The man de-briefing Harry seemed to be a one-man band. He was in civilian clothes, and they sat in a cubicle in the hospital, and he seemed to know medical terms and military terms and the phrases from the Communist lectures. He had forms beside him. When they came to a death, he had a form for that. It took two witnesses to establish an American death behind Communist lines, and after some of the disappearing and reappearing acts he had seen, Harry was inclined to think it was a good idea to require a second witness even though you had had the man die right in front of you.

They were talking about his first escape now, and Harry was telling about Lee and the little baby-carriage-wheeled cart and pulling the prisoner north. Harry's face grew angry as he told of how Lee would not help, and of the straw rope tearing his hands until they bled, and how he had yanked the helpless young Chinese across every bump he could find.

"What do you think happened to that boy after you left him off?" the man asked.

"I like to think he died," Harry said. "He'd had a pretty rough ride."

The man looked at him and said nothing.

Late in the afternoon the man was going through a list of names that earlier returnees had identified as collaborators.

"Nope," Harry said as the man would read a name, "No," "Didn't know that one," "Sorry."

" — Wuthers."

"Hold it. I can help you with that one." Harry's eyes closed and he began talking.

III

Harry sat chatting with the crew chief as the Medical Air Evac flight moved across the Pacific from Honolulu to San Francisco.

" — till now we been on Wounded Warrior," the pockmarked crew chief said, lighting a cigarette.

"What kind of a deal is that?"

"Down in Indo-China. We're not supposed to say nothin' about it. The French are gettin' pushed around down there pretty bad. We been flyin' supplies into Hanoi and Saigon."

Harry stared at him. "You mean they've got a war going on down there?"

"Hell yes. Communists really layin' it on 'em down there."

"God damn it," Harry said slowly, and walked back to his seat.

IV

Harry walked in the sunlight in Golden Gate Park. He had finished his processing for the day, and his mother was not due until tomorrow. The willows shone green-gold in the September afternoon.

Each time a child passed him, he smiled. The only children he had seen for three years were Asians, small and graceful and all the same color scheme, and these multi-colored awkward noisy energetic creatures were fascinating. Looking at them, he could see that they could not possibly survive on a bowl of millet a day.

Down in a meadow there were a lot of adults. The men were wearing slacks and sport shirts, and the women were wearing slacks and blouses.

Some kind of an outing, Harry said to himself. The people were laughing, and a man in a baseball cap was telling them to form up in two long lines, the men facing the women, about ten yards apart. Then a woman with purple hair came down the line of men, handing each one an egg. On a signal, all of the men tossed the eggs to the women, who caught them with a great squealing. Harry came closer. The man with the baseball cap shouted something, and both lines stepped back a few feet. Then the women tossed the eggs back to the men. One of the eggs broke as a man tried to catch it, and everybody shrieked with laughter. As Harry stood to one side, the women's line threw again. They were about twenty yards apart now, and each time the shower of eggs went through the air, a few more broke in the hands of the catchers, splattering on clean gaudy sport shirts and on slacks and cardigan sweaters. Person after person left the line, holding his hands in front of him, sticky and dripping from the broken eggs. There was a big green garbage can near Harry, and the men and women who had been knocked out of the game gathered about it, dropping the broken egg shells and pulling out handkerchiefs and laughing as they cleaned themselves off.

Harry blinked. For a moment he had seen filthy GIs on their knees fighting around a bucket of lukewarm water with some grains of millet in its bottom.

Harry opened his eyes. He watched them destroying food until a big handsome blond man and a fat little girl with upswept hair had won by keeping their egg unbroken. Then he walked on.

*   *   *

They had given him a little room by himself at the end of the transient barracks, but he could not sleep. At first he thought it was the foghorns in San Francisco Bay, but after a while he realized that he was alone in the room, and that he could not sleep in a room where there were not other people tossing and snoring. He gathered up his bedding, and installed himself on the bottom of a two-decker bunk halfway down the aisle. There were only a handful of men in here, but it was enough.

All right, Harry thought, wiggling down under the covers in the foggy San Francisco night, now sleep.

Still he lay awake. Once a man down the line came out of his blankets fighting, and the man across the aisle shouted in his sleep, "No! No!" Through Harry's mind there rolled the city's streets and avenues, endless banks of plate glass and chrome, and cars everywhere. People carrying crammed shopping bags. Anywhere you wanted, in a cigar store, a drug store, you could go in and buy a Hershey Bar. Big flabby pink women walking down the streets giving their husbands hell, or driving big cars as if they owned the earth. Everywhere colors, lights, rich silk dresses and jewelry and fat dogs on shiny leashes.

Suddenly Harry became aware that a kid was sitting on the edge of the bunk next to his. There was no mattress on the bunk, and the lights coming through the window shone on its steel netting. The kid was wearing a white T-shirt and fatigue trousers in the gloom, and he was just sitting there on the edge of the naked bunk. He looked like Interlicchio.

Harry sat up slowly, his hands moving across the rough Army blanket.

"Interlicchio?" he said in a small voice.

"Nah," the kid said. "My name's Forlenza."

"Oh." Harry sat back, leaning against one of the iron pipes that supported the bunk above him. The kid kept sitting there. Harry kept staring at him. Half the time he saw the kid, and then he saw GIs dead in the snow, green sacks lying in the snow.

Then the old one came floating towards him, just Interlicchio's head under the helmet, looking down the slope, waiting for the Chinese, but waiting for Harry to say something.

All right, Harry said. This is my last night in the Army. What do you want me to say, Interlicchio? I'll try to say it.

Harry sat up even straighter. Slowly his lips formed words. The kid on the other bunk remained motionless.

Interlicchio, I'm sorry you're dead.

The helmeted head kept on looking forward.

All right. Interlicchio, I'll pray for you.

The helmeted head kept staring down the snowy valley.

Interlicchio, I'll find your parents and tell them what you did. I'll tell them you were a hell of a fine soldier, and you and Tommy Quinn, with those machine guns, you held off the Chinese and let a lot of other guys get out.

The Florentine face kept waiting for the attack.

Harry sat up even straighter. He felt the West Point ring move on his chest. That's another thing, he thought. I have to get this back to Swann's wife and his father.

Interlicchio was still waiting.

Harry let out an impatient sigh.

All right, Interlicchio, I don't know what you want, but I'll tell you what I'm going to do. I'm going back to school and I'm going to start studying about what happened to us. I want to know why we were thrown in there so goddamn unprepared, and I want to form some opinions about what we ought to do over there from now on.

The helmet seemed to waver.

You listening? I am going to do everything I can to see that you guys didn't die for nothing over there. You'll have to give

me a little time to figure out where I can fit in on this deal. I
don't care if I end up a professor like my father, or in the State
Department, or back in the Army, or in jail.

The helmet moved closer.

I've got three years' back pay coming to me, Interlicchio.
That ought to buy me a little time to study and think. I know
what we think we're doing. Now I want to find out what the
Chinese think they're doing. Then I want to see if we can lay
down some ground rules. If we can't, then I damn sure want us
to be more prepared than we were the last time.

The helmet was almost on top of him.

And don't think I think the United States is so perfect. I
just had a bellyful of the United States this afternoon. I won't
sell us out, but I don't have any illusions that we're any better
than anybody else.

Harry took a deep breath. "How's that?"

Interlicchio turned toward him. "Thanks, Purdick," he said,
and vanished. Harry shook like a leaf. The kid on the bunk was
gone.

V

Constance's hands trembled as she put down the telephone in
her room at the St. Francis. The voice on the house phone had
been Harry's. He was coming upstairs. She glanced beseechingly around the white plaster walls, the white molding, looking
for strength and finding none.

She looked at her face in the mirror, hastily applying lipstick,
clumsily combing her hair. Please dear God help me explain
about Anne. He's back, he's here, that's all that matters, but —

There was a knock on the door. Constance rushed to it and
threw it open. A man in uniform stood there. His angular face
was like leather, and his eyes had a strange, far-off stare.

"Where's — " Constance began, and Harry's voice said from yellow teeth, "Mother?"

Constance sobbed and threw her arms about him, feeling these strange hard limbs, her face against a chest of ribbons and badges, her fingers running down the somehow sinister ladder of stripes on his sleeve. She was crying, and he was awkwardly patting her shoulder. Then he was closing the door to the room and she was standing, her hands smoothing her dress and then her face and still staring at this man, at the big black shield on his shoulder, with the embroidered profile of an Indian wearing a war bonnet.

"Where's Anne?" the man asked.

"Harry — why don't you sit down." She watched him move gracefully onto an armchair next to the bed. He sat on the edge of it, an expectant smile on his face, as she still stood, twisting her hands. Constance blinked as she looked at him. There was something terrifying, as if he were a wild animal who should be running under the sky instead of sitting in an armchair, his polished shoes resting on thick carpet. She lowered herself onto the little stool before the dressing table, her eyes still fixed on him.

I can't be afraid of him, she thought. I mustn't be. She saw a blue horizontal enamel bar above his ribbons, a silver frontiersman's rifle on it, and she opened her mouth and tried to speak. There were strange echoes of shouting and shrieking and skies opening and men tumbling into Hell.

"Harry," she said, "please don't hurt me."

Tears sprang from Harry's eyes.

"Harry — "

"Anne's dead," he said.

"No." Constance shook her head. "Harry — she married Bill." She choked, and leaned towards him, her hands coming to her temples. "We thought *you* were dead, Harry. About a year and a half after we thought you were dead — before we heard you were alive — she . . . married . . . Bill."

"But, Mother," Harry said in soft, reasonable tones, "she

wrote me." A little smile was flicking at his lips, as if there was an explanation to a joke here somewhere.

"Harry — " Constance rose and moved over to the side of the bed, near him. Sitting on the edge of the bed, she put both hands on his arm. "We thought it would *kill* you if you heard about it, then." She stopped and looked at what Harry was doing. His arm that was under her hands remained still, but with his other hand he was pulling aside his sand-colored uniform tie and fumbling with the collar button of his shirt. His hand went inside his T-shirt, and she had a glimpse of a thin metal chain and a ring that he was clutching in his hand. For quite a few seconds he stared at her as if he had never seen her before. Then he spoke.

"You're not going to get me now," he said. "I got through. You're not going to get me now." His hand dropped the ring back inside his shirt, and moved to his side as if picking up a weapon. "You people are crazy if you think you can get me now." He rose and walked to the window, and Constance gasped. She thought he was going to open it and jump.

Harry stood looking down at Union Square, the cable car merrily clanging past below, the women in silk print dresses and the men in light-shaded suits and summer straw hats, the big shiny cars. "They have any children?" he asked in a calm voice.

"She's expecting her first any time now."

Harry bent his twitching forehead against the cool glass. He saw the pigeons hopping about in the park in the square, and an old man feeding the pigeons, and a little boy running in the sunshine. "There were some good men over there," he said after a minute, his eyes half-closed. "I'm going to try to do something for them."

Constance nodded numbly. She stared down at her hands for a long time. When she looked up, Harry was still at the window, his face in thought. Through her wet eyes she saw his set jaw, and she saw that whatever else Harry was going to do in life, he was not going out any windows.

Time had stopped in the room. She stared at Harry's polished shoes, his uniform trousers, and now she heard echoes of feet marching on dirt, muted sounds, animals crawling through bushes.

Finally she rose and haltingly made her way to the window beside him. "Harry — I don't know if it means anything to you — " she put her face in her hands. "I'm so glad you're back."

Harry turned. Slowly he reached out his hand and lifted her chin. She saw his suffering, taut face, and closed her eyes.

"It's nobody's fault," Harry said. "That's just the trouble."